SECRETS OF THE SPHERE

HERMAN STEUERNAGEL

1

THE RUBBLE, which was nearly all that was left of the ancient city of Vegas, wasn't the worst of the aftermath of the Onyx attack. Neither were the hundreds dead or thousands displaced. Worse were the skeletons of Onyx lying in and among the ruins.

Most of the city's residents had never seen the vast scale of valuable components the giant robot orbs contained. Though the Onyx hadn't killed off all those who had chosen this city as their home, the remaining residents of Vegas were apt to destroy themselves.

Sierra Runar had missed the fight. She had missed the Onyx crashing to the earth. She had missed the spirit of unity that had overtaken those who had lived both above and below ground. She had been told it had lasted for a whopping four days before the seeds of disarray had exposed themselves.

Now, only suspicion remained. Distrust and sideways glances between people who had formed an unsteady alliance had hurriedly replaced any sense of community that had briefly existed.

The enemy, now defeated, left those who were already desperate in a cruel position. In the streets and within the buildings of their destroyed city, corpses of the Guardians spelled opportunity. Valuable pieces of them remained: electronics, plastics, metals, and more would fetch premium coin with any traveling merchant. Or—if someone were to be so bold—an even better price if they could smuggle it out themselves.

The city itself was barely a shadow of what it had been before the attack. When Sierra had been allowed out of the MedCenter infirmary, she had nearly cried. The city had been crumbling before, fading as the desert reclaimed much of it over the past two centuries, but now it had been all but leveled. Only a few buildings remained standing, and craters in the earth's surface revealed much of the Underground where most of the city's residents called home.

Sierra was well aware that if it hadn't been for her newly discovered power—the ability to activate technology by coming into contact with it—there would have been nothing left of the city at all. No residents to keep from one another's throats.

Days of tension and heated arguments had mounted until the leaders of both the Community and the Underground had to step in. Their respective leaders, Malachi and N'ara, had agreed to work together, in an unsteady partnership, to protect the objects until they could conclude what the best course of action would be.

At least both leaders saw the potential the fallen bots held for the city and the future well-being of their peoples.

Today marked exactly one week since Sierra had returned from activating the EMP blast that had caused the Guardian orbs to fall from the sky; a blast that had put an end to all the destruction—by bringing destruction of its own.

Her sole companion from the Sphere, Wil Underwood, had left with the Resistance. Ella had joined them as well, but Sierra suspected that had more to do with Wil's presence than the group's actual cause. The woman had trained her lustful eyes on Wil ever since they had arrived at the Outpost.

Despite being followed around like a puppy, Wil seemed to be able to keep Ella at arm's length. Both had been instrumental in staving off the Guardian attack on Vegas. Wil had unleashed a power of his own, which had taken out several dozen Sentinels, and could be credited, equally as much as Sierra could be, as the savior of what little of the city now remained.

Ella had been Malachi's right-hand warrior and had handled the hand-to-hand conflict with the Sentinels with ease. She'd been a cornerstone of the Community until deciding that accompanying Wil to the coast was in her better interest.

The Resistance had been eager to leave for their next destination: another city of the ancients that lay across the mountains to the west. Whatever the next part of their plan was, they had to restock and re-man their efforts.

Wil had visited Sierra at the Rio Grande Inn after she had awoken from the coma her powers had put her in. Unconscious for nearly a week, whatever she had unleashed from within herself to ignite the EMP blast had taken everything out of her.

"Just promise me I'll find you again," she had said to him. She'd gripped his hands, which were strong and calloused. They were different from before. Something had changed in him since they had left the Sphere.

In truth, something had changed in both of them, but, in Wil, it had been more dramatic. The mischievous imp she remembered from their childhood was fading. This version of Wil had a chip on his shoulder—and it was one Sierra worried he would never be able to satisfy.

Concern had flashed in people's eyes when Wil had told them he was joining Elizabeth and the Resistance. Sierra had never had time to meet the woman, but Malachi, Ella, and even Leo had cautioned against him enlisting with her. But they had no hold on him. There was nothing they could offer to hold him back. So, they had let Wil depart with only words of caution: *"Be careful, especially with that woman."*

And that was the last Sierra had seen of her friend.

Now, Sierra stood before N'ara, Queen of the Underground once again. Ruler of the dejected, N'ara reigned over the malnourished residents who lived beneath the city—or at least she had, until most of its chambers had collapsed under the colossal weight of dozens of Onyx crashing down on top of them.

Sierra was once again in N'ara's uncomfortably familiar command center, deep in the Underground, beside Malachi Riley, the leader of the group that called itself the Community. They were mostly outcasts and vagabonds, but under Malachi's leadership, they had decided to work together, for survival served them better than trying to fight alone for scraps on the street.

The Community and the Underground had been notoriously at odds, up until the Silent Zone had fallen. Once the energy field protecting the city from the Guardians had disappeared, a common enemy had united them, if only briefly.

The blue lights that had once lit the room had been extinguished by the EMP blast, leaving only dim torchlight to illuminate the halls. Flames licked the concrete walls, built from gray blocks that had withstood the test of time. Water dripped somewhere at the far reaches of the room, amplified by the silence as the three stared at each other. Ancient relics filled the room: machines full of colors, texts, illustrations, and numbers, many of which were attached to defunct monitors, their displays now dark. The colors attached to them felt out of place in such a dreary setting.

N'ara could at least have offered them a seat. Instead they stood while she sat on her makeshift golden throne. Unlike the last time they had been in this room, they sought no favors, only a path forward to peace.

The truce between the Underground and the Community was shaky. Word of some Community members having raised their own flag around the remnants of the city hadn't helped to ease tensions. The blue flag intertwined with three gold circles represented equality and cooperation for the greater good, but such a symbol could not resonate with those accustomed to following the orders of a supreme monarch. Not when the same symbol had represented so much imbalance before the attack.

"I'm saying," Malachi continued, "that if you're not careful, the people will turn on both of us. There was little for them to cling to before, and there's even less now. Even guards need to eat; they still need to feed their families. We can't expect them to protect the orbs forever; not while they're struggling to survive. No matter how loyal our people are, their allegiance will only last for so long. Sooner or later, they will give in to necessity."

The torchlight caught the green flecks in his eyes. The vest he wore must have offered little warmth in the cooler subterranean fortress, but he showed no sign of discomfort.

"Yes, Malachi, you've made your point," N'ara replied, rolling her eyes and baring her pointed teeth. Torchlight danced over her pale skin. Her pupils had dilated so fully, none of her pale iris was now visible. It was a common trait among those in the Underground.

Despite her best efforts, Sierra always shivered at the effect. And that wasn't the only thing about the woman that affected her nerves. Malachi might have found it within himself to put aside that the woman had tried to kill them, but Sierra hadn't found it so easy.

"How do you propose we proceed?" N'ara asked.

"We need to work together—and without worry of being stabbed in the back. Nobody will come out ahead that way." Malachi paused, pursing his lips. "We need to trust each other. Despite any misdeeds of the past."

N'ara returned his gaze, ignoring the slight. So far, Malachi had not directly mentioned that the woman had sent them stripped and bound into the desert heat, but he had hinted at the incident a few times.

N'ara glided over his words like desert glass. She wasn't taking the bait. "If you want me to simply roll over and give your Community free rein of the city, I won't. You may have defeated the Guardians, but the people of the Underground won't relinquish our customs."

Sierra was growing tired of the banter. The two leaders had been arguing for the last two hours, and the back and forth was far beyond tedious. "Enough!" she exclaimed, startling herself with the force of her own words and then taking a deep breath to regain her composure. "You have two options. Work together as equals, build trust with those in the city by treating them fairly, and use the wealth from the crashed units for the good of everyone—or let chaos reign. If you sit here arguing forever, then chaos *will* win, sooner or later. There will be no going back. Neither of you are going to let the other salvage the parts for your own gain; that much is clear. Quit arguing and do something. *Anything.*"

For the past few days, Sierra had watched while grown men squabbled over shiny bits of metal and plastic, as if there wasn't more than enough to go around. Clearly, they had lived in a world where they had been forced to scrounge for their next meal for far too long. Those in the Sphere might have been living under the watchful eye of the Guardians, but at least they had worked together, even if it hadn't been for their own benefit.

The effect of her words didn't hold N'ara captive for long. "What would you have us do, then, child? Divvy up the parts to everyone in the city? That would take far too long, and we'll have beggars from far and wide knocking on our gates, asking for a handout."

"You both claim to be leaders. So *lead*. Get a council together to decide the best use of the wreckage. The best use for *everyone*." It was her turn to raise an eyebrow at N'ara. "And decide soon. I'd start with getting the people something to eat. Food has been growing scarcer by the day."

The sound of dripping water continued to echo at the back of the chamber as both N'ara and Malachi sat quietly. N'ara drummed her fingers on the arm of her chair, her sharpened nails clicking on its surface.

It shouldn't have been a difficult task. But maybe it was. Maybe this was what became of humanity when left to its own devices, people at each other's throats until the strong overwhelmed the weak. How was it that a simple suggestion of cooperation left them speechless?

The situation was made all the more frustrating by Malachi being just as stubborn as N'ara. For all of his talk of cooperation within the Community, he had made it clear during this encounter that he wanted collaboration to be on his terms. Although she detested the woman, Sierra readily understood why that wasn't a solution for her.

"Why is she even here?" N'ara barked, standing up from her throne and walking toward them. "This girl claims to be the destroyer of the Guardians, but what if her actions were nothing more than coincidence? We're going on her word and that of a man who claims to be over *two hundred* years old?" She pointed her index finger at Sierra for emphasis, the torchlight bouncing off of her pale bald head and exposing the veins visible just beneath the skin.

"I trust her a whole lot more than I trust *you*," Malachi snapped back. "She's right, and you know it. This may be the chance we've longed for. We could finally unite our people. We could be the next San Francisco. A prosperous city for all."

"San Francisco has its own set of problems; you know that. But I see what you're getting at." N'ara lifted a thin hand to the back of her head, staring at the ceiling in contemplation.

"You need to put aside your own desire for power," he continued, pausing briefly before adding, "We *both* do."

She gave him a sharp look.

"Don't look so surprised," Malachi said. "The city will dissolve into chaos if we don't bring some semblance of order to it, and we can't achieve that by competing for authority."

"And I suppose you want to choose who is on this council?"

"This can be the first step in our new alliance. Let's set up an eleven-person council. You and I can each choose three representatives to sit alongside us; people whom we feel could provide strong insight into matters of the city. No games. Leo gets a seat too and can pick two. Each member gets a vote."

Sierra smiled at the suggestion. The Innkeeper had helped her to discover Terre's whereabouts. Everyone in the city had been grateful for the help Leo had given to all during the attack, and he was well respected for his impartiality.

N'ara crossed her arms and leaned back, considering his proposal. "Why Leo?"

"He has helped us both; he has no strong allegiances to either the Underground or the Community. He also has the most to gain if we can unite moving forward. His involvement will discourage you and I from each picking three biased candidates who will cause nothing but a deadlock. Forming a council will be redundant if we vote four to four on every decision. We'll be no further ahead than we are now."

N'ara paced back to her chair and stared at it, as if she thought it might hold the answer. "What if I don't like this idea?" she questioned. "What if I refuse?"

Sierra rolled her eyes. "Then we stand here and argue until the people decide to take matters into their own hands."

"Don't pretend you don't know the civility of our peoples is hanging by a thread, N'ara," Malachi intervened. "A thread that was already frayed, and now barely a strand of that remains."

N'ara nodded absentmindedly. Sierra guessed the Queen of the Underground knew the solution was the best way forward but didn't want to show weakness.

N'ara sat back on her throne, resting an elbow on its arm and her chin on her hand. The chair had been made from pieces of ancient relics. The parts reminded Sierra of Wil's collection of trinkets—treasures he had stashed away from the old world. It had mostly contained buttons, coins, and various odds and ends. He had brought them to school only once that she knew of, but they had made the adult instructors at the school anxious. Maybe that should have been a clue something was wrong, but as a child, it had been easy to overlook small warnings and clues as part of the norm.

N'ara hadn't moved and was still staring at them, seemingly pondering. Though it unnerved her, Sierra had to admit it was better than the nonstop arguing.

The silence highlighted the constant dripping of water in the recesses of the room, which seemed to get louder with each passing moment. It grated on Sierra's nerves, though she tried her best to keep her irritation at bay.

"All right," N'ara said, finally breaking the silence. "I'll consider this plan—for now. But if I think you can weight Leo's choices in your favor, I'll pull my support on the whole endeavor."

"Understood," Malachi answered. "I recommend we try to meet tomorrow morning. We've already let things go on for too long. Let's show the people we're at least moving forward."

The three of them were startled as the room's main door swung open, slamming against the wall, and an overweight, sweaty man burst into the room. His shirt was untucked, and the excessive perspiration streaming down his face had also stained his clothes.

There were few people Sierra had seen in the city who looked to have had more than enough to eat. This guard was the exception.

As he entered the room, he doubled over, struggling to catch his breath. He had sufficiently gained the attention of all eyes in the room. He gasped for air, as if he had run up several flights of stairs instead of down them.

"Sorry . . . for the . . . intrusion . . ."

"What is this about?" N'ara questioned, obviously irritated.

"One of the scouts has . . . *huff* . . . returned from the compound," the guard replied.

Sierra perked up. Rhys had been with the scouting party. The Sphere was a day's journey away, and they had been gone for nearly a week.

"Only one?" Malachi asked, his brow furrowed with concern.

"Yes, sir," the man wheezed.

"Don't *sir* me," Malachi replied. "What of the others?"

"He is reporting that none of the other scouts survived. He was barely able to escape with his life himself. He's in the infirmary with the Healers now."

Rhys!

Sierra pushed past the sweaty man, all but sprinting for the exit.

"Sierra! Wait!" Malachi shouted behind her, but she ignored him.

She and Rhys hadn't gotten off on the best foot. He had believed his mother had left him to seek the comforts of the Sphere and had held a grudge against its inhabitants ever since. Rhys's mother Greata had been Sierra's best friend. Sierra still had a hard time resolving that the same woman she knew and loved would have abandoned her family to live a comfortable life, whether by her own choice or not.

Sierra gripped the medallion that hung around her neck. The size of her palm and nearly half an inch thick, its imagery of a sun and waves was still a mystery to her, but it was the last gift she had received from her friend before the Guardians murdered her. Before they forced Sierra out of the Sphere and into this world.

Despite their rocky start, Sierra had warmed to Rhys, and vice versa. They had shared a kiss they never got to follow up on, and when they had last parted ways, Rhys had come to her defense, standing in the way of an Order member named Elana and a group of Guardians that had pursued them. Pursued *her*.

But by the time Sierra had woken from her coma, Rhys had already been gone for two days. She was told he had joined the scouting party, which had been sent to assess the number of those in the Sphere who would need help after its fall. Her former neighbors who, for the first time, would learn the world around them was inhabitable. It was the hope of Malachi and the rest of the Community that they could help those who would be lost in a world without their technology or their Guardians.

It had surprised Sierra that Rhys had chosen to be on the scouting mission. He had made it clear that he wanted nothing to do with the Sphere. In fact, Sierra clearly remembered him calling those who lived there lazy and soft.

They hadn't even had time to discuss how they felt about each other.

Maybe that's why he left.

She worried that she might never know; that it might be too late. Rhys could be dead. She had to find out.

Her mind raced along with her footsteps. Dodging those who continued to do what little they could to put the city's structures back together, her heart ached as she pushed herself, both physically and emotionally. Sierra was still not used to running. Her legs had finally begun to feel relief after days of trekking through the desert. After fleeing the Sphere, it had been a blessing to rest for the past week. She would pay for pushing them to their limits again, but she didn't care. She had to get to the infirmary.

Only a few blocks away lay the Rio Grande Inn. It had been the first stop she and Wil had made when they'd arrived in the city with Malachi and the other members of the Community.

She eased her pace only slightly as she approached the

entrance. A man she didn't recognize was waiting at the door, blocking her way. The man's pale eyes studied her; they had no color whatsoever. The irises lacked pigment, his pupils sitting in a sea of white, narrow and dull. The man's dark robe was covered in deep blue patterns that circled the hood, the sleeves and the hem. His face was as pale as a resident of the Underground, but he stood out in the harsh daylight without the protection of either sunglasses or his hood. His robes reminded Sierra of those of the Order, the cult that chose to follow the Guardians, although the pattern was unlike any she had seen.

"Are you the girl they speak of?" His voice was scratchy, as if his throat were as dry as the desert surrounding them. "Are you the one that took down the Guardians?"

"I suppose I am," Sierra answered, hesitant. There was something about the way the man had phrased the question that told her he wouldn't be offering his congratulations.

The man's eyes flitted back and forth, as if unable to focus, and his hand trembled.

"Who's asking?" Sierra inquired.

The man surged toward Sienna, the glaring intensity in the whites of his eyes striking her too as she felt a searing pain in her stomach.

Sierra looked down in horror—and saw the knife embedded in her gut.

2

———

BLOOD FLOWED over Sierra's hands. She cradled the hilt of the knife protruding from her belly, unable to process what had happened to her, and unsure if she should pull it out or not, she froze.

Her attacker had already retreated down the street.

Sierra's vision waned, and a chill coursed through her. Several people rushed to her side, but through the dizziness, she couldn't make out who they were.

Terre Hoffman was the one figure she recognized, and he appeared out of nowhere. He wasted no time in chasing after the assailant. Despite Terre being over two hundred years old, there was no contest. The stranger didn't get far before he was tackled to the ground.

Sierra was reeling, but she couldn't bring herself to look away from the brawl occurring on her behalf. Terre didn't hold back, slamming the attacker's head against the ground, and the man answered with a swift punch to Terre's face, causing his head to fly back. Terre stumbled and lost his grip.

Once again, the man tried to flee, but he only made it another hundred yards before being set upon by two guards who had joined the pursuit. The two muscular men each grabbed an arm and lifted the perpetrator off the ground as though he were weightless.

Sierra fought against her clouding vision, but it was to no avail. Hands prodded her where the knife met her flesh. Her black shirt had been torn, revealing the wound and the bright red blood flowing over her white skin. Sounds of consolation around her faded into faint murmurs, the words incomprehensible.

The dull ache in her gut worsened in its protest. Each beat of her heart threatened to explode through the wound as Sierra looked at her blood-stained hands and tried to comprehend the events that had just transpired.

She realized this could be her end. Cold metal had torn a hole in her abdomen, and she had no guarantee those around her could reverse the action. Strong hands set her down on the concrete as calls for help broke through her consciousness.

Above those cries, a gut-wrenching, inhuman call broke through her haze. "Demon child!" yelled the man who had stabbed her.

Sierra struggled through the fog of her consciousness, only vaguely aware of the man being carried away by the same guards that had tackled him.

"You've been damned to repeat the sins of the ancients!" he continued. "Sins which cannot be forgiven." His ranting continued as he disappeared down the road.

Terre was suddenly by her side, along with a woman she didn't know. The two were deep in a conversation Sierra could only hear fragments of.

"She's losing blood. We need to get that dagger out of her!" Terre said, the frustration evident in his voice.

"We're working on it," someone replied. "But if we just pull it out, we could make the damage worse."

"Who was that man?" Sierra asked, the world spinning around her.

"Don't worry about that now," Terre replied, his dark eyes filled with concern. "Do you think you'll be able to stand if we help you?"

Sierra didn't get a chance to answer: the pair hoisted her up. Her stomach burned, but a chill overtook the rest of her. She held on to those on either side of her as the world spun.

Who was that man? What were the sins of the ancients? Who wouldn't forgive her?

Her eyes fought to close. She continued to move, more with the help of others than of her own strength. She barely felt her feet touching the ground as everything else around her continued to spin. The two blocks to the Inn had never seemed further away.

Although the Rio Grande Inn had fared quite well during the Guardians' attack on the city, the main foyer had been completely destroyed. As a result, the pub had become the main entrance to the building. It still amazed Sierra that the hotel had received as minimal damage as it had; there was so little in the city that now remained in one piece. As she passed through the entranceway, the noise of the pub surrounded her; an assault of sound she was unable to comprehend.

"What are you doing bringing her here? Get her to the MedCenter!" A voice that sounded a lot like Leo's cut through the noise. Then she was moving again.

Bile rose in her mouth, and Sierra feared she would vomit. Flashes of pain gripped her as she was half carried down the hall.

The room they entered was bright, and she closed her eyes against its glare. She nearly smiled as she did so; it gave her the sensation of floating. Someone grabbed her legs, and before she knew it, she was lying on a table.

Sierra could feel the blade within her; the cold steel against her burning hot flesh.

Someone cut away the remnants of her shirt.

Her hands, now resting on the table, were wet.

Was that blood?

She gasped. Her body temperature oscillated between burning heat and ice cold. She shivered uncontrollably.

Panicked voices continued all around her.

She didn't want to die. Not like this.

An unknown person held her arms to the table, and she couldn't move her legs either. Breathing deeply, she tried not to panic.

Pain struck anew, jagged in the pit of her stomach. She gasped and tried to sit up, clarity striking her in waves as she struggled to see those around her. Someone pushed her back down on the table and her head hit a pillow, but it wasn't thick enough to provide complete protection from the metal underneath. A powerful hand on her bare shoulder held her down.

A woman Sierra didn't recognize stood above her, pressing down gently on her stomach. Two other women worked to sew up the wound to her midsection. The knife lay on a nearby table, dripping with blood.

My blood.

The woman, wearing what had once been a yellow dress, rubbed a wet cloth on her wound, and the resultant stinging caused Sierra to convulse involuntarily. Terre's grip on her strengthened.

"Sorry!" said the woman with the cloth. "This may sting now, but it will help prevent infection. You're lucky; I don't think the knife hit anything vital. But it won't matter if the wound gets infected."

Sierra tried to grip the table for support, but her hands had been bound.

"You're going to be okay," Terre said comfortingly.

Her gut burned furiously. It sure didn't feel like she'd be okay.

"Who was that guy? Why would he want to stab me?" Sierra could hear her own voice, ragged and hoarse.

"Now's not the time," Terre replied.

Her mind burned as hot as her stomach. "Tell me!" she barked through the pain.

Terre's eyes went wide, and he sighed, unable to mask his annoyance. "He was of the Order." he said, leaving the statement to hang as though it explained anything at all.

"I don't understand . . . We saved the city." Sierra winced as the women lifted her midsection to finish bandaging it. "Why would they want to kill me for it?"

Terre nodded at the other women as he let go of Sierra's shoulders, and the remaining attendants gently cleaned the blood off of her and the table.

"Everything the bots told you in the Sphere," Terre began. "How they saved humanity and kept it safe after the wars. The Order believes it. Despite them knowing the Sphere is an illusion, the Order believes the Guardians are protecting the greater good. To them, the bots are gods. They are waiting for the time when the Guardians will take their rightful place as rulers of the world. You initiating that EMP blast has halted their ascendance. They won't take that lightly."

Sierra sighed as she closed her eyes again. Elana, one of the members of the Order, had led a group of Sentinels against them, in an attempt to prevent them from launching the EMP. To prevent them from saving Vegas.

As if it weren't enough they had to deal with the looters, the bandits, and those trying to kill each other over parts of the downed units—and never mind the remaining Guardians circling the new Silent Zone, now aware of the city's presence— there were now crazy cultists trying to stab them. Well, stab *her*, anyway.

Sierra's blood now covered the woman in the yellow dress, who unbound Sierra's arms from the table and helped her to sit up, providing her with additional stability. Another woman, short and about the same age as Sierra, brought her a cup of water. Sierra drank greedily and was offered another when she finished it.

"You're going to need a lot of water," the woman in the yellow dress said. Her blue eyes sparkled as she gave Sierra the second glass. "This injury will take its toll on your body. You'll need fluids and rest if you are to recover."

Sierra sighed. "For how long?"

"Preferably a couple of weeks."

A couple of weeks? So much time had been wasted already.

Rhys.

"What happened at the Sphere?" Sierra croaked, her mouth bone dry despite the two glasses of water she had just swallowed. "Is Rhys okay?"

"Rhys will be fine," Terre answered. "He's here, but he needs to rest as well. No more questions."

Her heart leapt. *Rhys is here? He must have been the scout who made it back alive.*

She had already lost too many friends, and losing Rhys would have been especially devastating.

The excitement caused the pain in her gut to flare, muting the thrill of her friend's survival. She lay back down in an effort to allow the pain to subside.

"What of the people of the Sphere?" Sierra asked. Her mother was still there. The scouting party was supposed to have brought her back, along with the remaining residents.

"I haven't received enough details yet," Terre answered. "But there's nothing you can do for anyone right now except rest and recover."

The door to the room opened, and a younger man poked his head inside. "Ancient One," the man said, addressing Terre.

"Call me Terre, please." He rolled his eyes as he protested half-heartedly. No matter how much he pushed against the nickname, he couldn't shake it. A living legend, Terre earned the amazement of all who had heard his story. Which was likely everyone in the city by now.

"Ancient One," the man continued, completely ignoring Terre's request. "Malachi and Leo would like to speak with you. They said it's urgent."

"What about me?" Sierra asked.

"You rest," Terre cautioned. He nodded to the messenger and followed him out.

Sierra let out a frustrated sigh. She was tired of being confined to a bed. The effort she had exuded by firing up the EMP had knocked her out for nearly a week, and she had only regained consciousness for a few days before finding herself once again incapacitated.

She also resented being left out of the discussion. The people of the Sphere were her kin, and she felt at least partially responsible for the new reality they were being forced to face.

When the pain had subsided once again, Sierra took a step onto the tiled floor, her bare feet connecting with its cool surface. Still uneasy, she leaned against the table to gain her balance. The woman in the yellow dress seized the opportunity to wipe the blood off Sierra's back. Sierra was then handed a fresh shirt, which she pulled over her head.

The woman held onto her with a stark white arm; Althea's skin was not quite as pale as those in the Underground and was decorated with freckles.

"Thank you all for your kindness and help," Sierra said. Her mind was clearing, and gratitude toward her medics filled her.

"You're welcome," the woman said. "But we are the ones who that should thank you. Without you, none of us would have survived the bots' attack."

"Hey now, that's not necessary." Sierra put her hands up in protest, despite the twinge of pain she felt at the sudden movement. "I was just lucky."

"No, you have done great things for us. The bots haven't seen a defeat like that since the wars. I want you to know how grateful we all are."

"Trust me," Sierra answered, trying her best not to roll her eyes. "Nobody will let me forget."

She hadn't been expecting the celebrity status invoked by activating the ancient device. For reasons still unknown to her, Sierra had been gifted with visions of the past and a means to help, so she had seized the opportunity. For that, she had been nothing more than lucky.

For the first time, Sierra gazed around the medical room. Oversized picture windows opened the room up to receive natural light, likely providing the brightness needed to perform delicate tasks like slicing someone open. Unlit torches decorated the walls. Once the sun went down, their light would do the job if needed.

How many bodies had these women had to stitch up after the attack?

"What's your name?" she asked the woman.

"My name? I'm Althea."

"Have you lived in the city your entire life?"

She shook her head. "I believe you know Ella Torres. My story is much like hers."

Sierra nodded, raising an eyebrow. She had been wary of the woman, a member of Malachi's Community who had taken a fancy to Wil. Something about her had rubbed Sierra the wrong way.

"Malachi freed you?" she asked.

"Yes." Pain reflected in Althea's blue eyes. "Ella and I both grew up in the Sphere outside of San Francisco. It's hard to tell now, but we were best friends. We were both kidnapped, meant to be sold. We never understood why we were taken away from San Francisco; we would have fetched a higher price out there. But there isn't a day that goes by that I'm not thankful we weren't. After Malachi rescued us, we were free to pursue our own passions. Ella is a leader; always has been. It's no wonder she became Malachi's right-hand woman. I wanted to help others. Since I was a little girl, healing was all I've ever wanted to do. I'd take in wounded birds and help them to fly again. Now I help injured people."

"Well, thank you." Sierra stepped away from the metal table, but when her balance wavered, she had to grab on to Althea's shoulder for support. "I'm still a little shaky, it seems."

Though she felt weak, Sierra was surprised at how little pain she felt. The area was warm and sore, but she felt able to move more than she had even a few minutes ago.

"Just don't overdo it," Althea cautioned. "We've done what we can for you, but you'll still need to rest."

Rest could wait; she really wanted to know what urgent news had pulled Terre away from her bedside. With a new energy, Sierra stepped out into the hallway—just as dizziness overtook her, and she collapsed.

3

————

THREE DAYS LATER, Sierra was finally able to get out of bed.

She recalled little of anything after her conversation with Althea, other than bursts of tossing and turning in her bed, her Keeper, Ember, at her side. As Sierra learned of her situation, she cursed. More days had been lost while she lay incapacitated, and she was still unaware of what had occurred at the Sphere.

Rhys lay in a bed across the room from her. Despite Terre's assurances that Rhys would be okay, he had barely hung onto the edge of survival. In the Sphere, computers and datapads would have monitored the boy's vital signs, checking numbers and stats to ensure they knew how best to address his condition. Here, the medical staff crudely monitored his temperature and tried to keep him warm or cool depending on the time of day. Other than dressing and cleaning his wounds, there wasn't much else they could do.

Ember had told Sierra that Rhys was stable, though.

At least he had survived, but it didn't feel like that was enough. Rhys had been the first person to look at her the way he had. The first guy she had danced with. The first she had kissed. The first she felt truly connected to.

It was strange; he was someone she had known for such a short amount of time, but Sierra knew she wanted to be with him. She wanted to spend time with him and longed to be next to him.

It was frustrating that, for the first time in her life, there was someone she'd be willing to have a relationship with, but for three quarters of the time they had known one another, at least one of them had been unconscious.

Did Rhys hold the same feelings toward her, or had the kiss simply been an impulsive move before heading into a deadly situation? They hadn't had time to explore the possibilities.

She sighed as she considered how close she'd come to nearly losing him. They had very nearly missed their chance.

Sierra tried to rise, unsure of what her body could handle, testing her limits. Some of the injured in the facility groaned in their sleep. The putrid smell of blood and death struck her nostrils. If she had anything in her stomach to retch, she likely would have done so. She struggled not to dry heave, but bile rose in her throat before she gained control of her senses.

The concrete floor was cold, and she prayed she wouldn't pass out again as she tried to stand.

"Easy now, Sierra!" Ember called out cautiously as she entered the room.

"I feel better," she responded. "And I'd like to see if I can find Althea to get this dressing changed."

There were thousands of questions swirling around in her head, but she felt as dirty as the city, and she was sick of her own filth.

Although there were probably many people who could rework her dressing, Sierra wouldn't mind finding the woman who had helped her the other night. She had liked Althea and appreciated the common link they shared from growing up in a Sphere, and Sierra was keen to learn more about her and other

Spheres and what they were like. That way, perhaps she would find more clues about the world she had left behind.

"You are moving well, considering your injury." Ember's orange eyes glowed in the shadows of the room; her head cocked to one side, as if studying her.

"Well, I did sleep for three days."

Sierra smiled at her Keeper. She still marveled at how lifelike the robot's skin appeared, despite its bone-white color. Her qualities were soft and approachable. Until they had left the Sphere, Ember was the only humanoid Guardian Sierra had ever encountered. The Sentinels had changed that.

"You received a significant injury," Ember continued. "Are you certain you are not still in pain?"

Sierra straightened up and twisted slightly. There was a tightness in her stomach and a bit of an ache where the knife had struck, but otherwise she felt okay.

She shrugged. "Maybe it wasn't as serious as we thought."

Ember pursed her lips and frowned. "That's not what your vitals indicated when you were brought in. You were fortunate."

"Well, I'd still like to get cleaned up. Althea can assess my progress."

"Sometimes I wish you had access to the MedBots, Sierra."

Sierra paused and furrowed her brow. That was the first time she had heard Ember make reference to other Guardians since she had disconnected herself from their network.

"What's that supposed to mean?" Sierra asked.

"Their analysis is much more in-depth than that which humans can perform."

Sierra raised a questioning eyebrow. Yes, the Guardians did have better equipment, but they had also tried to kill her. They'd killed her friends, Greata and Ed, and they'd tried to take out Terre and Rhys as well. Not to mention destroying most of the city, now left in shambles in the wake of their attack.

Was the Keeper having doubts about that action?

"Those bots wanted us dead, Ember."

"The other Guardians have no understanding of the programming they follow, Sierra. MedBots were built to heal and evaluate human medical conditions. There is no grand ill intent behind them."

"And what of Titan? He's out to kill me!"

"I was not speaking of Titan. But we will speak more on that later. Please ensure your wound is attended to."

Shadow covered the room as a cloud passed in front of the sun. Ember's orange eyes and light panels provided the room with an eerie glow to compensate.

"Sure, I'll go talk to my lowly human healer. I hope she doesn't decide to shoot me if she doesn't find me of value."

Sierra stormed out of the room, albeit slowly on account of her legs still shaking. She gave the door a good shove behind her, letting it slam back.

The residents of Vegas had managed just fine for the past two hundred years.

In the desert, before the attack on the city, Ember had disconnected herself from the Guardian network out of self-preservation. If she hadn't, they would have tracked her down, reprogrammed her, or dismantled her altogether.

No ill intent indeed.

At the time, Ember had questioned the Guardians' decision to destroy thousands of humans within the City of Vegas. Because of those questions they determined there was a flaw in her programming. A flaw Ember and Sierra had later realized to be sentience. The ability to think for herself, to feel and express emotion. It shouldn't have been possible. But it was a change Sierra had miraculously birthed in her friend. Had enabled Ember to think as a fully conscious being.

As far as Sierra could tell, it was the same power that had

enabled her to set off the EMP, enabling her to stop the Guardians that had launched an assault on Vegas.

The MedStation was situated on the ground floor of the Rio Grande. It had initially been set up underground in the hopes that damage from the Guardian invasion would be kept to a minimum, and they had been lucky. While many of the Underground residences had either collapsed or been exposed, the Inn's basement had remained mostly intact. Its concrete walls had provided the entire building with stability, and a lot of luck had prevented the building from being struck directly. The infirmary had since been moved to the ground floor after the attack to make it easier to carry the bodies in and out.

Sierra worked her way down the stairwell, passing several attendants and guests moving back and forth throughout the Inn, before arriving at the makeshift medical room.

The room was expansive, but still barely contained the hundreds who had been injured in the assault. And this was only one room of many in use. With the amount of damage the rest of the city had suffered, the Inn was full.

Leo had been more than generous in accommodating as many survivors as he could. A few other buildings had also been set up as temporary shelters. In addition, overflow housing had been established in rudimentary tents along the side streets of the city. The damage across Vegas was so extensive that residents were being held in almost every room and space still standing.

"Sierra! What are you doing up and about? You should be resting!" Althea's short, bright red hair bobbed as she approached Sierra and put an arm around her waist, as if worried Sierra would topple over under her own weight.

Sierra moved Althea's hand off her back, turning herself around to face the woman who had treated her.

"I'm okay," she said, lifting a hand in the air as she steadied herself with the other. "I'm fine. A little shaky, but nothing to worry about. I just need my dressing changed. It's kind of gross."

"All right." Althea nodded nervously, seemingly unconvinced.

Sierra pushed herself onto the table and removed her shirt. The healer grabbed a pair of scissors and gently cut the dressing, and Sierra lifted her arms in the air to make the task easier for her. She could feel the pull on her skin where her attacker's blade had gone in and her stomach muscles were sore, but the wound was no longer painful.

Althea gasped, causing Sierra to jump slightly. Sierra worried the woman had accidentally nicked her with the scissors. She hadn't felt a cut, but she instinctively looked down to assess the damage. It was hard to tell how bad the injury was with all the dried blood caked on her stomach, but Althea wiped it clean with a wet towel.

Sierra watched as the healer's eyes grew wide and her mouth fell agape. She glanced down again and ran her hand across her belly. Although moist from the cloth, her midriff was completely smooth. There was no damage, not even a scar.

"Wait, what's happening? Why is there no mark?" She twisted and turned, trying to get a better look.

The bandages lay on the floor beside her, brown with old blood, as proof the wound had been real.

Althea stood, pale as a Sentinel, and stepped backwards, her eyes on Sierra's stomach. She shook her head, mouthing as if desperately wanting to say something but unable to find the words.

"Althea?" Sierra asked. "What's wrong?"

Althea shook her head, her eyes fixated on where the wound should have been.

Sierra pushed herself off the table and reached out a hand to the healer's shoulder, hoping to snap her out of her shocked state. Instead, Althea's hands went to her face, and she ran out of the room in tears, leaving Sierra standing there, confused.

What just happened?

Sierra glanced around the infirmary. No other healers were

present in the room, and the patients who lay on the few remaining beds weren't in good enough shape to have witnessed the bizarre exchange.

She put her shirt back on, wishing she had brought a clean one. The putrid stench clinging to the fabric made her eyes water. Clearly she could also have used a bath.

Sierra wandered into the hall. The sound of nearby sobbing informed her she didn't have far to go. Althea sat on the floor, her arms on her knees, her head resting on her arms.

"What's going on?" Sierra asked.

"Why now? Why *you*?"

Sierra sat next to her, her back against the wall. "What's going on? Maybe there's something I can do."

Althea's words were muffled as she spoke. "No, there's nothing you can do."

"You need to help me understand. Why don't I have a scar?"

Althea let out a sniff and rubbed her eyes. "I told you I escaped the Sphere with Ella," she said, her gaze still focused on the floor in front of her. "I'm guessing that since she didn't tell you about me, she also didn't tell you what happened that day."

Sierra shook her head. "I barely know her. Ella didn't even tell me she lived in a Sphere. I found out from Rhys."

Althea looked at her, her eyes red. "We came across a man lying in the street, just outside the Core. The man had been severely burned. He was bleeding, his shoulder seared, and he mumbled something about the Guardians and the Outside. Ella happened to have some water with her. I had just written my LPE's, and although I had yet to be placed, I had already been assigned duties at the MedStations."

Sierra remembered her own Life Placement Exam vividly; she had written hers the day she had been forced to flee the Sphere as well, but she allowed Althea to continue uninterrupted.

"It had only been a few weeks, but I had already seen some strange injuries. They taught us not to question what we saw.

Our task was to heal the injured, nothing more. The man was in such bad shape that I wondered how his state of health hadn't triggered a wellness detector. Orbs should have been surrounding him, bringing him help. I could tell he wasn't going to make it. His burn was so fresh, it was still warm. He mumbled something about the Guardians having shot him, and Ella and I looked at each other in disbelief.

'The trees,' he kept saying. 'They lied to us. I saw the trees.'

"It was strange, but he had lost a lot of blood and it's not uncommon for someone dying to hallucinate.

"As we treated the burn, we noticed he was holding something green. We pulled it out of his hand just to get it out of the way, and it was then we saw that it was a handful of leaves. Luscious green leaves.

"We realized there was something more to what he was saying than a mere hallucination, even though we didn't fully understand what it meant. You know what it's like in the Sphere, Sierra. The signs pointed to a scenario far beyond what we could comprehend. But we knew we shouldn't be found there with him."

"We pulled him away from the road and found what looked to be an abandoned shack. Something you'd never come across in the Sphere. Once we were inside, we realized this man had been staying in the building. There was a bed, and a kitchen. It was well lived in. We cleaned him up the best we could, but his shoulder was badly scorched. I didn't think he'd ever be able to use it again. His face had been burned as well; severe enough that it should have been horribly scarred. We were pretty sure the man wouldn't make it through the night, but we couldn't take him to the MedStations as he'd claimed the Guardians had caused his wounds. It seemed unbelievable to us, but somehow we knew there was truth to it from the extent of the damage and the way he was talking."

Sierra nodded, mesmerized by the woman's story. Althea

paused briefly as another healer walked by. Embarrassed to be interrupting their conversation as he passed, he quickened his pace. Once he had disappeared, Althea continued.

"Well, this was one of those times Ella and I just knew something was out of line. We knew the man wasn't making it up, and we had to keep him hidden. We agreed to take shifts to watch over him. Ella went home that night; the LPEs had designated her to work at the Core for which she needed to prepare. I stayed with him, keeping him hydrated. I just wanted to make sure someone would be there with him.

"He murmured in his sleep. I didn't understand half of what he was talking about—not back then, at least—but I knew he had seen things that weren't supposed to exist. At one point, I heard him mention a path to the Outside. He explained precisely where it was, and even though I didn't understand how it could be possible, I made a mental note of it."

Althea took a deep breath. The tears had stopped, but her eyes were distant.

"The next day," she continued, "Ella took over, and I went to the MedStation for my shift. I stole some antiseptic and antibiotics that I thought would help stave off infection. I risked being interrogated, or worse, but the secrets the man held were too incredible to ignore.

"I was in for the shock of my life when I got to the tent to find him sitting up and chatting with Ella. His arm had completely healed, and his face was young and beautiful. There was no trace of burn marks, and the scar tissue was gone.

"We couldn't explain it. Something had happened overnight while I was dressing his wounds. I had felt a fiery sensation come from within me, and I knew his miraculous recovery was something I had caused."

"That sounds like when my power activates," Sierra said. "Then it bursts from my body like I can't contain it."

"I didn't want to believe it," Althea replied. "I didn't want to be different."

"Your hesitation is understandable. The Order and the Guardians have always discouraged anything 'different'. Tell me what happened next."

"The man was eager to share what he had discovered but was vague on so many other things. He implied I had somehow been part of a program; that whatever had been done to me had allowed me to heal him. But he left suddenly, before he could elaborate. Ella and I came to a crisis of faith over the coming days, and that's when we decided to follow the directions he'd murmured in his sleep. To see for ourselves."

Sierra sat in awe. The story of the Sphere, the crisis of faith—it all brought her back. She couldn't believe she had only left the Sphere a matter of weeks ago. It felt like a lifetime.

"So, you discovered you have the power to heal? I'm guessing that's what happened to me? It sounds like a wonderful gift. Why did you run out of the room?"

Althea shook her head and looked Sierra in the eye. "The only time it happened was years ago. I have doubted it ever had anything to do with me. There was no reason for me to believe there was anything within me to possess that ability, as I could never repeat the result. Then you come down here without a scratch and it all came flooding back, and I knew it was real. But I still don't want to believe it."

"I don't understand why this is a bad thing?"

Althea looked at her, finally composed, her eyes intense. "That day, my entire life changed. I've grown comfortable in my role here with the Community. I'm needed. I can contribute."

"You're not making sense. You can still contribute. Maybe if you can learn how to harness this gift, you can contribute even more so."

Althea laughed nervously, shaking her head again. "No, Sierra.

I can't. Everything is about to change. I can feel it, just as I felt it that day when I knew there was something out of place. I'm meant to join you. I don't know what your plan is, but I'm a part of it. I can feel it in my bones."

And as Althea spoke the words, Sierra knew she was right.

4

———

THE HEAT of the day permeated the Inn. Sierra missed the relief of temperature-controlled buildings. It wasn't just the heat inside she had to get used to, though. As Sierra stepped outside, the intensity of the bright midsummer sun struck her. The air was dry, but her sweaty T-shirt stuck to her skin, leaving her damp and uncomfortable. The morning air had only just warmed up, but she could tell the afternoon heat was going to be near unbearable. If the barrier of the Sphere and the fake toxic cloud surrounding it provided anything, it was a reprieve from the desert sun.

Besides the heat, the intensity of Althea's story, which so closely mirrored her own, was also making Sierra sweat. Like herself, Althea had been a woman who'd lived her entire life entrenched in one reality, only to have it suddenly ripped away. A woman who had been forced to realize the entire world around her had been a lie. How many more like her were out there?

At least Althea had continued her work, healing others. The career path the young woman had set out on hadn't altered. Whether or not her circumstances had been a lie, Althea's healing talents had remained a constant.

But what did Sierra have? Ember, her only connection to the Sphere, seemed to be reminiscing about MedBots and the days she had spent connected to the network. The Keeper had been acting strangely ever since they had arrived in Vegas.

Only then, under the harsh glare of the sun, did it strike Sierra that she hadn't discovered the results of her Life Placement Exam the day she'd left, or where she would have been assigned. She had always assumed it would be the Core, though she supposed it never really mattered.

As strange as it was to consider, Sierra didn't even know what her parents had done there. She knew they worked in genetics, but what that entailed was nothing she was privy to. Her mom didn't like to talk about work, and she was too young to remember any detail her father had ever shared, if any.

It was odd that she'd never put much thought into it before. Working at the Core, to her, had always been an inevitable end; a rite of passage, growing up and fulfilling her role in society. There were many aspects of the Sphere that were taken care of there, ranging from genetics to maintaining the force field to the MedStations and probably many tasks she hadn't known existed.

And now what was she to do? The Sphere was down. Who knew what had become of her mother, and her friends were dealing with their own demons.

The medallion that hung against her chest—the last heirloom of her friend Greata—provided some semblance of cool relief against her skin. Rhys had hinted that he knew more of its origin, but with Sierra having had so little time to chat openly with him, he had thus far kept his secrets to himself.

Terre would likely know its story, as well, but as cryptic as the man was, she was doubtful an attempt at getting more details from him would be successful. If it hadn't been Greata's dying wish for Sierra to find him, she guessed Terre would have left long ago.

The noises of the city that greeted her as she stepped out onto the street seemed to be livelier this morning than they had in days prior. People were gathered along the sides of the street, laughing and talking. The skeptical air seemed to have lifted from their faces; joy had replaced stress, and a fresh energy filled them. Whatever the reason, Sierra welcomed the shift after the fighting, hostility and anger that had been building.

The sound of merriment grew as, unsure of where she would find Malachi or Terre at this time of day, she made her way into the heart of the city.

Among the scattered ruins of an old enormous hotel stood stands of fruit, vegetables, and other foods. Someone had decorated a large square with colorful banners. Flags and decorations lined the sides of the crumbled building, a glimmer of new life in a ruined city. Jugglers and dancers performed in the central square while both children and adults clapped and danced alongside them.

The transformation was astounding. Back home, they would have festivals of sorts, but this seemed natural and spontaneous, and it seemed like everyone was getting in on the action. It reminded Sierra of the spirit she'd found in the Inn on the day she had arrived in Vegas with Malachi, but on a much grander scale.

Those who had lived in the Underground donned sunglasses and coverings to protect their delicate skin from the sun, but they could still be found dancing right alongside those who typically spent their days on the surface.

Several of the orbs lay nearby, still lodged in the ground amid the now-derelict buildings. Guards still stood at their side, ready for would-be looters, but instead of suspicion, they wore smiles, seemingly jovial to those who interacted with them.

Sierra could hardly believe what she was seeing. This scene would have been inconceivable merely two days ago.

She made her way through the crowd. Various vendors called out to her, offering her food from their stands. The bounty on display was more plentiful than anything close to what she had seen outside of the Sphere. She politely accepted an apple from one seller and rubbed it on her sleeve before taking a bite. It was crisp and sweet and much larger than the fruit she was typically allotted.

"Sierra!" Malachi's voice cut through the crowd, and she strained to find him within the sea of people.

"Malachi!" she replied, spotting his ponytail bobbing among the other heads. He was tall to begin with, so he appeared to be a giant next to those who had suffered malnourishment in the fringes of the Underground.

"What on earth has happened?" she shouted above the cacophony of noise. "What's going on?"

"The Council has proclaimed today a holiday." Malachi's face was as stoic as ever, but his green eyes betrayed a smile behind it.

There is hope there, Sierra thought. *Even if it is hesitant.*

"It's a celebration of our new leadership," he finished.

The sound of music continued from somewhere behind the vendors, toward the back of the square from a source Sierra couldn't see.

"These people were at each other's throats a few days ago," she observed. "They were about to tear each other apart."

"It's remarkable what *hope* can do," he said as he pointed toward the stands. "We've sent convoys out to bring in a bounty of food. It's perhaps a fragile hope, but we've reassured the people that tomorrow will be a brighter day than the ones that have gone before."

"Where did this come from? Supplies have been so scarce . . ."

"I suppose we have you to thank," Malachi answered. "Our scouts determined the new Silent Zone stretches out to the growing lands. We now have an unencumbered path most of the way. There's nothing to attack our merchants other than rogue bandits, and even they have been rather quiet."

"What of the Prowlers?"

"Those who couldn't be bribed into guarding the Onyx fled to other centers. They smelled no profit here. I don't think we'll have problems with them for weeks, maybe longer. Unless they grow desperate and try to take on the guards. But that is unlikely."

Several children filled their pockets with fruit from a nearby stand while others played between those who were dancing. Sierra couldn't remember seeing this many children on the streets of Vegas since they had arrived.

"Can we talk for a bit?" Sierra had to raise her voice above the growing intensity in the clapping and cheering of the crowd. "Somewhere a little quieter?"

Malachi looked back in the direction from which he came, as if he had left someone behind. Not seeming to find who he was looking for, he turned back to her and nodded, following her lead toward the street.

They traveled for a couple of blocks, but it was slow going. People packed the street. It wasn't shoulder-to-shoulder like it had been in the square, but the party had filed out onto the main boulevard. This road had once been known as the Las Vegas Strip.

In the vision Sierra had of this place, as it used to be, the streets had a hundred times as many people, bursting from buildings that were now barely shadows of their former selves. This place had been a city unlike anywhere she could possibly have imagined.

The surrounding mood was so upbeat that Vegas felt like a completely different place. Sierra hadn't realized how heavy it ordinarily felt. Without realizing it, she had become immune to the crushed souls that had haunted its streets and alleyways; the hollow eyes that had wandered around the Inn; the souls that had lost what little they had.

The upbeat atmosphere nearly mitigated the devastation still surrounding them. Members of the Community and the

Underground had done a good job of removing what rubble they could, but there was still much that was simply too big to be moved by hand. Fragments of the Onyx still sat lodged in the buildings on which they had fallen. Metal beams from ancient structures jutted into the sky, barely clinging to the concrete structures that once towered above the streets. They stood as a haunting reminder of the cost of the surrounding jubilation.

To be fair, the eyes of most of the populace had been empty before the attack. Food had been a scarce commodity in this place for a long time.

But in the three days she had been asleep, the city had transformed into a shinier version of itself.

Sierra crossed the street with Malachi and pulled into a side alley to get away from the hustle.

"You must be feeling better," Malachi proclaimed as they stopped, as if only just realizing she had been unconscious. "I am surprised, though. I thought Terre had mentioned you would be bedridden for two weeks."

"I've had an exceptional healer working on me," she said, not wanting to get into the finer details of her experience. "I'm feeling better than ever."

Skepticism marked his face, but he carried on. "Does your healer know you're wandering the streets?"

"Althea gave me the okay to be up and about. I'm a bit sore, but I'll live."

Malachi was silent for a few moments, but his shoulders eased and his face relaxed. "Good," he continued. "We've missed your presence these past few days."

A smile crept over his face. Despite his skepticism, she couldn't remember Malachi's mood being this good since she had met him. Plagued by one calamity or another, this was as much of a needed break for him as it was for the rest of the city. Maybe even more so.

She hated to be the one to bring that mood down.

"What have you learned about the man who stabbed me?" she asked. She was happy the city had found a piece of its old soul, but there was still someone out there who wished to see her dead.

The smile left Malachi's face as he shook his head and sighed. "We know he's a member of the Order. We can only guess they aren't happy about you destroying the Guardians that attacked the city, but other than that, we're not sure."

"Are your men still questioning him?" she asked.

Malachi crossed his arms and looked across the street to those enjoying the festivities, perhaps wishing he was among them again, instead of answering her questions.

"He got away."

Sierra raised an eyebrow, cocking her head in disbelief. "What do you mean, *'he got away?'*"

"We think he must have had help, likely from someone we trust. The guards didn't see anyone suspicious come or go, but when they went to check on him yesterday morning, his chains were on the ground."

So, one man wanted to kill her and at least one other within the city was sympathetic to the same cause. How nice it was to have saved the city, only to have a target painted on her back.

Sierra stared incredulously at Malachi, waiting for him to volunteer more. His green eyes locked upon her, offering no hint of what was to come.

"Do you have an idea of where he went? Does he walk among us?"

"We think he's fled the city, but we have no way of knowing for sure."

Partygoers walked the streets, clearly enjoying themselves. A few children had lifted multi-colored kites into the sky. For the moment at least, the city dwellers seemed to have forgotten how full of hardship the world around them truly was. All it had taken was a little assurance of food. Yet, among them was someone who wanted her dead.

"Are there others?" she asked. "Am I in danger?"

Malachi sighed again, crossing his arms and leaning back against the wall that lined the alley behind him. He clearly didn't want to tell her, and that was the only answer she needed.

"Not all who are members of the Order wear robes. There are many others who are sympathetic to their cause. There are some who will have issues with you for being Sphere-born."

Sierra groaned. Until she had left the Sphere, she hadn't realized people could be so at odds with one another. Part of her had hoped they could at least band together to build something better for themselves; that maybe with time, there would be a way.

All Sierra could do was hope the would-be assassin had fled the city, but it was likely this would not be the last she heard of him or the rest of the Order.

There was no point in dwelling on it; it was time to change the subject. "It appears assembling the Council was a positive step, at least," she said, nodding toward the crowd. "I didn't think I'd ever see a celebration like this in Vegas."

"Nor I," Malachi answered. "But like I said, it's fragile. Perhaps if this can help us build trust with each other . . ." He trailed off, as though he wasn't sure how to end the sentence. "Well, we have a long way to go."

A warm gust of wind lifted nearby kites higher into the sky, to the delight of the children holding the strings. They laughed as they ran with the wind, trying to see how much height their makeshift toys could get. The children were obviously from both the Underground and the Community. Sierra guessed some were from even further away, based on their clothing alone. They ran through the torn-up streets, as if oblivious the world around them had come tumbling down.

If they can unite, why can't the adults?

A subtle furrow on Malachi's brow indicated he had missed the example of the children playing. He surveyed the celebration with something else on his mind.

"You don't think it'll happen, do you?" she asked.

His eyes met hers, and she knew she had guessed correctly.

"Do you think N'ara's the type to share power and credit with the Council?" he replied.

"She seems to have worked to bring some good," Sierra answered, nodding toward the surrounding celebrations.

"I have known N'ara a long time. She won't plan on allowing the Council to carry on longer than it suits her. Greed is a jealous lover, and once you've let her into your house, it's hard to get her to leave."

Sierra wasn't sure if the comment should insult her or not, but she understood what Malachi was saying. "Surely she'll look at what we've achieved in such a short space of time and reconsider the way she's ruled?"

"Sierra, I love how innocent you still are to this world. I wish I could believe that, but N'ara won't look at any of this and see success. Her entire life, her quest has been for control. Someone who names themselves the Queen of Vegas won't relinquish her title easily."

Sierra thought back to her first encounter with N'ara and how the woman had betrayed a prior pact made with Malachi. He had no reason to trust her now.

"Besides," he said. "Even without N'ara, the people here have known nothing but suspicion and fear their entire lives."

"You've managed," Sierra answered.

"My road is one I hope no other will have to take."

Sierra nodded, staring into the heart of the city, past the revelers to the ruined buildings. Black orbs littered the streets and wreckage, their circuitry visible and valuable metals hanging from the more damaged of them. Malachi had told her there were enough riches in the fallen machines to build the city back to greatness. It could change the lives of everyone in the city forever. Not since the time of the ancients had man had so much access to this many of the black orbs. Not even close.

"Why go along with it, then?" she asked. "Why form an alliance with her at all?"

The corner of Malachi's mouth lifted in a subtle snicker. "A fool's hope."

"It's more than these people have had in a long time," Sierra replied.

"If nothing else," he continued, "this truce buys us some time. We need to figure out what other threats are out there now, and we can't waste our resources fighting among ourselves."

"What do you mean?"

Malachi looked away as his face darkened. "Rhys barely made it back. The Order killed the rest of the scouting party. They attacked them after rampaging the villages. There was nothing left. The Order burned it all to the ground."

Sierra stepped back, finding herself against the remnants of a brick wall. She leaned against it, at risk of falling over. She was afraid to ask, but she needed to. "What of the residents?"

Malachi shook his head. "Everyone they found was dead. They wouldn't have known what was coming."

The desert sun seemed to intensify as the world around Sierra spun.

"Is there a chance anyone escaped?"

"Rhys believes there are a few that remain captive under Guardian control. The blast didn't knock out their power station on the edge of the lake."

"Power station?"

"You know it as the Core."

"So, what we did was for nothing?" she asked.

"I wouldn't say it was for nothing. We have set the bots back; extended and secured the Silent Zone. We're definitely no worse off than before. The fallen machines give us a chance to restore this city. But the bots still have the power to rebuild their capabilities. It's only a matter of time."

Sierra's heart sank. Dizziness threatened to knock her over, reminding her she hadn't yet fully recovered from her injury.

All to buy strangers more time. More time for what? And at what cost?

Those from the Sphere were supposed to be here now, safe. Instead, they were dead. The scouting party was dead. The Guardians still had control over those left alive. Those in the city were still largely entrapped within the Silent Zone. And her mother . . .

Sierra hadn't thought of her mother much over the past two weeks. She had left the Sphere in anger, and she hadn't had time to dwell on that fact until the last few weeks, as she relived her experience over and over. She'd had a sense of hope, knowing the Community would bring her in.

She had left the Sphere believing her mother was safe. She hadn't worried about her, trusting that leaving was keeping her out of harm's way. Now that wall of protection had fallen. And it was her fault.

If there was a chance Sierra could help her, if she could make some small amount of right in this fiasco of a wrong she had created, she had to take it.

There were still people she cared about here—Rhys, for one. He was unconscious now, but Althea had convinced her he was on the mend. At least he would not die because of her, too. Not yet.

Sierra craved some sense of normalcy, but she wasn't even sure what that meant anymore; if normal was even real. Her entire life had been a fantasy.

Her thoughts drifted to Wil. Her friend had been bent on revenge. Maybe that was the answer? Maybe the only way to bring humanity together was to convince them they had a greater enemy. They had won a battle against those who had held them hostage. The immediate threat had been removed. Maybe all they needed to see was that the greater threat was still out there. Maybe they needed someone who could channel their frustrations at those who had been the cause of their suffering for two centuries.

But first, Sierra had to find out if her mother was still alive. She had to know. Even if her mother hadn't made it, there were others who could still use her help. Sierra had been the reason their homes had been removed from the Guardians' protection; the reason why the Order had decided to decimate them all.

She tried hard to push down her anxiety and the hopelessness she felt. Each breath was becoming an effort. What other choice was there? She had to do something to help, even if it meant putting herself in harm's way once again.

"I want to go to the Core. I need to know if my mother is still alive."

Malachi's face hardened. The man usually betrayed no emotion, but alarm now contrasted with the surrounding revelry.

"There's something else you should know," he said. "The Order member who attacked you was sent by Titan. He still wants you dead."

5

Titan.

Sierra only knew the Guardian by name. She had tackled a Sentinel when she had first left the Sphere, and from what she could tell, her power had transformed him, giving this robot the power to choose, as she had done for Ember. He had become self-aware; self-determined. But whereas Ember was dedicated to protecting Sierra, Titan seemed intent on killing her.

Through everything that had transpired over the past few days, Sierra had almost forgotten about him. *Almost.*

She hadn't linked the robed man to the rogue Guardian.

It wasn't enough to have been flung from her home; to have lost everything. It wasn't enough that the Guardians appeared determined to destroy humanity. For reasons she could not imagine, this particular machine was fixated on killing her.

Sierra inhaled deeply, allowing the warm desert air to fill her lungs. The mid-afternoon sun beat down as she surveyed the surrounding crowd. Those who had been used to the darkness of the Underground had covered themselves from head to toe, sunglasses masking their faces. Her attacker could be any of them. His accomplice—if there was only *one* of them—could be anyone.

At the thought of the attack, she put her hands to her stomach, reliving the trauma it had induced. "What is he after?" she asked.

"I don't know," Malachi replied. "But until we know more, Terre and I think it would be best if you stayed here, under our protection."

Their protection. She had taken down an entire Guardian army and survived a stab wound, and somehow they thought she needed *their protection?*

"My mom could still be alive, Malachi. If she is, I need to find her. I never intended for her to die, and definitely not by my hand."

"Getting yourself killed won't help anyone. We sent a half dozen scouts just to investigate, and only Rhys made it back alive. What makes you think you have a better shot? You're not trained to fight."

He was right, of course. Sierra didn't even know how to hold a sword and had only fired a blaster once by chance. She had triggered the EMP, but even that felt like a lucky coincidence. She hadn't been able to replicate her abilities since returning to the city. It was as if whatever well she had been drawing from had suddenly dried up.

Each of the scouts dispatched to the Sphere had been far more prepared than she could ever hope to be, and they had been slaughtered. In addition to whatever they had faced, there was also the added complication of a Guardian with a mandate to kill her; a Guardian who had apparently gained avid followers willing to stab her if presented with the opportunity.

And then there was Rhys. The boy she had barely gotten to know. The young man had been a jerk to her when they first met, but he'd then come around as he got to know her better; as he got to know what she was really like, as opposed to the stereotype he had conjured up. He had fended off an attack in order to help her take down a Guardian invasion.

For Rhys alone, she'd consider staying. Maybe the two of them could ride triumphantly into the Sphere and take out the remainder of the Guardians and the Order. A power couple to defeat them all.

But that was fantasy.

She had every reason not to go; every reason to stay in the city, as Malachi had suggested. But she refused to wait around for the next person to kill her. She might as well bring some good for the damage she had done.

Malachi maintained his gaze, waiting for an answer. The leather vest and belts he wore always gave him the appearance of being a rebel, though his sacrifices for the Community suggested otherwise. He was their protector, and it made sense he wanted to watch over her as well. But she would not sit back and let the men decide for her.

Regardless of all the reasons for her to stay, there was one pinnacle reason for her to go: her mother. Despite the differences they had, Sierra's mother was the last surviving member of her family. Sierra had felt little remorse in having to abandon the woman, but she wouldn't be the one to cause her death. Not if it wasn't already too late.

Thousands of people were potentially dead as a result of her actions. She tried not to think about her role in their slaughter. Everything she had done, she had done with the goal of saving lives. She had worked to save a city of strangers, and as a result, possibly everyone she had grown up with was dead.

Had she done the right thing?

Her mother's survival was the only sliver of salvation she saw; a glimmer of hope she desperately needed to cling to. If her mother had been at the Core when the blast went off, perhaps she had been spared. Perhaps there was a chance to find and rescue her.

"I have to try," she said finally. "My mother is the only family I've known for the last ten years. If there's a chance she's made it, I need to try."

"It's not safe," he replied. "You are too important to our cause. The people here will listen to you; you brought the bots down. Don't underestimate the power your voice will hold here. We can send trained men able to defend themselves to bring out any captives safely."

Sierra snorted. "It is not your place to say whether or not I go. I will not sit here and wait for you to manipulate me in order to keep the peace. This began with me. Greata set me on this path. I thought it would be done when I found Terre, but it seems I need to press on and finish what I started. Titan is after me. Let *me* worry about what is safe."

Malachi crossed his arms and leaned back, clearly unimpressed, but Sierra didn't care.

"I wish you'd stay," he relented. "But your life is your own; I can't force you. That said, please consider taking someone with you, at least. Someone who is more familiar with the land and its dangers."

Sierra nodded. "I'll let Terre know that he can join me if he wishes. Ember will accompany me, but perhaps a few more will, too."

"Just remember there's a bounty on your head. The Order has many members and a far reach. If Titan has convinced them to follow him, life could become very difficult for everyone."

THE CORE. It was a place she had always thought herself destined for. She had just never pictured her journey there to be like this.

Both her father and her mother had worked there. Her dad had been some sort of biological engineer, and that was the extent of what she knew. The most anyone would answer of her questions about his work was helping to prepare those born into humanity for a newly terraformed Earth, whenever that was supposed to happen. So she'd stopped asking. Her mother had never spoken of her work, and, as such, Sierra had always assumed she'd taken over her father's role. After her dad and sister, Izzy, died, they never discussed what happened at the Core. Her mom would leave for weeks at a time, only to come back and sleep or retreat into her room.

The years wore on, and once the time came for Sierra to take her Life Placement Exam, she had assumed she would follow in her parents' footsteps. The adults seemed to think there were other possible outcomes for her, but she had deduced otherwise.

That was all in the past now. The Sphere was no more, and whatever she had thought her predestined lot in life might be had evaporated like a bad dream.

On the streets of Vegas, the revelry hadn't died down, despite the setting sun. Instead, the square had been lit with torches, giving the celebrations an eerie glow. The markets had closed, but that did not seem to have discouraged anyone.

Surprisingly, there hadn't been people trying to take advantage of the wealth of goods available. At least, not yet. Sierra had to admit she was a little skeptical of bringing free food for everyone. She wanted to hope for the best and things were good now, but what would happen when the wealth of food dried up? How long could they feed everyone for free?

She knew little of the economics of this world, but Malachi seemed to believe N'ara would use the current situation to her advantage, and as much as Sierra wanted to believe the best in people, Malachi had much more experience with people than she did.

Cheers erupted from the crowd, drawing Sierra's attention. It appeared someone had pulled out a set of swords, lit with flames, and was now proceeding to juggle them. Despite feeling unsettled about everything, she couldn't help but watch the magic unfold. A smile even crept over her face. Maybe all the people needed was a brief distraction; a break from the grim realities of both the recent battle and their normal day-to-day hardships that were likely far from over.

If it was possible, the crowd actually seemed to have increased in size now that the sun was fading. Former residents of the Underground were out in full force, their sunglasses removed and body cloaks cast aside. The light and cool evening provided a reprieve for those who, for more than a century, had lived out of the harsh desert sun. Some had even removed pretty much all their clothing. Some wore nothing but a translucent shawl, leaving nothing to the imagination.

Sierra often felt like a sheltered prude in this world; many had given up the luxury of modesty generations ago. For her, the Guardians had established a strict dress code, and as everyone followed it, she had never questioned whether people might choose to dress otherwise. Or that they could be comfortable wearing so little.

Sierra stood on the periphery of the party. Part of her longed to join in, but the feeling was fleeting. She couldn't shake the uneasy thought that there was someone out there who wanted her dead. She had no way to be sure they weren't among those in the crowd, waiting for another opportunity.

The street was full of people she didn't recognize. Large pupils of Undergrounders reflected light from both the moon and the torches.

Their faces displayed elation that many of them hadn't known for a long time, maybe ever. Small children watched the flame throwers with mouths agape, mesmerized by the moving flames but unsure how to process the wonder they were experiencing.

Sierra's friends kept her waiting. Despite their recent argument, Ember had been eager to join her. The Keeper would prove useful as a guide in navigating around the Core. Ember's earlier quips about the MedBots still disappointed her. After the years of lying, destruction, and murder the Guardians had committed, Sierra would rather put her life into the hands of a human Healer, even if it meant they wouldn't be as precise. If they could inject something to make a patient forget an interrogation, what else was a MedBot capable of?

"Are you ready?"

Sierra jumped at Terre, who had appeared suddenly beside her.

"You scared me!"

"On edge?" Terre asked, a sly smile on his face. The moonlight highlighted his prominent features, casting strange shadows across his face and reflecting in his dark brown eyes.

Sierra shivered against the chilly breeze of the evening, but it was a welcome change from the heat of the day. Leaving at night would have its advantages, but she was going to be watching over her shoulder the whole journey.

"Can you blame me?"

Terre shrugged.

From what Sierra understood, Terre had kept mostly to himself since arriving in the city. There was a certain type of celebrity that came with being named a living ancient, and he wanted no part of it. He spent most of his time with Leo instead, playing cards in the pub, and when Leo attended to his own duties, Terre retired to his room. Malachi occasionally sought his counsel, but he was reluctant to offer much direction.

Terre's outfit was as rugged as its wearer. Forest green sleeves and hood emerged from a black tightened vest. He had concealed a weapon on his belt, hidden underneath the light cloak that hung from his shoulders. A couple of small chains hung from the vest, and Sierra wasn't sure if they were functional or purely decorative. Attached to the only chain which hung from his neck was the silver robot medallion that sat atop his tunic. The emblem intrigued her, but Sierra dared not ask him about it. Its image was that of a Guardian, or a crude representation of one, like something a child might have drawn. The piece looked as if the color had faded away. Sierra also imagined that he didn't realize he clung to it whenever he tried to make a tough decision.

"I'm surprised you joined me," she said, attempting to gain her composure. "What interest do you have in a journey to the Sphere?"

"My quest is my own." He put up the hood which also blanketed his face in shadow. "There are sins in my past I have yet to pay for."

Sierra took a deep breath, trying to bring her heart rate down; it was still pounding after his sudden appearance.

One down, two to go.

She must have arrived earlier than she realized. Ember was never late.

Only a few moments passed before both Ember and Althea arrived. Ember had covered herself in a heavy robe. Neither the heat of the desert, nor the cool of the evening would affect her, but the thicker fabric hid the lights that accented her frame. Travelling at night, the lit panels on her body would alert anyone within a few hundred yards of her presence.

Ember had received her fair share of abuse in the city. Being a Guardian, free to roam around unencumbered within the Silent Zone, was not something that went unnoticed. Those who didn't curse at her, stared. It didn't appear to faze Ember, but it tortured Sierra to see her friend being subjected to such cruelty and disdain.

The humanoid's orange eyes provided a faint light themselves. There wouldn't be anything she could do about the glow without being completely blind, so she hid her face as best she could beneath a traveler's hood. Unless someone was looking at her head-on, they wouldn't notice.

Althea's shawl was light yellow, which stood out in sharp contrast to the outfits worn by the others. Whereas her other two companions had been trying to conceal their presence from those around them, Althea's yellow shawl, white button-up shirt and tight brown pants were much more conspicuous. Even in the dark, her attire was easier to see. The large brown duffle bag on her back hopefully contained something that would be a little less of a beacon if they needed to keep out of sight.

Malachi had questioned Sierra about her request for the Healer to come along. Althea was among the most talented in the city, and there were many residents still recovering from the attack. He didn't want to lose her. But Sierra had asserted herself and told him he was the one who was insisting she take a party along with her, and she'd take along whomever she chose.

Malachi had grumbled a bit but ultimately let it be.

Her three companions stood before her. Terre looked indifferent; other than the large pack on his back, he could have been going for a leisurely evening stroll. The only emotion betrayed on his face was perhaps mild amusement.

Althea's eyes were wide, looking at others in the street with worry. Was the medic also thinking about her would-be assassin?

"Are we ready?" Sierra asked, adjusting her own pack. It felt like a lifetime since she had last made the journey. It was incredible how so much could change in such a short amount of time.

Suddenly, the ground shifted beneath her feet. She reached out to Althea, but as her hand was about to make contact, it fell through empty space.

Nobody was there.

People were yelling, but the city and its celebration were gone. The sun was high in the sky, as if it were mid-afternoon. Her eyes had to adjust to the shift.

She knew instantly what was happening.

Another vision.

Instead of the ancient pavement that lined the city streets, Sierra felt hot sand in its place. The ground continued to tremble beneath her feet, and it took her a moment to realize the cause.

An army had amassed before her. Sentinels and humans. They appeared to be on the same side. Above them, several orbs circled —some Onyx, some Scanners—along with other orbs she either couldn't make out or couldn't recognize. The periphery of her vision faded, as if she were in a dream, and it made many of the details fuzzy.

Irrespective of the distortion, one thing was clear: the black cloaks with luminescent crack-like lines in the distance were unmistakably those of the Order. Others stood alongside them, wearing similar cloaks to the ones her attacker had worn, their patterns more like mazes running along the length of the fabric.

To her right, a woman sat on a horse, overlooking the army before them. The woman seemed familiar, but Sierra wasn't sure why.

The woman lifted a hand above her face to block the sun as she continued to survey the crowd before her. Sierra followed the woman's gaze across the landscape. The Guardians and members of the Order assembled before them seemed endless. Thousands of people marched alongside thousands of Sentinels. Some were wearing robes of the Order and some seemed to wear clothing of the Sphere, while others wore clothing closer to attire worn in the city of Vegas. Still others wore clothing that looked nothing like any she had ever seen.

Before them all stood a giant beast. Metallic and cold, the beast resembled a horse, but it stood nearly three times as large. Its rider appeared to be a Sentinel, and it looked out over the army it led with eyes glowing a dark red.

Titan.

The bot had undergone a transformation; he'd changed his lighting and the markings on his frame. He had transformed himself into a demigod. But it was the same machine she had seen in the desert. She was sure of it.

Beside Titan, a second bot sat astride a second beast. This one was slighter than a Sentinel, but the details blurred, and Sierra couldn't make out anything further.

The woman beside her spoke. "And so, it begins."

Her voice was familiar. A memory itched at the back of Sierra's brain, struggling to surface. She knew this woman.

"Who would have known this is how it all ends?" the woman said.

"We've seen these events unfold countless times," Sierra heard herself say. "It shouldn't surprise us."

"This was only one possible outcome," the woman replied. "It's too bad more weren't willing to join us."

"You know I tried," Sierra heard her voice say. Her voice, but she didn't say the words. The edges of the world around her pulsed and faded.

Sierra concentrated on the woman beside her, trying to hold onto the vision. The woman's long black hair. The purple eyes.

Realization hit her.

"Izzy!" she called out.

The last time Sierra had seen her older sister was ten years ago, on the day she died. But here she was, all grown up, and apparently in charge of an army of her own. Thousands of men and women lined up behind them, ready for battle. War was coming.

Sierra yelled, trying to get her sister's attention, to test her substance. She couldn't seem to make the body she inhabited react the way she wanted.

Izzy remained steadfast in her attention on the battle that was about to wage before them.

Although Izzy didn't seem to hear her cry, in the distance, Titan's head whipped around, his red eyes zeroing in on her own. Despite the leagues between them, Sierra felt the gaze of the bot, heavy and murderous, and she struggled to breathe, thinking the weight of it would strangle her.

The edges of her vision folded in around her, fading away to the periphery of what she could perceive. She struggled to keep the solidity of the scene before her, but it was like fighting against waking up from a dream. Her sister, the army, and the desert sun faded away. Titan's eyes lingered the longest, until even those disappeared.

Her feet gave way beneath her, and Sierra fell. The world dissolved, and she spun downward.

Until she felt a pair of arms catching her from behind.

"Sierra! Are you okay?" a voice called out from beyond the emptiness.

She consciously reached out with her mind to feel where her legs were; to feel the concrete path beneath them. The hands under her arms supported her weight, but there was solid ground below her.

She was back in Vegas.

The sound of merriment surrounded her once again, and she opened her eyes to see Ember and Terre standing over her, both evidently concerned.

"She's not ready for this journey," Terre announced. "We should wait at least another day."

"No!" Sierra exclaimed, pushing herself upright. Althea had a hold on her that had prevented her from landing on the earth below. "I'm okay."

"You're not fully healed," Althea said. "It's all right if we rest another day."

Sierra shook her head. Their plans would not change. "It's not the wound. I had another vision."

She leaned into Althea, who still had an arm around her to support her weight.

"What's going on, Sierra?" Ember was beside her, holding her hand. This was the second time Ember had been present while Sierra had experienced visions of another time.

"I saw her!" She returned her Keeper's gaze. "Izzy. She's alive!"

6

———

Sierra used the support Althea provided to compose herself before finding her footing. She tried to hold onto the images the vision presented before they slipped away like a dream.

Where had she been? Had she seen the future? Was she seeing something through her own eyes? Sierra was sure it was her own voice she had heard.

Either way, if she could trust the vision, her sister Izzy was alive. Her big sister, who was supposed to have been dead for ten years. But how?

The woman Sierra had seen in her vision was a leader; a confident warrior on her way to fight a battle against an enemy Sierra didn't recognize. An army composed of both people and Guardians.

"It was just a glimpse," she said. "Just like the first time I saw Vegas. Ancient Vegas. I don't think it was the past this time, though. What I saw hasn't happened yet."

"Am I the only one who doesn't understand what's happening right now?" Althea asked. "Has this happened before?"

Sierra nodded and closed her eyes, trying to orient herself. She didn't remember being dizzy the last time. She held onto

Althea once again, her hand on her shoulder for support. Sierra took a deep breath and felt another hand on her side, and she didn't have to look up to know it was Ember.

She shrugged off the assistance of both protectors and forced herself to support her own weight. She would not give them any more reason to believe she should stay.

"Weeks ago, I saw this city," she said to Althea, motioning at the faded empire around them. "Las Vegas. What it used to be. And Terre." She glanced to the man, who didn't visibly react.

"Because of my visions," she continued, "I knew I was to find the device to defeat the Onyx." She shook her head. "But I didn't stop to think the visions might continue."

"And who is Izzy?" Althea asked.

"Izzy is my sister. I was told she'd died ten years ago, along with my father . . ." She trailed off, her gaze cast into the distance. If Izzy was alive, was it possible . . .?

"Sierra?"

"My mom and I were told they had died in an accident at the Core. They sent Ember to us to help raise me. She acted as my Keeper while Mom worked."

Sierra looked to Ember. The robot's orange eyes were studying her, her warm smile both lifelike and yet utterly lifeless at the same time.

"Did you know?" she asked Ember. Her words sounded more accusatory than Sierra had intended, but her suspicion wasn't without merit. The Guardians were supposedly interconnected through their network. It was the reason Ember disconnected herself, so they couldn't track her down. If Ember had known Izzy had really survived . . .

It would crush Sierra.

Ember's eyes flickered and danced in emulation of thinking. Was she scanning her memory or faking it? Sierra hated being suspicious.

"I had no idea," she answered.

If Sierra hadn't known Ember, she wouldn't have caught the lapse in time between the question and the answer. It was only a split-second, and had it been anybody else, she wouldn't have noticed. But Ember wasn't human, and over the years, Sierra had grown to know her Keeper extremely well. There was something behind that pause.

"All of my records show your sister and father having died that day. I don't even have details of what the accident entailed. I'm sorry, Sierra. That is all the information I can share."

Ember was hiding something. Behind those glowing eyes and the caring smile, there was something she was holding back.

If she couldn't trust Ember, who could she trust? Her mother might be dead. Wil, though he had his issues, was the only other person left from her past, and he was now hundreds of miles away, on his way to San Francisco.

"Maybe these have a purpose, too," Althea offered. "Whatever you're seeing now, maybe it's meant to help you on your way, or warn you of a fate to come."

"Perhaps," she replied. "For now, I'll take it as confirmation that continuing is the right decision. If I am to find answers, that's where they'll be."

Nobody moved to argue with her, so Sierra continued. "Let's get moving. No sense in wasting any more time."

"You can't be serious?" Althea pushed back, looking to the other companions for confirmation. "You just about passed out! You're seeing visions and reliving past trauma. You're pushing yourself too hard!"

Sierra looked her new friend in the eye and grabbed her shoulder. She had been right; this woman would play a part in whatever was to come.

"I've sat here for too long already. I need to get back, Althea. My sister is probably alive, and I need to find out what really happened. If these visions have a purpose, I don't think it's coincidence that we're heading to the place she supposedly died.

For the second time in the last few weeks, I'm looking for answers to questions I didn't know I had. Let's hope these visions point the way to them once again."

Not willing to wait any longer, she walked toward the city's outskirts. The last glow of the sun had faded. Her friends followed, with no more questions. There would be time for those later.

Despite traveling through the night, it felt like no time at all before the sun crested over the horizon and Sierra and her party stood on the fringe of the new Silent Zone.

The entire valley had a haze to it, and she could tell it only thickened ahead. She didn't need to ask to know it was the physical representation of the aftermath of her home's destruction.

Ember surveyed the landscape. What could the Keeper sense that the rest of them couldn't? Ember, the lone exception to technology that could function within the Silent Zone's grasp.

Ember's enduring ability was a question that demanded an answer. The humanoid was a constant reminder of the threat Titan posed; a Guardian that could reason, unconstrained by the boundaries that had kept humanity safe for generations.

Now, they sat mere yards from the border of two worlds. There was nothing marking the shift, but Ember could detect it. She had explained the change their human eyes couldn't see, but none of it made any sense to Sierra; to her, they were nothing more than fancy words to let them know their presence would be detectable to the Guardians once they crossed that line. She accepted Ember could determine what was happening.

"Are we setting up camp here?" Sierra asked. The yellows and oranges of the rising sun highlighted the red rock around them. The morning air was still crisp, but as soon as the sun hit them, its heat would follow close behind. She wouldn't mind a few hours' rest before continuing on the next leg of their journey.

Terre shook his head. His dark brown eyes showcased yellow highlights as the sunlight reflected within them. He used his black staff as a walking stick. It was taller than he was and made him seem a much more intimidating figure when paired with the dark green robe he wore for their journey. His hood was also down, exposing his thick, wavy brown hair.

"We have no protection here," he answered.

"What do you mean?" she asked. "I thought we're still in the Silent Zone?"

"We are," he nodded. "But that won't protect us from bandits. Or *them*." He pointed down the slope, just south of the Core. She hadn't noticed the small encampment, dwarfed by the canyon beside them.

A few dozen tents were aligned in even, orderly rows, with six larger tents encircling them in an outer perimeter. A flag marked the center of the camp, but it was too far away for Sierra to discern its markings. Several men on horseback stood guard around the campsite, and there was no other movement at this early hour.

"The Order," Terre continued. "Normally they'd leave us alone, but this close to the Core, I wouldn't put anything past them. They definitely wouldn't take too kindly to discovering you are an escaped resident of the Sphere they just razed."

"I still don't understand. Why would they torch the villages?"

"They call us The Oathbreakers," Althea said. "Once you leave the Sphere, you're considered a betrayer to the Guardians. If a member of the Order uncovers an Oathbreaker, they see it as their duty to either convert or kill us."

"Is that why I was stabbed?"

"No," Terre replied. If Sierra didn't know better, she'd say he had a slight smirk on his face. "You and Wil each took down more Guardians than anyone else since the Robot Wars combined. You, my young friend, have a bounty on your head."

"How do they know I was the one who activated the device?"

"Their eyes are everywhere. Not much happens that doesn't get back to them."

Sierra paused, taking in his words. When she'd activated that machine, it had never crossed her mind there would be those sympathetic, even reverent, to the Guardians.

Back in the Sphere, the Order were its political leaders. They were the Guardians' human counterparts, but she had never considered their influence would be so widespread. Even when a handful of them had chased after her as she set out to fire the EMP, Sierra had assumed it was the lot of them; a couple of Spherians sent specifically to hunt her down and bring her back.

Sierra took a deep breath. The smell of burning hung in the air as the wind shifted to the west. A dark haze loomed to the north. The Order held a much bigger presence, and perhaps a much bigger threat, than she had imagined. Maybe more than she still imagined.

"We can't stay here. They're bound to see us." Terre motioned. "Let's keep moving."

Sierra looked to Ember, who had been quiet through the entire exchange. In fact, she had been silent for most of the trip.

"How much did you know of the Order and what they do?" Sierra asked her. "Did you know they would hold me responsible?"

Ember's orange lights lit up, processing her reaction to the question. "The Order has worked as our human eyes and ears for centuries. They started out as a small band of survivors willing to do anything to stay alive, but their influence grew. The ancients built our programs to have a human counterpart. I had no special insight to tell me they would specifically target you, but considering their reverence of the Guardians, it's not out of character."

Cold and calculating, Ember's responses had become more and more detached from the loving Keeper Sierra had grown up with. Was her strange behavior a byproduct of the EMP, or perhaps of disconnecting herself from the network? Something else within the bot had changed, and it made Sierra uneasy.

They carried on, and it wasn't long before they crossed the invisible barrier that marked the end of the Silent Zone. There was no physical sign of its cessation, but Sierra could feel the change in her bones. The moment they crossed the divide, she could feel both a weight being lifted and the distinct feeling she was being watched. She looked to her companions, who seemed to show similar shifts in their demeanor.

Terre, ever the stoic, shifted his tunic uncomfortably, but for someone who kept his cards close to his chest, he may as well have been dancing in discomfort.

Althea had her eyes closed and was letting out soft murmurs. Her eyes darted from one spot to the next, as if expecting an ambush at any moment. Sierra grew tired just watching her.

At first, Sierra believed Ember was continuing as if nothing had changed. Ember of course knew precisely where the field disappeared and wouldn't be beholden to the uneasy feelings experienced by the rest of the party. But the robot, too, looked to the sky, as if expecting orbs to be flying overhead.

Sierra couldn't help but scan the sky herself. Knowing the Guardians could detect them was unsettling, but nothing appeared among the wispy clouds forming overhead.

The wind picked up, and Ember's long orange hair blew back. "So many . . ." she whispered.

"So many what?" Sierra queried.

Ember brought her head down from the clouds and eyed Sierra with a raised eyebrow, as if momentarily confused by how the human had heard her, but realizing what she had said, her face relaxed.

"So many lost. I don't think either of us realized the impact the EMP blast would have. Thousands of Guardians fallen. There's a sense of emptiness here. Without access to the network, I can't tell an exact number, but I know I should be able to detect many more. So many are gone."

Sierra exchanged a worried look with Terre. For the second time in two days, Ember had expressed sympathy for the Guardians. She had known Ember her entire life. She had done nothing but look out for her, even when threatened with deactivation for the sake of Sierra's cause. Something had changed since then. A worrisome strand underlined the cracks in the Keeper's behavior. Her aloofness wasn't helping matters.

"Machines." Terre clamped a hand on the Keeper's shoulder, causing her to whirl around. Sierra tried to hide a smile. If robots could be startled, she was sure that was the closest she would ever come to seeing it.

Ember blinked several times as she glared at Terre. Her reply was cold. "I am a machine as well."

Sierra quickly erased her smile.

"Just because I've gained consciousness," Ember continued, "doesn't mean I'm suddenly something else. I can sense the loss of those that used to exist here. My consciousness forces me to experience that loss. Imagine being intimately attached to thousands of your kind, and then losing that connection overnight. There is no one, bot or machine, that has experienced this level of emptiness."

Terre loosened his grip. Sierra studied her friend, trying to decide if she should say anything. Ember's eyes were still distant, downcast and vacant, and her face had never been so human-like. Her eyes were downcast and vacant. Her white frame appeared hunched and dejected.

Terre's face mirrored her concerns. "Don't be so sure, bot," he finally replied.

"Are we going to take a break before we get the Core?" Sierra asked, deciding to change the subject.

Ember's behaviour concerned Sierra, but the humanoid had proven her loyalty. At least, she had so far.

"Yes," Terre answered, taking the cue to move on. "We'll follow the edge of the SZ to the north. The scouts set up a camp not far from here. We'll sleep there."

7

———

A GENTLE HAND shook Sierra back into consciousness.

They had arrived at the camp mid-afternoon, just as the heat of the day had started to get to her. The camp the scouts had set up was quaint, with a few small tents and a canopy to block out the sun. It surprised Sierra that it was still standing, but Terre informed her it wasn't on any well-used routes. It was likely nobody had come across it.

The smoke was thickening the closer they journeyed to the Core. The entire desert was locked in a haze.

They had walked for nearly eighteen hours straight, so Sierra had fallen asleep as soon as her head had hit the pillow.

Sierra was prodded again, and she reluctantly opened her eyes. The faint smell of distant burning lingered in the air.

"Sierra, wake up," Althea whispered. Her skin was showing redness from the previous day's sun. Maybe she was as sensitive to its rays as she claimed.

"What's going on?" Concern reflected in her friend's eyes as Sierra bolted awake. She was on her feet in seconds and then had to steady herself as the motion made her lightheaded.

"Ember's missing," Althea said.

"What do you mean?" Sierra asked.

"Get dressed. I think it's best if Terre fills you in."

Sierra scrambled into her day gear and jumped outside. How could Ember have disappeared? Perhaps she had gone to find food or something useful for the party. It wasn't like her to leave and tell no one.

"What's going on?" she asked, her head barely out the opening to the tent. "Wasn't she keeping watch?"

"Supposed to be," Terre said. "I knew I shouldn't have agreed to let her keep watch the entire night."

"How long has she been gone?" Sierra asked.

"Your guess is as good as mine. It's early morning now. I woke up several hours ago and saw she wasn't at her post. I took a quick look outside, and down toward the Order camp. They appear to have disappeared into the night as well."

"You think they took her?" Sierra asked. "We've got to go after her!"

"No," Terre said. "That's not what I'm saying."

Irritation had replaced the tiredness that had been on Terre's face. He had at least gotten some sleep that night.

"What are you saying, then?" she asked.

Moonlit shadows bounced off his face, masking part of his expression, and Sierra couldn't tell if he was mad or concerned.

"She's left, Sierra. She's gone to join the rest of the Guardians, or maybe to find Titan. I knew we shouldn't have trusted her."

Sierra pushed him with both hands on his chest and nearly fell over herself. Terre seemed only slightly more fit than many of the athletic men in the Sphere, but pushing against him had been like pushing a wall.

"Ember would never . . ."

"Don't tell me what a bot would or wouldn't do! You grew up with them telling you nothing but lies; an ancient program made for another planet, corrupted to keep humanity protected from itself. What you have seen of this world so far is only a fraction of what's out here and yet still you choose to believe this bot won't follow its program."

"She's my friend." Sierra couldn't believe what she was hearing. Ember had been acting strangely, but she wouldn't leave her. She wouldn't help those who intended to harm Sierra.

Would she?

"She was *programmed* to be your friend, Sierra. She has known no other way to be. With that programming disrupted, who knows how she'll act now."

"No! I will not accept that!" Sierra yelled.

A firm hand suddenly gripped her mouth, muffling her cries. "The camp is gone," Terre said, "but there are still others who I'd prefer not know we're here."

He removed his hand, and she stared at him with icy daggers.

"It makes no sense! Ember helped us, even when she knew she would be sacrificing herself. Why would she leave us here?"

"That's the only reason I have kept her around. Maybe the EMP scrambled something in her circuits after all. Maybe being disconnected from the network triggered a dormant command. There could easily have been a homecoming program that activated on close proximity to the Core. I don't know. All I can tell you is there's no sign of a struggle, and she left without saying anything to us. It doesn't appear she's betrayed our location, though, so just because she's left us doesn't mean she's turned on us." He took another long look into the desert. "*Yet.*"

"She won't. And it is not up to you to decide if we 'keep her around.'" She used air quotes to mock his condescension. "She may be artificial, but she's still one of us."

She paused. It was the first time she had ever considered the limits of her friend's consciousness.

Terre scoffed, revealing his feelings about the statement, but he left it at that.

Sierra pushed past Terre. There had to be something he'd missed. Maybe there was a clue he hadn't seen.

The man shook his head, putting his hand to his forehead. "I'm wondering if we should continue at all. This is becoming too risky."

"Too risky?" she questioned. "Or do you mean 'put it on hold' while we search for Ember? Because I will find my friend, and then I will find my mother."

"Look, I was barely on board in the first place, and I didn't bring you out here to get yourself killed, either."

"Nobody forced you to come. I would have come regardless of you joining me, and I will continue regardless if you choose to leave."

Terre threw up his arms. "You're right," he continued. "Nobody forced me to come." He didn't lose the tension in his back or the flaring of his nostrils, but the arguing stopped. He pointed in the direction of the Order camp. "If you see something I didn't, we'll go look for her. But I won't let you die chasing the ghost of something you want to be there."

Sierra would have looked regardless, but she took the opening he presented. She nodded and studied the ground where Ember had stood while Sierra slept. A solitary pair of footsteps led in the direction of the Order camp, made it halfway, and then simply disappeared, as if someone had plucked her from the earth. No other footprints led to their camp, not even their own from the day before.

"The path ends." Terre smirked behind her. "She wanted to cover her tracks."

"Or someone else did," Sierra replied.

Why does Terre seem so pleased about Ember being missing?

They descended down the road to where the Order camp had been and spent close to an hour combing the area. All traces of the camp had been wiped clean. It was like nobody had been there the day before, except for the imprint of a giant square flattening the dirt.

Terre watched her, amused. Althea watched the sky, worried

that reconnaissance orbs might surprise them at any moment. Sierra searched nearby desert shrubs, hoping something would reveal itself.

Nothing did. Any piece of cloth or trace of a footprint had been meticulously erased.

The desert was unforgiving; during the best of times, the wind blew over most tracks within a matter of hours. With everything intentionally scraped, it was hard to have any sense of what was going on at all. The flat pad of red dirt was the only sign anyone had actually been there.

Almost the only sign. At its edge, a mass of footprints emerged, revealing that the Order had traveled west. Sierra scanned the tracks, hoping for a wayward mark; something dropped; *anything.*

Nothing materialized.

"You could help, you know!" Sierra said. The heat of the sun was creeping into the day, and they would have to get moving if they were going to complete their task before nightfall. "You couldn't have searched that thoroughly in the time before I woke up!"

The smile faded on Terre's face, and he uncrossed his arms, nodding slightly. He strode to the far end of the camp where Sierra hadn't yet reached and began a search of his own.

Turning to the medic, she asked, "Althea?"

"What? Oh, I'm sorry. I would feel better if I could see the orbs coming before they get here."

"We'll hear them before we see them," Sierra said, and she carried on with her search.

Althea had never looked more uncomfortable. How long had it been since she had stepped outside of the Silent Zone? From the way she acted, it was possible she never had after Malachi rescued her. She'd simply escaped one prison only to confine herself in another.

"They did a thorough job of cleaning," Sierra continued.

"Ember couldn't have done this alone. But why would the Order sweep her tracks leading to our camp? And if they knew that's where she came from, why would they leave us be?"

Terre studied the tracks showing the Order's exodus. Hundreds of footprints of both men and horses and the ruts of wheels marked the dirt. All headed toward Vegas.

"Any sign of Ember's tracks among them?" Sierra asked. The morning sun had been rising steadily; their hour was up. If they were going to get into the Core and out again before nightfall, they were going to have to leave now.

Terre stopped mid-stride, looking at a spot on the earth. "There was a droid with them," he announced.

"Can you tell if it was her?" Sierra took a spot next to him. The footprint was clear in the dirt. The perfect barefoot shape and the zig-zag pattern on the heel made it clear the print originated from a bot, but any other distinguishing markings on the bottom of the robot's foot had been lost in the shifting sand. It surprised her the print had remained as clear as it was. But there were no others accompanying it.

Terre shook his head. "It wasn't a Sentinel; their metallic feet would leave a different print. I'm sure it was a Keeper, but a lone footprint doesn't tell us much. And whether it was Ember or another Keeper bot is impossible to say." He tried following the direction of it, but any other sign became lost in the surrounding prints.

Terre shrugged. "Assuming it was her, I can't tell if the bot was acting under its own volition or not. Sorry, Sierra."

The shifting sand was quickly covering the shallow prints that stretched out to the west. To what end remained a mystery.

"Should we worry about the city?" Althea asked. "Should we warn them?"

"They'll likely not bother the city," Terre answered. "Groups of the Order traveling through isn't anything unusual." He looked to Sierra. "It's your call. If you want to pursue them in the hope she's with them, we can. But I can't promise she is."

Sierra could feel the weight of her companions' eyes on her as they waited for her decision on which direction to go. Her heart longed to follow her friend. But what could they do against a party of Order members? What if the droid footprint wasn't Ember's? There were too many unknowns. Her stomach was in her throat as she weighed her options. There didn't seem to be any clear path.

They could follow the Order and hope to catch them. The three could likely overtake them without issue. But what then? Sneak into the camp searching for someone who may or may not be there? Likely get captured themselves in the process? Terre might be up to the task if his heart was in it, but she didn't have any illusions that her stealth skills were adequate enough. Althea, still searching for monsters in the sky, would definitely not be up to the challenge.

Before them, a canyon opened up. The rocky ravine worked its way through the desert. A well-trodden path on its banks would lead them to the Core. Smoke masked most of what lay ahead in the distance, including the people who had suffered because of her.

Sierra sighed and shook her head. Nothing seemed to be the right option. Nothing seemed like a definite smart option. But she had brought her friends this far.

What would Wil do in her situation? He'd probably rush into something without thinking. It had gotten in him into trouble more than once. But she was not Wil, and she couldn't sit there thinking about it forever.

"You're right, Terre." She might as well admit it. "We don't know what happened to her."

Terre nodded slowly, cautious about what she might say next.

"I'd like to continue into the Core. I need to know if my mother is alive, and if there are other survivors, we need to get them out. Ember is a friend, but she is capable of taking care of herself. If my mom is still alive, we have to find her."

"All right," Terre said. "Do you have a plan on how we do that?"

"As much of a plan as I've had until now. Get in, find them, and get out."

"Losing the bot makes that a harder task."

She nodded. "I know, but we've come this far. I'm not going to turn back now. You can come with me, or you can go back. Both of you." That caught Althea's attention, and she finally met Sierra's eye. "I won't hold it against either of you. But *I* need to do this."

Terre rested a hand on her shoulder. "We came here because we believed it was the right thing to do. I don't think that has changed. Where you go, we all go."

Althea looked at him warily, but she didn't disagree.

8

—————

THE STENCH of death hung in the air, and the odor of burnt metal and flesh stung Sierra's nostrils.

The devastation was still fresh. Bile rose in the back of her throat as she tried to choke through the smell.

The air was thick. Smoke, mixed with the dirt and filth the wind picked up, meant they couldn't see much more than fifteen feet in front of them as they trudged across the desert terrain.

"How will we know we're getting close?" she asked, fighting to keep the stench out of her mouth as she talked. It was a losing battle.

"We're close," Terre replied.

Luckily, Terre had thought to pack goggles for them all to wear. Flashes of red and orange embers in the distance broke through the haze. The villages still smoldered.

Could she have done something to prevent the decimation? Could she have arrived sooner? Could she have prepared them in some way?

"How far will this destruction spread?" she asked. "Will they attack the city as well?"

"The Order would likely have done this because they all

became Oathbreakers," Terre answered. "I've never seen them attack on this scale, though." He shook his head.

"But it's not like these people chose to leave the Sphere's protection!" Sierra protested.

"To the Order, it doesn't matter. The people defied the Guardians' will. They would have recognized no other option."

"It makes little sense. Why does the Order get to live outside the Sphere and not those who had lived here?"

"Things don't always need to make sense for them to be true," Terre answered, still surveying the burning hellscape before them. "The Order believe what they have decided to be true, and they act on that belief."

Sierra didn't have to ask again how they'd know if they were close. The debris and bodies strewn across the ground made it clear. The Order hadn't bothered to clean up the aftermath of their destruction, instead leaving the dead to rot in the heat. She wanted to retch, but it was impossible to avert her eyes.

They had gutted homes, and some they had knocked down completely. Some were now no more than piles of rocks. The Order had been thorough.

"This is awful," Sierra said, holding up part of her robe to her nose to try to stop the stench. "How could anyone have done this?"

Althea hadn't said anything since the smoke had thickened. Perhaps the woman was trying not to vomit, as well. She had covered her entire face with her hood, and only her goggles popped out.

"In the early days after the wars, atrocities like this had been common. One group of people trying to destroy another," Terre said. "Humans can be awful to each other when desperate or convinced they've found a better path."

"Do you think anyone could have survived this?"

Terre nodded. "There are always survivors. For better or worse."

"The Guardians protect us," Sierra whispered to herself. The irony filled her lungs along with the putrid air. How many of those she had grown up with had said those words with their final breath?

The walk had given her time to think; maybe too much time. The weight of her actions plagued her. Sierra had been so preoccupied with saving the city that she hadn't considered the effect it would have on the place where she had spent her entire life.

It had been naïve of her to think the people of the Sphere could adapt and carry on. She had thought they would just meld into this unknown world and be comfortable with the consequences. Having been hand-fed by the Guardians their entire lives, even without the attack, most of them would likely not have fared well. Malachi had been willing to lead them, to guide them. Now, there was a good chance there was nobody left.

The smoke and ash masked the sun, but its heat still assaulted them, cooking the smell of devastation that seeped into her pores and lungs.

Lights in the distance marked the buildings that made up the Core. Despite the haze, they shone through the shadows, faintly revealing the large circular structure that made up the central hub of the Sphere.

"I've never seen the Core before," she thought out loud.

"Then you probably haven't seen what's next to it, either?" Terre asked.

Sierra paused, trying to process what she was looking at. Descended into the valley floor was a giant wall. It had to be hundreds of yards tall, and just as wide. Lights illuminated both the base and the top of the structure. Dots moving along the top told her that people walked across it, emphasizing its size.

"What is that?"

"It's a dam," Terre answered. "We built it to power our cities. The bots co-opted it to power the Sphere. The EMP should have taken it out, but there was obviously a miscalculation. Perhaps the centuries weakened its charge."

"It's massive! Did the ancients do anything small?"

"Not if they could help it."

From their perspective, Sierra could just make out four towers standing behind the wall, their tops lit up, revealing their presence in the mist.

Closer to where they stood, enormous concrete structures jutted out from the rock on either side of the ravine, nearly as impressive as the wall itself but not nearly as tall. Small windows lined their walls, allowing small glimpses of the screens, lights and sparks within.

"What's happening in these buildings?" Sierra asked as they approached.

"Those are the rebuild operations," Althea answered. "We didn't have such an elaborate facility back in San Francisco, but I'll never forget the way the sparks light up when Guardians are being created."

"Your facility is just as big," Terre interjected. "It's just dispersed around the compound. You wouldn't have seen the whole thing at once."

"It seems quite active," Sierra said. "Are they rebuilding after the fight?"

"It's likely," Terre nodded. "Since we're here, I'd like to take a closer look."

She gave Terre a sideways glance. "What about the Guardians? Won't they see us if we venture down there?"

"We're going to need to risk bumping into a bot eventually. If we can gain a sense of the scale of their rebuild, we'll have a better idea of how much time you've given us."

Sierra winced. She still didn't like the idea that she had merely bought them time. She had risked everything and sacrificed so much.

"You've got other ideas," she said. "What are you thinking?"

"I'm wondering if there might be a way to shut them down."

She nodded hesitantly. He was holding something back. "How likely do you think that is? Why wouldn't the ancients have pulled the plug if it was that simple?"

"I never said it would be simple. But you have a way of making the unexpected happen. Fate has led you here for a reason. If those visions led you here, maybe there's a purpose behind it. Cleaning up the leftovers from your last vision would be a good start. You seem to have a habit of being led to the right place at the right time."

"All right," she said. "Let's have a look."

Buffeted by the wind, the three of them ventured down a rocky path that led to the side of the cliff face. It felt strange for them to be descending when the Core was just up ahead, on the top of the ravine, but Terre promised there was another way to get where they needed to if they followed the path that led to the dam.

"How do you know your way around here so well?" Sierra asked. There was so much mystery surrounding the man and she had resolved to peel away his layers. Greata had seen something in him, and it had to be more than simply surviving for two centuries.

"I used to work here," he replied.

Sierra turned to look incredulously at him, but Terre's gaze remained fixed straight ahead, his expression unchanged.

"You worked at the Core?"

"It wasn't the Core back then. The buildings you know of as the Core didn't exist. The dam was here, though, and the army tried to protect it. I worked here for a brief period. I was just the tech guy, but they brought me in anyway. We thought we had gained the upper hand, but we were only fooling ourselves. Although, if we had been able to launch that EMP in time, things might have been different."

"What happened?"

"Let's just say we got in our own way."

"We've heard so many amazing stories of the ancients and their technology. How were you not able to stop them?"

"We could have," he replied, agitation marked in his voice. "But we waited too long. Our government thought it was more important to protect their investment, to protect the economy, than the lives that were at stake. They wanted to salvage them, get them to work properly rather than wipe them out. If our leadership hadn't been so stubborn . . . well, it could have changed everything. By the time they made the call, the bots had figured out what we were up to and—well, you saw the rest in your vision. They took out our command centers, took out our cities, and our means of transportation. It was too late."

By this time, they had descended to the bottom of the valley. The edges of the buildings towered above them, and Sierra had to strain her neck to see the tops of them. Beside them, the river rushed by, flowing violently from beneath the giant wall that shut out everything at the valley's end.

The smell of burning metal punched the air as they got closer to the structures, overwhelming the smell of the burning villages above them.

Grinding, clanking, and buzzing echoed from within the buildings. Glimpses of flying sparks filled the windows, but they would need to get higher to see what was happening.

"Up the stairs." Terre pointed to a metal balcony that hugged the side of the building. "We'll get a closer look, but be careful. Don't allow yourselves to be seen."

They crawled nervously up the stairs behind Terre, carefully placing each foot to make as little noise as possible. Not that Sierra thought they'd be heard above the racket coming from the building's interior.

Althea's wide eyes frantically scanned the windows alongside the buildings and the path ahead. Terre's wide strides and barely masked grin made him look excited to be there, like he was going to uncover something amazing.

What was happening within these walls was obviously important enough to pique Terre's interest, but Sierra could see the Scanners flying in the distance. She prayed they wouldn't come near enough to detect them.

Both Terre and Althea scanned the edge of the building, looking for something. Cameras, maybe.

Sierra peeked through the first set of windows. It was hard to see through the darkened glass, but the sparks and dim blue lights within gave her enough of a glimpse to know what was happening. Sentinels were lined up. She couldn't tell how many, but there had to be dozens. Each was connected to a large interface within the wall, and mechanical bots rode up and down between them. The bot plugged into each of them for a few seconds, then moved on to the next and repeated the process.

She moved along the platform a little further and peered into another set of windows. The same process was being repeated over and over. Sentinels, Scanners, and Onyx were all lined up, fresh from the assembly line. There were dozens of each of the units in this building alone. She could only guess the same scene was duplicated in the facility across the ravine.

"It's true, then," she said. "All we fought for was only temporary. The bots will rebuild, and Vegas will be no better off."

"That's not entirely true," Terre responded. "The SZ is larger. The people have safer passage to the growing lands."

"Still," she continued, "the Guardians will rebuild. They'll move on, and Vegas will still be trapped. All I've done is destroy my home and everyone in it."

"We might yet be able to do something about these," Terre said.

"Like what?"

"Let's find out who's left here first. Let me know if you have any more visions that might provide some more insight."

"Terre," she said, trying to come to terms with the questions forming in her mind. "How many Guardians did Ember say we had taken out? Dozens fell in the streets of Vegas, but how many went down out here? How big of a hit did they take?"

"It's hard to know for sure, but Ember said thousands had gone down. Why?"

Althea had come from a Sphere like her own. It was safe to assume Althea's Sphere had a station like this, for rebuilding Guardians. They had taken thousands of Guardians down with the EMP blast, but she remembered Malachi telling her there were *hundreds* of Spheres. The pieces were only now falling into place.

"How many are left? We've bought ourselves some time, but how many more are there?"

"In the area? Likely a few hundred, maybe twice that. It's really hard to say. I can't remember the exact stats . . ."

"No, not here. How many are there in total? Everywhere? Althea's Sphere and the ones elsewhere. How many Guardians are there?"

Terre's eyes narrowed as he pursed his lips.

Althea interrupted before Terre could answer. She was pointing skyward.

"Guys, we've got trouble."

9

SIERRA FOLLOWED her line of sight to the top of the dam. A couple of dozen people had gathered on the wall. At this distance, they were hardly more than dots on top of the massive structure, but it was clear that something had sparked their attention.

She froze, as did her companions. The figures on top of the dam were looking in their direction. After studying their movements, Terre determined it hadn't been them that had drawn their attention, but their party was still in a position where they could be seen.

"Let's go! To the wall!" Terre grunted. Crouching, he moved swiftly, not waiting for an answer, stepping carefully as if afraid he might step on a stick and draw attention.

As they got closer, Sierra could make out that the figures were members of the Order standing guard above them. If they had been looking, they would have easily seen the party that had been scanning the inner workshop of the machines.

Despite the smoke that muted the sun, the heat of the day crept in, and sweat ran down Sierra's face. Terre was dripping. For everything else Terre seemed to know about the world, the heat hadn't been something he'd learned how to deal with.

"Why are we going toward them?" Althea hissed behind Sierra. "They'll see us for sure!"

"If we can get to the base of the wall, they won't see us unless they are looking straight down!" Terre said.

At this distance, even through the haze, their movement could easily draw the eye of the guards above. Even though they appeared not to have looked directly at them, Sierra would not take that for granted. The quicker they could get out of the guards' line of sight, the better.

As they ran, Sierra cringed at the yellow cloak Althea wore. It was like a beacon against the red dirt. Nothing could be done to help the wardrobe choice now, but Sierra made a mental note to convince her friend to wear something that would blend in with the featureless landscape a little better next time.

Every step on the dry earth crunched ten times louder than it ever had in the past.

They followed a path that overlooked the river flowing out from the dam's base. It was nearly twenty feet across. She had only ever heard of bodies of water like this. Like so much of the world she had discovered, they were no longer supposed to exist. She wanted to pause for a closer look, but instead of stopping to marvel, she was forced to press on in her crouched half run.

It wasn't until they were at the base of the dam that Sierra realized the full scale of the structure before them. Taller than any building left standing in Vegas, it would have rivaled the buildings of the ancient city.

The dam curved inward, which made it seem even more spectacular. Sierra and Althea both breathed heavily, but Terre seemed unaffected by their brief jog, other than the thick sweat that clung to his brow. It now ran down his face as he came to a standstill. He took a cloth from within his robe to wipe it away.

"What now?" she asked. "They're blocking the way to get in, aren't they?"

Terre nodded. "We need to climb up, but it's going to be difficult without them seeing us."

A small path wound its way up the rock beside them; stairs carved into the side of the riverbank.

Terre eyed up the wall. "We're going to have to go up to get in."

"Won't there be guards blocking the entrance there as well?" Althea asked as she leaned against the wall. She still panted, trying to catch her breath from their near sprint.

"You'd probably have a better idea than either of us at this point. You're the only one who's actually been inside a working Core."

"Didn't you say that you worked at the Core?" Sierra asked.

"I worked at the dam," Terre said. "It's only the power source for the rest of the place. I could give you a tour of the ancient facility, but it wouldn't do us much good. I was here long before the Guardians took it over and modified it for their purposes."

Althea's gaze flitted nervously as she took in the structure's enormity. "Our Core looked nothing like this. And I heard little about the Order until I had already left. There was nothing but trust in the Guardians."

Terre shook his head. "Remember, the dam isn't actually the Core; it's just part of its power source. The power station for your Core would have looked different. North of San Francisco?"

She nodded in reply.

"The ring-shaped building we saw earlier is the Core's primary structure. The layout inside will look nearly identical. I was thinking you might know a way to get in that wouldn't be as obvious."

"Not every Core is the same?" Sierra asked, confused as she assumed each one would be.

"The Guardians built them based on the power supply available. This Sphere is located here because of the dam. They designed the bots to be resourceful; to use what the land around them provided."

Thousands of questions danced in Sierra's head, but only one mattered, and there was only one Terre would answer right now.

"So how do we get up without being seen?" she asked.

"We might have to take our chances," Terre answered, warily surveying the dam.

Althea's eyes were wide as she looked up at the stairwell with dread. Sierra wasn't sure if it was the climb or the chance of being caught that scared the Healer the most.

Sierra pressed her hands against the wall, feeling the pulse she recognized as the heartbeat of the Core. All of those years she had thought the Guardians provided life to their refuge, and in reality it had been the ancients. The Guardians had just tapped into what they had already built.

The stone was cold and slightly damp as water from the raging river below splashed up and licked the structure.

"Wait here," Terre said.

A platform hugged the side of the dam, stretching out across the river. It looked solid, though unused for a couple centuries. Terre stepped out onto the ledge, unconcerned with its integrity. He continued to look up, surveying the dam as if it might hold the answers to getting past the guards.

Terre made it to the other end of the bridge and then disappeared. Perhaps he had discovered another way up. Sierra could only assume he would come back for them.

She rested a hand on Althea's shoulder. The woman blinked rapidly, her gaze to the sky. Her mouth was agape, her finger pointed upward.

Sierra followed her gaze up the side of the wall. Something at its center appeared to be bubbling—a dark, silvery mass. She stared, trying to comprehend what she was seeing. It took a few moments to realize the bubbles weren't liquid at all. There were objects coming out of a small door. Bugs of some sort, maybe.

She tried to focus in on one of the moving pieces. Not bugs. *Scorpions*. Based upon how small the guards at the top had appeared, these creatures must have been monstrous.

One dislodged itself, falling several hundred feet through the air. The platform shook violently as it landed directly in front of Terre, who had begun to make his way back to them. It was about twice as tall as the man and four times as long, its shining pincers easily as large as him.

Its body in the dam's shadow was a dark silver. Whatever this was, it was a machine.

Terre was on top of the beast before it had time to orient itself to its new surroundings. He wound up his staff and made contact with the side of the shiny beast. The impact knocked it off balance and into the rushing waters below.

Staff still in hand, he turned back toward Sierra and Althea. "*Run!*" he shouted.

They could hardly hear the words, but they could see the strain in his throat, the panic in his eyes, and after seeing how many of the monsters now crawled above them, they didn't need to be told twice.

Sierra broke into a sprint to the side of the ravine, Althea close on her heels. She pushed harder than she ever had in her life, trying to avoid more of the metal beasts as they fell from the sky. The ground shook from their impact, causing her to stumble. She only briefly looked back to ensure they weren't being pursued. Two more of the beasts had fallen in front of Terre.

"Don't stop!" Althea was in her ear, pushing her along. Sierra didn't have the resolve to argue, so she continued to push hard.

It wasn't until they had reached the edge of the stairwell that she dared to stop and look back.

Four of the beasts now surrounded Terre. Two more floated in the stream beneath him, quickly disappearing in the rapid current.

Terre swung at the machine closest to him, but they had the power of numbers behind them. He couldn't take them all out before they gained their balance. Terre ducked just in time to miss being struck by a metallic tail. He took another swing at the creature's legs with his staff, knocking it off balance, but only for a moment.

He needed their help.

Sierra turned around, intent on running back toward Terre, but Althea met her with her arm, holding her back.

"You'll only get yourself killed!" she yelled into her ear over the sound of crashing water around them.

"They're going to kill him!" Sierra responded.

"How do you plan to help?"

Sierra paused. Althea was right; she would likely run to her death, but she didn't want to just stand here and watch the scorpions sweep Terre into the river.

The beast Terre had struck was struggling, its legs fighting to push itself upright once again. In the meantime, another beast behind Terre swung at him and stabbed him in the back with the sharp tip of its tail.

Sierra gasped, and Althea let out a strangled yelp.

They couldn't hear him, but Terre's mouth opened wide as if screaming in agony and he fell to his knees. His hands and staff scrambled behind his head in attempts to dislodge the metal from his flesh. Without pause, the scorpion picked up its conquest in one of its giant pincers and scurried up the wall toward the rest of the swarm.

Terre, by this time, had gone limp in its grasp. The other three on the bridge crawled back up the wall. The swarm parted for the beast carrying Terre. It passed them and slipped into the entryway, and the rest of the scorpions followed into the opening.

Within minutes, the beasts had disappeared.

10

Sierra knelt in the red dirt, staring at the dam.

It could have been seconds or hours. She had no idea how much time had actually passed, but her knees ached as they pressed into the jagged rocks that made up the edge of the riverbank. Her cloak provided little relief from the stones she knelt on, but she didn't care.

Althea knelt next to her, breathing heavily, in a similar state of shock.

Both of them watched the entryway and waited for the metallic beasts to return. Or for some sign of their friend. Or for what to do next.

The pair had once again put considerable distance between themselves and the dam, in case the creatures re-emerged. The guards above had appeared to move on. Her gaze continually scanned the top of the dam above them to ensure they weren't being watched.

Sierra's heart was in her throat. Its ragged beat slowed as the minutes ticked by. She had yet to catch her breath.

Terre was gone.

First, Ember. Now, Terre.

Gone.

They had set out for the Core as a party of four and were now down to two, and they hadn't even reached their destination yet.

It had all happened so fast; all Sierra could do was play those few minutes in her head over and over again. She looked for something that could have been useful, that could have helped in the heat of the moment. Perhaps there had been nothing they could have done differently.

She fought back the tears that threatened to appear. She would not cry.

Beside her, Althea seemed small and pale. The woman had insisted on coming with them. She believed something had tied their fates. And now it seemed the two of them were the only ones left of their little party.

They'd come here to discover if there had been any survivors of the attack on the Sphere. Now they were the ones who needed help.

"Have you ever seen anything like them before?" Sierra managed to say, realizing as soon as she said it how heartless it might have seemed for this to be the first thing she asked.

Althea shook her head slowly, her eyes never leaving the door.

Sierra had never even imagined anything like what she had just seen. Were those scorpion-like things Guardians? Controlled by the Guardians? Some sort of trap left by the ancients? Or something completely different?

"They're Serkhet." Althea answered her unspoken questions. "But this is the first time I've ever seen them for myself. I didn't believe they were real. There are so many rumors of desert creatures. Myths and legends. In the MedCenter, you just dismiss fantastical stories. People hallucinate about many things in the desert. Mothers tell children of the Serkhet to keep them from wandering off alone. Occasionally, a madman would stumble into town, swearing he'd been attacked by them."

Althea's head dropped, looking toward the red earth beneath

her. "Despite the strange wounds these men had, nobody ever believed they were real."

"Why not?" Sierra asked.

"The patients were always deranged from the sun and had so many wounds that they didn't survive long. We always wrote them off as mad. Well, maybe they weren't after all."

"Are they of the Guardians? Or the ancients? Or something else?" She voiced her questions as if it made a difference. Whatever they were, they had taken their friend through a door twenty stories in the sky.

Althea shrugged. "In the legends, they were always described as mythical beasts. But these were made of metal. Nothing of nature I have seen looks like that. Whether the Guardians or the ancients created them, I don't know."

"Why only Terre? Why didn't they come for us too?"

Althea frowned. "That's all I know of them. Unless you count tales of them taking children lost in the desert to their lair to decorate their walls."

With everything she had seen in the past two weeks, Sierra wouldn't discount any possibility.

The two sat in silence for a few minutes. Sierra regretted coming. She regretted setting out on this disastrous mission and putting her friends in danger. They'd warned her. Only one member of the scouting party had come back, but she'd thought she would do better, and now two of her friends had suffered an unknown fate. It wasn't fair Terre had been taken. He had done nothing but help her. And he had pushed the hardest for them to turn back.

"We can't stay here," Althea finally said. "The guards will come back. We need to decide what we're going to do."

Sierra stood, her eyes on the wall; another barrier in this world that did its best to keep everyone apart from each other.

"We should head back," said Sierra. "I've already lost two of my friends today. I'd rather not lose a third."

Althea stood and brushed the red dust from her yellow cloak. "We can't go back just because you're scared I'll get hurt. I chose to come, knowing there would be risk. There's more at stake here than just us."

Was it worth it, though? Sierra had come here to find her mother; to maybe find a clue about her sister still being alive. And to find out what had happened to her home. But as much as she appreciated Althea and valued her coming along, she'd offer little help in an attack. Terre and Ember had accompanied her to offer protection. Her protectors were now gone.

If they went back to the city, they could at least come back with reinforcements, provided Malachi would risk more of his fighters to come back for Terre.

That didn't seem like the right solution, either. Even if she could convince Malachi to send a handful of Community members, they wouldn't stand a chance if they ran into an army Order members, especially if they were planning to attack the city. Despite Terre's belief they wouldn't bother themselves with an attack, the last two weeks had proven to her that anything was possible.

In reality, she had been stalling. Deep down, she knew the answer.

"Let's continue," she sighed. "If others survived the attack, I still owe it to them to try and find a way to get them out of here, including my mom."

Althea nodded, but her face betrayed her apprehension.

Sierra took a deep breath and trekked to the stairs that lay nestled within the hillside. Someone had carved out a trench into the side of the rock face. Each step was heavy and uncertain.

It was a long haul to the top, and Sierra couldn't help but continually look back to ensure the bots hadn't returned for them. She had all but forgotten the Order guards on the top of the dam, but they seemed to have avoided that threat, at least for the time being.

The top of the staircase marked the beginning of where the Sphere had once stood.

What remained of the buildings in front of them had been the southern tip of the South Village. The Core itself had been the hub of the community and of the entire Sphere. Now that they were close, Sierra could make out the enormity of the ring-shaped building. Multiple halls and chambers jutted out into the red dirt around it, housing hundreds of offices, labs, and facilities that had kept the Sphere running for over two hundred years.

The South Village maintained the Core and its workers. They would scrap metals from ancient devices the Guardians brought in, and they did much of the electronic assembly within the village. Anytime someone needed a new appliance or an old one repaired, the South Village made the updates and sent it back. At least, they had done so before it had been destroyed.

The rest of the buildings beyond the Core itself were similar to the ones she had been used to growing up: red squat dwellings, built by the Guardians from the soil below. She could only make out a couple that lay on the edge of the canyon above them. Most no longer remained standing, and the rest vanished into the smoke.

Their interest wasn't within them, though; their interest was within the Core itself. It was unlikely anyone would still be inside these homes. Rhys had told Malachi the survivors had all gathered at the Core.

Sierra suddenly felt a pang in her heart for the young man. There had been so much left unsaid between them. He had put himself in harm's way for her. Despite her initial misgivings about him, he had come around and helped her in the end.

Now, Rhys' father Terre had disappeared because of her. The two men didn't see eye to eye, but she knew the connection between a child and a parent, even when they didn't always get along. It was why she was here now, looking for her mother.

The status of both parents were now uncertain. Because of her.

She selfishly wished Rhys was with her. Not because she thought she needed his help, but because she enjoyed being around him. But part of her was also glad he was safe, back in the city. It could just as easily have been him the Serkhet took instead of Terre, and she wouldn't be able to forgive herself if Rhys died because of her.

Althea stood behind her, seemingly unaffected by the effort of the climb, as she surveyed the ring of the Core that seemed to stretch on forever.

"There will be a few ways in," Althea began. "The closest will be directly across from the dam."

"Close is good."

"The only problem is, if there are still guards along the top of the dam, they'll see us for sure. And that's if the entrance to the Core itself isn't guarded."

"OK," Sierra said. "So, now what?"

"I don't know. If there's any chance of finding Terre, that's the door we want to use. Those machines took him into the wall of the dam, and we're going to need to find our own way inside."

"What are the odds he's alive?" Sierra asked.

"From what I've seen of those who've stumbled into the MedCenter, not good."

The edge of the dam wasn't far from where they stood. The only problem was there was no cover between them and the entrance. If anyone was standing guard, there would be nowhere for them to hide.

"Tell me about the other entrances."

"There should be two relatively close by. One would be a worker's entrance not too far from here. It would be a great option, but it's probably locked."

"Okay. And the other?"

Althea sighed. "The main gate. Which is the entry closest to the genetics department, where your mom will be if she's stayed close to her work station."

Sierra stared at the facility, considering their options. She couldn't see anything beyond a small tower at the entry to the dam's promenade. "And there's probably just as good of a chance that guards are waiting there?"

"There will probably be Guardians on watch duty there. Either Sentinels or orbs."

"Let's stick to the closest access point. From there, we'll see if we can determine if anyone is blocking the way."

Althea nodded in agreement.

Dry red rocks crunched under their feet, every step like a warning beacon to those who might be on the lookout. It couldn't be helped. They kept as low as they could, intent on keeping out of sight.

Wide pillars extending up from the dam and over the path across it partially blocked them from view of whoever might be atop it. Sierra kept a wary eye on the spaces between the pillars, crossing her fingers that nobody would step out and look in her direction at precisely the wrong moment.

She didn't waste any time; it was now or never. Sierra approached the break in the wall and peered nervously around the corner.

Not a soul was there.

The crashing of the waves far below them was now a mere whisper. The hum of the Core vibrated the ground they stood on.

Her father had talked about the hum of the Core when she was a girl. Its pulse took some getting used to, but once you were inside its belly for weeks on end, it spoke to you. He'd told her he could tell when something was wrong by how it felt. It was the Core's heartbeat.

The Core's heartbeat sang to her. A heartbeat without a body, and her body gave it a temporary place to belong.

Except she no longer belonged there. The world she once knew was literally up in smoke.

She took a step toward the door at the end of the path, and then another, expecting with each movement an alarm to sound or shots to be fired.

"Where did they go?" Althea asked.

"I don't know," Sierra answered. "But let's not wait around to find out."

Two solid doors stood before them. Most of the doors in the Sphere were transparent, made of glass. These were older, made in an ancient time.

Below them, white stone replaced the red earth, decorating the walk around the Core and leading up to the doorway. Every step they took was an exercise in caution.

A wave of panic came over Sierra, and she forced herself to push it down. How they expected to get in and out unseen, she didn't know. But she would find a way. She had made too much of a mess to not try and clean it up.

They crept up to the building, just as the doors creaked open.

Sierra froze.

11

THERE WAS no escape for them.

A small lip of wall beside the door would give them some protection, but not a lot. They rushed around the thinly veiled corner. It would only take a glance in their direction to blow their cover. With no other option, Sierra pressed herself against the thin barrier as best she could and motioned for Althea to do the same.

The wall between them and the pathway was a couple of feet wide at most. They pressed their backs as far in as they could.

"We will dispose of the rest of them," a man's booming voice echoed down the corridor.

"That's over three thousand people!" a second voice said.

"They will all accept the way of the Guardians. They can become part of Titan's army or protectorates of us, but if they refuse, that's all we can do to ensure they don't become Oathbreakers."

"It seems like a waste."

Sierra held her breath. The speakers had stopped next to their hiding place. One wrong move, the slip of an arm or a leg, would give them away.

"They are only being shown mercy because Titan thinks he may have a use for them," the first man said. "The ten thousand who were eliminated weren't as lucky. Titan will finally bring the Guardians to the reign they were meant for."

"I know. I'm just surprised at the slaughter of the Chosen. We have always believed they would join us in the end."

"Remember, these Chosen were released before their time. Whatever that Oathbreaker girl did decided their fate, not us. This Sphere should still stand. Vegas should be under Guardian reign. Instead, we're left to clean up her mess."

"Yes, I'm well aware."

"We need to get them sorted out before nightfall. Titan wants us to follow the others west as soon as possible."

"They are all spread out in the holding cells for now. We'll see what Titan will have us do with them."

Sierra could hear the two men breathing. Which meant if the men were paying attention, they could hear her and Althea as well. That was, if they didn't hear her heart pounding first.

The two continued past them, thankfully in the opposite direction from where they stood. Their voices faded as their distance from them increased. Sierra tried to gauge their location along the path without sticking her head out into potential view, but she couldn't tell. She waited for several long minutes before risking peeking around the corner.

The path was empty once again.

"Are you okay?" She turned her attention to Althea, still huddled behind her. The woman was shaking, her eyes closed.

"No," she replied in a whisper. Althea straightened her cloak and her posture. "But I insisted on coming. So here we are."

"If what those two were saying was true, there are survivors. For now, at least."

Althea nodded. "One thing at a time. We came here to find your mother. If we're lucky, we'll find out what happened to Terre. We'll figure out the rest on the way."

Sierra cringed inwardly. That didn't sound like a plan at all. Who knew if her mother was still alive? It was just as possible she had been at home when the Order had gone through the Sphere murdering anyone in their path. Even if she was here, the guards had mentioned that they had split the survivors up around the compound. Finding her would be like rolling the dice.

Sierra shook the thought from her mind. There had to be hope her mother was still here. And regardless of whether she was or not, there were over three thousand still alive who needed her.

"Come on," she said.

Sierra crossed the gap to the entrance, tugged at the handle, and slid the door open enough to slip through with Althea behind her.

As the door closed, darkness enveloped them. She reached for Althea to ensure she was still there, then felt for the adjacent wall. Maybe she could follow it to find a light source. It only took a few moments for her eyes to adjust, however, revealing the dark cavern they had entered.

The floor and railings were both made of metal. They stood on a small platform that seemed to float in the chamber's darkness. Only faint beacons of light lined the walls, producing enough light to make out where the walls were but not much else.

The hum of the Core was strong here. The vibrations rattled her bones, and she felt nauseous if she thought too hard about it.

She walked over to the rail and peered below. To her left was a vast pit that descended into infinity. Steel stairs crisscrossed back and forth from one platform to another. It was a long way down.

She would never have guessed the metal beams of the facility extended so far below ground. Sierra looked back at her friend, wide-eyed as she surveyed the surrounding cavern.

Sierra pointed to the stairs, and Althea nodded. There was

only one way for them to go, and she hoped it wouldn't be all the way to the bottom.

Sierra did her best to keep her legs steady despite the vibrations. The first flight of stairs was short; a mere twenty steps. A door greeted them on this level, also made of solid metal. She crossed her fingers and tested it, and it opened with ease. A beam of light from the other side greeted them.

Sierra poked her head through the opening and, satisfied with what she saw, entered, motioning for Althea to follow.

The door closed gently behind them, blocking out the bulk of the vibrations.

"I was worried we were going to have to go down the whole way," Sierra said, grateful they didn't have to climb back up those steps. The room they had entered appeared to be a buffer room of some sort. Plain white brick lined the walls, and another metal door led further into the Core. It was cooler and less humid than the cavern of the other room.

"I believe it'd be mostly mechanical pieces down there," said Althea. "From where we were, my guess is it descends to the base of the dam. It's likely we'd run into Guardians maintaining it."

"Good thing we could get out on the first floor," Sierra said.

"They'd be maintenance drones. They'd probably ignore us."

"You seem to know a lot about what's going on here. Did they have a dam like this in your Sphere?"

Althea shook her head. "No, our Core was run on solar panels. But the concept would be the same. Maintenance Guardians would man them; they'd have no other purpose."

Sierra nodded as if she understood and decided to let it go.

"What about Terre? Those things took him into the wall. I thought he'd be in there."

"We could take a chance on the descent to find out. They could just have easily traveled through the wall to another part of the Core, though. I had hoped going through that door would have given us a clue, but we'd just be going in blind."

"Aren't we going into this whole thing blind?"

"True," Althea reluctantly agreed. "But we could walk down a hundred flights of stairs only to find nothing and have to come back up."

"Right." Part of her wanted to go down the stairs; wanted to explore any chance there was of finding Terre. If he was alive. But they had to use their time wisely. "Where to now, then?"

"The genetics lab. If your mother had been in the Core during the attack, that's where she would have been stationed. I think we should start there."

"Okay. Lead the way."

Althea took a deep breath and seemed to gather her confidence before stepping to the exit. She opened the door slowly and poked her head through.

The hallway beyond was empty, but both women assumed that could change at any moment. Those two guards had likely come this way, so surely there were more.

They inched their way forward, trying hard to stay quiet. The floor here was a dull gray concrete reminiscent of the Vegas Underground. Construction built to last millennia. The hallway was long and came to a 'T' intersection in front of them, forking to the left and the right.

A light hum stopped Sierra dead in her tracks. She grabbed Althea's shoulder and crouched down. The other woman followed her lead.

The hum grew louder, and a look of recognition crossed Althea's face. A mechanical tapping down the hallway accompanied the approaching noise.

There was nowhere for them to hide. The hallway was barely five feet wide, with no recesses or archways to speak of. She glanced back down the hall. They were halfway from where they'd entered. It was a good hundred yards, and if they sprinted now, they would definitely attract the attention of whatever was headed toward them.

The ticking grew louder, echoing down their chamber. The rapid footstep-sounding noise could only be coming from one thing.

Sierra slunk into the shadows as much as she was physically able. Althea mimicked her, pressing her back to the wall. Her eyes were closed, her breathing ragged.

The light of a gray orb crossed the hall in front of them. It didn't appear to be in a hurry, but it wasn't hovering slowly enough to be scanning, either. It continued past, and its hum faded. The ticking, however, grew louder, until Sierra was sure it was right on top of them.

A metal scorpion crossed the hall, following the orb. The ticking slowed as it passed, and it stopped in the hallway crossing. It stood motionless.

Sierra panicked, but she was frozen in place.

The Serkhet's pincers were held out, slowly opening and closing, while its metal legs twitched. It appeared to be processing something. What little light the hallway provided reflected off its plated exterior. Now that the surrounding light was dim, blue light patterns were visible on the Serkhet's frame. They mimicked the Guardian's light patterns, but not exactly. The patterns appeared stationary; they didn't move like lights on a screen, as the Guardian designs appeared to do. These were built in.

What purpose would either the Guardians or the ancients have had for the mechanical beasts?

"Keep moving, Lexa! You don't have to wait for me!" A woman's voice echoed down the hall. The voice seemed familiar, but it was distorted by the corridor and Sierra couldn't quite place it.

The scorpion turned its head back, and Althea gasped. Sierra winced; they would be directly in the creature's line of sight if it was paying attention. But its head didn't linger long enough in their direction; instead its focus was to the source of the voice.

"Get going, then. I'll follow you to the Pit. We'll see what delightful treat your brothers collected for us. Come on, though. Get on with it."

Althea looked to Sierra. She didn't have to say anything for Sierra to know what she was thinking.

Terre was the treat.

The Serkhet continued on without another glance in their direction. Following close behind the machine trailed a tall woman in a white robe with the glowing cracked glass pattern of the Order.

The woman's hair was dark, and her features were striking. She walked with the confidence of someone who was in charge and determined. In her hand was a familiar staff. A green gem attached to the top of it matched the pattern in her cloak. The stone's luminescence reflected off the solid gray walls around her.

Sierra knew this woman.

Headmaster Claudia crossed the hallway without so much as a glance in their direction.

Head of the Order—within the Sphere, at least—Claudia had overseen Sierra's Life Placement Exam on the day that drove her Outside. Sierra used to think this woman represented the highest of high society. Now, she understood the Headmaster was at the forefront of the fabrication of the world she had grown up in.

The woman didn't slow, oblivious to them crouched in their dark corner.

The two stayed stationary for a few minutes. The ticking of the Serkhet's feet against the floor faded and eventually disappeared.

"We should follow them," Sierra said.

12

———

"Are you crazy?" Althea's wide eyes reflected what little light the hall provided.

"They'll lead us to Terre," Sierra answered.

Althea shook her head. "We'll just get ourselves caught. Terre will be guarded. We're no match for an orb or an Order member and a horde of Serkhet, never mind anyone else who might be in the Pit. We need to carry on, find your mother, and then come back for Terre and the others. Maybe with some Community members from the city."

It wasn't that bad of an idea.

Claudia hadn't exactly been warm toward her during the best of times. Now that Sierra had exposed the secrets of the Sphere, Claudia wasn't likely to change her opinion.

"Look, no matter what we do, we risk being caught," Sierra said. "Let's at least have a look at what we're up against. If Terre's alive and we're able to release him, we'll have him with us for additional help."

Althea looked at her as if she had two heads.

Why is she so hesitant to look for Terre?

"Are you afraid of the Serkhet?" Sierra asked.

"Aren't you?"

"Not any more than orbs, Sentinels or Order guards," Sierra replied.

For some reason, that didn't put Althea at ease.

"Come on," Sierra said. "We're here. Our fates are tied, remember? We're both here and alive. Let's work through this together."

That earned a smile from Althea.

"Like we said before, one problem at time," Sierra continued. "Let's at least find out where Terre is."

Althea gave her a hesitant nod and took a deep breath. "Okay," she said.

As they reached the fork in the hall, Sierra looked both ways to ensure there were no other surprises waiting for them. The hallway to the right, from which the woman and Serkhet had come, stretched on before banking again to the right. The path to the left looked identical; Claudia and her companions had already turned the next corner.

They were going to have to be careful not to get lost in here. It was a maze.

"Let me guess, we would need to turn right here to get to the genetics lab?"

Althea paused, considering. "I believe so, yes."

"So the opposite direction of where they went, of course." Sierra sighed. In order to find Terre, they had to potentially journey farther away from her mother. That was if she was in the lab at all. "I hope you're able to get us back."

Claudia had seemed quite pleased that the Serkhet had brought Terre in. Was she talking to the beast? Was the beast talking to her? At some point, she hoped she would understand everything that was happening around her; that someone could finally provide her with answers.

So far, the only person who had come close to doing so was Terre. They had to know if he was okay. Greata had given Sierra the charge to find him. And she wasn't done with the man just yet.

"I'll be able to guide us back," Althea confirmed. "But I still think this is a bad idea."

Sierra pressed on in the direction Claudia had gone.

They turned the next corner, and Sierra finally felt like she was home. Well, what used to be her home, at least.

The floor slowly ramped up, bringing them to ground level. The tunnel they had been in must have been a subterranean passage connecting the dam to the rest of the Core. Small windows along the lifted ceiling allowed the muted light from outside in. Large pots on the floor contained trees reaching to the sky; greenery that would have been placed throughout important buildings to remind residents of the hope for the future and a renewed Earth.

Large blue banners hung from the ceiling. Gold stitching framed their borders and decorated them with various images, the most common being the orbs she was familiar with. Other images, such as that of the Sentinels, Sierra realized, had always hung in the buildings around the Sphere, and she had never questioned their meaning. The irony smacked her in the face. This entire time, there had been clues all around her. Only now was she able to put the pieces together. What else had laid hidden under her nose?

Other banners included the lightning crack pattern, similar to that depicted on the cloak of those in the Order. One banner pictured the Sphere itself, while another depicted what the Earth would look like from space. Another was of Mars. A final banner at the end of the hall showcased a myriad of stars.

Until a few weeks ago, Sierra had never even seen stars. The stars on the banner would have only reflected ancient tales. Symbols of the ancients, hidden in plain sight her entire life.

A mezzanine opened up above them. An open staircase led up to the second level, where another wall lined with windows led into an adjacent room. The concrete floor had transitioned to a more familiar hard rock tile.

"Wait here," she whispered to Althea. Movement in the windows above had caught her eye.

Sierra stepped carefully up each stair, still crouched.

Everything here was pristine. The floor and the walls were pure white, cleaned daily by maintenance bots. The grime of the desert clung to her skin, its presence now amplified. A bath would do her wonders.

She put the thought out of her mind for the time being. The level of cleanliness the Guardians demanded in the middle of the desert was just one more layer of their mirage.

Through the window lay what appeared to be a medical room. Someone had restrained several poor souls to surgical stations. There were three people who lay still, the rise and fall of their chests the only sign that they lived.

Sentinels stood to attention on either side of the room. Their eyes were dark, their bodies inactive.

All except one had its back toward her. Its panels were lit up dark red as it monitored the individuals strapped to their chairs.

A machine held a large needle above one man. Sierra didn't recognize him.

Then it all came back to her. The lights. The needle. The questions.

She had been in that room, interrogated by orbs and Sentinels. It was a memory so hazy it could have been a dream. In fact, she had written it off as a dream. She had relived it while she was in the desert. She had seen this room; these lights. They had drugged her so she wouldn't remember and so she would tell them the information they wanted to know.

They had asked her about Izzy that day. About Izzy's visions. She had known nothing about them. Not then, and *not now.* Only after Greata had mentioned her sister possessing the same ability was it something she had been aware of.

"What is this place?" Althea whispered behind her.

Sierra jumped at the sudden interruption to her thoughts. "You're supposed to be keeping watch!"

"You never said anything about keeping watch! You just told me to wait. I was curious."

Sierra sighed and glanced down the stairs, scanning for anyone that might have entered the atrium.

"Sorry, I didn't know what you were doing." The woman looked around nervously.

"It's okay," Sierra assured her. "You've never seen this place before?"

Althea shook her head. "No, this isn't anything like the rooms I had access to."

"I have."

"I thought you hadn't been to the Core."

"Me neither. The Guardians did something to my memories of this place. What I remember, I had hoped was only a bad dream." Sierra shook her head.

"Well, what are they doing?"

"To these folks, I don't know. But they asked me questions about my sister. They wanted to know if I had had any dreams or visions, or if she had told me anything about any dreams she'd had."

Sierra caught her breath, and she nearly screamed as the thought struck her. "They knew!" She worked hard to control the volume of her voice; to keep it low enough to prevent those in the next room from hearing. "They knew she was alive!"

"How can you be sure?"

"I can't. The memory is so hazy,"

Sierra ducked lower as an orb flew across the room behind the glass. If they had interrogated her about her sister's disappearance all those years ago, what did the Guardians want from those currently in the room?

"We've got to go," Sierra said. "We can't risk being seen here."

Althea didn't argue. They descended, heading toward the exit, but no sooner had they gotten off the last step than the door to the room above them swung open.

The pair crouched behind a group of potted plants. Once someone came down the stairs, their protection would be insufficient, but it would have to do.

A voice came from above them. "Bring the mother. Two of her daughters have left this facility, and I want to know how and why."

Her suspicions were confirmed. Izzy had left. And the Guardians had known. Had Ember known the truth? Who else had known? Her mother? Sierra hoped she would somehow find a clue of what had happened to her sister, and where she'd be able to find her.

Althea visibly shook. The poor woman was going to make herself sick.

"Yes, Lord Titan," a second voice replied. "I will fetch her at once."

Sierra froze at the mention of Titan's name.

"Why was she not questioned previously?" Titan asked, his metallic voice grating on Sierra's nerves.

"The Guardians questioned her and the daughter after the husband's death, but they found nothing. She possessed the necessary acumen to replace her husband, so she continued to work in his place."

"Under what pretence?"

"The same as the others. To improve humanity in order to survive the outside world once the Sphere fell."

"Was she questioned again after Sierra's disappearance?"

Sierra gasped. They were talking about her mother!

"The collapse sent the Guardians into chaos before we had a chance. If the Order hadn't come and slaughtered . . ."

"Excuses. But the Order has caused considerable disruption."

"Sir? We followed the ancient texts. The Sphere's fall wasn't the Guardians' timing."

"I could have utilized them, but it does not matter now. Prepare the woman for interrogation before she is disposed of."

"Yes, Lord Titan." Footsteps echoed down the stairs and a member of the Order passed through the room and out a side door. Behind him, slow methodical steps and a light hum that Sierra recognized followed.

The Sentinel crossed the room. Sierra pressed as far back behind the plant as she could manage. She was practically sitting on Althea's lap, but the young woman held her close as if desperate to prevent Sierra from leaving her.

Titan's white cloak was like those of the Order members, but the patterns on it were gold. The dark red lights of its paneling and eyes created an eerie contrast of both leadership and destruction. She couldn't help but notice his arm had been repaired since their last encounter.

Sierra shared a confused look with Althea.

Her mother was alive. In any other situation, she would have leapt for joy at the news. But the opportunity to find and prevent her from being killed was narrowing.

The sound of closing doors signaled both the man and machine had left.

"Was that the same Sentinel you saw in your vision?" Althea asked. If it was possible, her face had gone even more pale than normal.

Sierra nodded. "That was Titan."

"What does he want with your mother?" Althea asked.

"I'm guessing he wants to use her to find me," she replied. "We've got to find my mother, preferably before that Order member does."

Althea nodded and looked toward the empty chamber with trepidation, before convincing herself to continue her lead.

Four doorways appeared down another short hall.

"The deeper we go, the more likely we'll encounter Guardians," Althea said. "The orbs will hopefully leave us alone if we're not doing anything illegal or access a restricted area."

"I have a feeling this constitutes a restricted area," Sierra said.

Althea muttered something under her breath before saying, "Nothing seems to be operating normally, anyway. It's best if we avoid being seen regardless."

As they continued, the hallways became shorter, punctuated by doorways and laboratories, tech centers and mechanical rooms.

Screens decorated the walls as they ventured deeper within the structure. Some screens were lit with images of the Guardians' promised reconstructed Earth, while some bore images of the Sphere as it once was. The transition was jarring. Sierra had been away from the Sphere for nearly a month, yet her time in the Silent Zone felt like a lifetime. Those living on the Outside could likely never imagine a place like this one. Live video; pulsing lights along the corridor; electronic doors. It was a different world here.

In most ways, it seemed like it was a world that should have been so much better. Those who lived here wanted for nothing. She had grown up never once needing food. She had never known anyone to have been kidnapped or stabbed. Nobody she had ever known had gone without anything they needed.

And yet it was all based on a lie.

Terre had told her the ancients had programmed the Guardians. Somehow this world had been designed for another purpose. But some things still didn't make sense to her.

She had grown up believing the world outside had been destroyed and needed to be rebuilt. Terre had told her they had been following an ancient program to keep them safe, yet the Guardians consistently murdered those who lived on the outside. Or murdered those on the inside who didn't follow the rules. Those like Greata.

How could they be programmed to both kill and protect?

A screen flickered to an image that caused Sierra to stop in her tracks. No matter how much she thought she had prepared herself, it wasn't enough. The image on the screen was a punch to the gut.

Home. Smoke rose from the remains of what the Order had picked through. The rubble of where she had lived. Gone.

She recognized her street. Fragments of the shell of her home stood, but only barely. Few surrounding houses had faired any better. Most had been leveled.

There would be no going back.

13

WARM DESERT AIR drifted from outside, carrying the stench of Sierra's incinerated childhood along with it.

Sierra tried not to retch as she thought of the bodies that had been piled up and were now burning along with the rest of her village. Everything from her past was now gone for good. Lie or not, it had still been part of who she was. Part of where she came from.

She had done her best to harden herself to what she had seen on the displays. They had to press on. She was now more determined than ever to find some way to right the wrong she had committed.

Sierra and Althea had made their way a little farther through the facility when they came across another stumbling block.

The smell of death drifted in through an opening in the wall near to where they now hid. Members of the Order stood watch in the entryway, and it was a wonder they hadn't seen the women wander into the room. Sierra had been so lost in thought she almost forgot where she was. It hadn't been until Althea grabbed her and yanked her into the corner that she realized the error that had almost cost them detection.

The break in the building led to a wide but short stairwell that overlooked what remained of the residences of the Core workers.

She could count six members of the Order in the entryway, gathered in a circle, laughing and chatting. From the few words she heard, she had a feeling she didn't really want to know what about.

Past them, orbs swept past the Core's entrance. They were regulatory units standing guard, scanning those that had entered the premises. Althea had told her they would have been in place before the collapse. Only a few red buildings still stood outside. They lined the street, defiant of the world that had come crashing down around them. A memory of what had been.

The room they had stumbled into must have been the Core's main foyer. Sierra was thankful they hadn't tried to work their way around the building to the main entrance. Dozens of robed men and women wandered around outside. Some led bound prisoners to an unknown destination, although Sierra could guess what fate would meet them if she couldn't find a way to help them.

The beauty of the Core's foyer was undeniable. While most of the Core felt clinical, the Guardians had designed the foyer to be warm and inviting and to provide a glimpse of what the Guardians promised their terraformed Earth could be. Greenery, marble, and decorative sculptures and designs filled the room. More banners lined the ceiling.

One wall had been completely exposed to the outside, allowing smoke to filter in. The doorway had been filled with glass at some point, but it appeared to have recently been shattered.

They would have to cross about thirty feet of open space to follow the path Claudia had taken. Without something to distract the Order members away from the entrance, Sierra didn't see a way for them to get through.

The occasional Sentinel also marched past, adding an extra

obstacle they'd have to maneuver around. Guardians focused outwards toward the settlement, likely keeping an eye out for more survivors seeking refuge.

One wayward glance toward her and Althea, and they would surely be detected.

Althea remained surprisingly calm. She had spent the entire morning quivering in fear, but something had now enabled her to steady her breathing and find her resolve.

Only an hour had passed since Terre's encounter with the Serkhet, but it felt like days. Ember's disappearance seemed like a month ago, not that same morning.

It all rested on them, and they still had to get into the heart of the building.

"Do you have any ideas?" Sierra whispered to Althea.

"No."

Sierra had been afraid of this moment. She had known they would eventually run into someone they'd either have to confront or evade. If they got caught here, they wouldn't discover anything, except for maybe where the rest of the residents were being held.

Their plan to follow Claudia to Terre had been a complete disaster. They had lost sight of their target after being halted by eluding Titan, and they were now crawling through the Core with no clear sense of direction.

She studied their surroundings for what felt like the millionth time. They were running out of time. Every moment they wasted here was another in which Claudia could be ripping Terre apart, or in which the Order could be dragging her mother to interrogation.

Her heart was pounding so hard, she could feel it in her skull. Her palms were sweaty. She tried to decide if she should make a run for it or try to creep by without being noticed. Neither seemed like a good plan.

Maybe they didn't need a good plan. Maybe any plan would do.

"Step aside," a commanding voice barked from an unseen corner of the foyer.

Those who guarded the gate shuffled over.

Sierra could just make out the Sentinel approaching the entrance. Unlike Titan, this machine's eyes were the standard blue. The lights along its body stood out against the dark haze of the smoke behind it, and a brown cloak hung loosely from its shoulders.

Sierra did her best to duck down further, attempting to press as much of herself into the floor while still being able to see what was happening.

Behind the bot, a group of twenty people, tied and bound, were being led. Each of them was dirty and battered, and soot marked their many faces. Their eyes were cast to the ground in defeat, but some still looked to the building before them in hope.

"Follow my lead," she whispered to Althea. Sierra expected to see her wide-eyed uncertainty return, but it surprised her when the woman simply nodded.

The Sentinel led the group up the steps toward them. The Order guards in the entryway had turned their attention to the street outside.

Sierra took another look at Althea and cursed the bright yellow shawl the Healer had worn. At least they were both dirty. It would have to be enough. This might be the only chance they had.

The group followed closely behind the Sentinel, and within moments, they passed the alcove where Sierra and Althea hid. Sierra stood and scurried to the back of the group, keeping her head down, and Althea followed in her wake.

Nobody in the group seemed to notice or care that the two newcomers were tagging along. The stench of smoke wafting from the survivors was putrid and strong, as though they had been among the flames. Perhaps some of them had been. It turned Sierra's stomach, but she did her best to ignore it.

It seemed strange the Sphere had a sudden influx of additional Order members. There had never been more than a couple dozen in the Sphere as far as she had known, and it now seemed like they overran the place. It boiled her blood to think they had destroyed most of the Sphere and then moved into the Core, assuming charge.

The Guardians might have been following a program, but the Order had chosen to kill.

Who here are the true monsters?

Sierra did her best to look as dejected as the rest of the group. From where the guards stood, they wouldn't be able to discern her and Althea weren't bound. The packs on their back may have set them apart, but she prayed they wouldn't draw any undue attention.

They entered through the doorway with the rest of the group into a lobby of sorts. Several orbs hovered above them. Members of the Order walked by, intent on another destination, not paying any attention to the group being brought in.

Sierra glanced at the orbs floating above them. A simple scan could have detected her and Althea were unbound. But every man, woman, and bot around them appeared to be preoccupied.

It was hard to tell through the dirt and the grime, but Sierra didn't think she recognized any of the faces that walked alongside her. What did they think of their saviors capturing and detaining them? She hoped she would get the chance to ask them about it.

How she would get that chance would be another story.

A large semi-circular desk sat in the center of the room. A curved wall of monitors sat behind it. A person typically sat in the chair, now left empty. This would have been the front desk of the entire facility.

Scenes on the monitors overlooked different areas of the

Core. Sierra quickly scanned the rooms on display. Most looked empty, but a large room caught her eye. Hundreds of people were huddled in a large holding cell. A pit in the center of the room bubbled and roiled with activity.

Serkhet.

The bubbling metal appearance of a mass of mechanized scorpions was unforgettable.

A couple of Order members could be seen on the outer edge, but from what Sierra could see, there were few guards for the amount of people in the room. She could also tell there weren't three thousand people there. There were three hundred at the most. She hurriedly scanned the other monitors but found no other prisoners being displayed.

One monitor displayed a room containing a few people working. Three women in lab coats were surrounded by highly technical equipment, conducting what appeared to be some sort of research.

One of them was her mother.

"Top right monitor," she whispered to Althea. She got as close as possible given their situation. She didn't want to draw attention, and there wasn't much opportunity as the guards hurried their group along.

"She's there?" Althea whispered.

Sierra nodded.

"That's the genetics lab all right."

"Do you think you can get us there?" Sierra asked.

"Yeah. Keep quiet, though!"

They received a few dirty glances from the prisoners next to them, but none said anything.

Althea was right; it was best not to push their luck.

A large corridor led them out of the foyer. Sierra needed Althea to make the call on where to break off from the group. She tried hard not to hold her breath. There were so many things that could go wrong. A Guardian orb could detect who they were; a guard could spot they were without bonds; a prisoner could call out when they broke from the pack. Or something else she hadn't even thought of could enter the equation. They had already encountered Serkhet wandering these halls; who knew what other surprises there might be?

Althea subtly slowed her pace as the guards led the group down the corridor. A half dozen doors on either side led to various chambers, perhaps to more hallways.

Sierra's heart sank as she surveyed the rest of the group and silently promised she would do what she could to help them. It was hard to believe these people were being taken captive for surviving an attack on their own homes. She tried hard not to think of the reason behind these people's plight, but it was impossible not to.

If she hadn't activated the EMP device, thousands of Vegas residents would have died by the Guardian waves that had rained down on the city. But fate enjoyed irony, and instead she had caused the death of thousands of people she had grown up with. Thousands who were oblivious to the Guardians' intention to do anything but protect them. Her people had been slaughtered instead.

It was enough to make her want to curl up on the floor and cry. Why should so much rest on her shoulders? None of these people had asked for her to be their savior. Nobody had asked her; it was just thrust upon her.

Althea glanced over her shoulder, and Sierra stopped herself from looking back as well. No need to draw extra attention.

Content with what she saw, Althea kept their pace a half step slower than the group but moved slowly to the side.

Sierra kept her head down and a wary eye to ensure they hadn't attracted notice.

Despite her concerns, nobody paid any attention to them. They had fallen behind the rest of the group, and the leading Sentinel hadn't looked back once.

As they approached a staircase, Althea made her move. Walls on either side of the stairs quickly provided a barrier between them and the group, and Sierra breathed a sigh of relief. One step closer.

"The lab's just up ahead," Althea said.

Sierra leaned on the wall to catch her breath. What had they gotten themselves into? Perhaps her mother would have some ideas, but, as it stood, she couldn't see a way to get her people out of this mess.

A series of office doors lined a narrow hall at the top of the stairs.

Althea continued to lead them forward.

Another desk sat empty in a small reception area. More monitors decorated the desk and the walls, but they were all turned off. As they got further into the room, the pulse of the Core returned. It was subtle, a vibration Sierra could feel in the essence of her being. Something nearby was producing a large amount of energy.

They tiptoed past the desk and through a set of glass double doors. The room on the other side was nearly pitch black. Dim blue lighting provided some guidance as to where the edges of the floor met the walls.

Sierra's pace quickened as she pushed into the darkness. Shadows played games on the walls of the corridor, bouncing off of any outcrop or mantle they could find.

They wound through a few twists in the hall before a white archway led them into another dark chamber.

Sierra let out a gasp, nearly tripping over her own feet.

14

———

HUNDREDS OF COLUMNS stood before them in a room that appeared as if it had no end in any direction. On the floor, a strip of carpet, the width of the archway, stretched into the darkness of the room.

On either side of its path, the cylinders stood, each only a foot and a half wide. They rose from the floor and disappeared into the shadow above. Sierra could only guess they reached as high as the ceiling, but there was no way to be sure. Hidden in shadow, the ceiling could have been twenty feet high or a hundred.

Within the middle of each column sat a three-foot section of glass, a window into its belly, which glowed a deep blue.

Sierra couldn't tell if the rest of the columns, above and below the glass, were dark blue or black. They took on the color of the light embedded within them.

A similar ring of blue light encircled the base of each column, creating a patchwork of circled lights along the floor that stretched endlessly on either side of the path.

It wasn't until Sierra was several steps into the room that she noticed there was something within the glass sections of the columns. At first, it wasn't obvious what they were: small blobs suspended in some sort of viscous fluid, possibly a gel.

"They're babies," she said aloud. Her voice, though quiet, echoed through the chamber, bouncing off each pillar.

Althea tilted her head, puzzled. "You didn't know?"

"Know what? What is this place?" Sierra asked.

"This is where we're born."

Sierra's jaw dropped as she scanned what had to be hundreds of fetuses in various stages of development. Some appeared to be only a small ball of cells, while others looked to be fully formed babies.

The Guardians gifted parents with children; that was the extent of what she had been told. Of course she had questioned where babies came from growing up, but as she grew older, she thought the Guardians bringing them was a way for parents to get around awkward conversations. But perhaps it had just simply been true.

"Gifts of the Guardians," Sierra whispered. "I knew they claimed to create life, but I had no idea this was what they meant." She walked up to one of the columns and placed her palm on the glass, studying the life that rested within its case.

"I remember when I first learned of this place," Althea said. "We were told the Guardians gift parents with a child, but we were never told where they came from. It wasn't something I learned until I stumbled on a room like this by accident working in my Sphere's Core. Until then, it was never something I questioned."

"Me neither," Sierra replied. Her fingertips skirted the edge of the glass. It felt wrong to touch the artificial womb, but she couldn't resist the draw.

"Your parents both worked here," said Althea. "They never told you what they did? That a place like this existed?"

"I knew little more than anyone else." Sierra laughed. "Maybe less. I knew my parents worked to give us the best genes to survive once the Earth was habitable again. They weeded out sickness, birth defects, and disease that used to rattle humanity. But I was very young when my father died; too young for me to understand anything about what he did here. My mom didn't like to talk about her work. Ever since Dad died, she didn't tell me much of anything."

"Yet you still came back for her."

"She's still my mom. And I feel responsible for the situation she's in."

"You know this isn't your fault," Althea said. "You couldn't have known the Order would have reacted this way. You didn't choose this outcome. Don't blame yourself."

Sierra nodded, but she didn't mean it. No matter how much Althea wanted to sugar-coat it for her benefit, Sierra's actions had led to this result.

The smell of the room was a blend of ammonia and cleaning fluid. The sour stench lingered over them, adding to the nausea Sierra already felt.

Aside from the smell, there was something else, intangible, about the room that made her stomach turn.

Sierra didn't know why the room bothered her so much. She had spent her entire life believing the Guardians developed and brought beings to life. Natural methods of childbirth were no longer practiced, or at least they weren't supposed to be. But this didn't seem like the way human life was supposed to start.

But, then again, nothing in the Sphere was how it should be.

It struck her as peculiar that the cylinders were stationed where they were. Rather than being tucked away in a back chamber, they were on full display; a reminder to everyone who walked this hall where each member of the Sphere came from, of where life originated, and what the work they did produced.

"I wonder how much of this Izzy knew? If Dad had brought her to see his work, she would have had to walk through this room."

Sierra pulled herself away from the stations of the unborn.

They turned a series of corners designed to keep the room separate from the next. Intense white light crept in from the next room.

It took a few moments for Sierra's eyes to adjust as they entered. The room was blindingly white.

The three women they had seen on the monitors worked within this room. Two of the women at the back were enclosed behind a glass wall. Behind them was a giant monitor, its image flipping from one column to the next. Various numbers and graphs overlaid a close-up of each fetus.

Between the glass wall and where Sierra stood was a larger space, which would have held over twenty people at various workstations. Display tablets set up at each station also held images of the cylinders and other documents and data.

A familiar figure stood in front of one of the datapads.

Long blonde hair flowed midway down the woman's back, frayed and disheveled. Though the woman looked to be in better shape than the prisoners, it was obvious she hadn't been taking care of herself. Even during the devastation of her husband's death, her hair had been silky smooth and well maintained. Sierra almost didn't recognize her, like she couldn't place the woman who had been an absent presence in her life for nearly eighteen years.

Her mom's shoulders slumped in her white lab coat, seemingly with the weight of the world upon them, hunched over her computer, working on something Sierra couldn't see.

"Mom?"

Nancy Runar turned around and Sierra had to keep herself from letting out a gasp. Next to her, Althea didn't succeed, but it was soft enough that her mother hopefully didn't notice.

Her mom's pale face was bruised, cut, and worn. She had recently been beaten; that much was clear. Whether it had been at the hand of a machine or a human, Sierra couldn't tell.

"Sierra?" Confusion marred the woman's face. "Why are you here?"

Sierra blinked at the question. Immediately, her past pain at having a mother who was never there for her rushed back.

Her mother hadn't asked how she was or showed any relief or joy at seeing a daughter who, in all likelihood, could have been dead.

"I came back for you!" Sierra began. "Don't you want to know where I've been?"

Her mom's face twisted like Sierra had said the dumbest thing she had ever heard. Monitors beeped around the lab, amplifying the silence she received.

"You shouldn't have come."

Sierra's mouth moved wordlessly. She looked to Althea, who looked just as confused as she was.

The two women in the glass room continued working on their screens, oblivious.

"I came back for you!" Sierra repeated. She didn't want to cry. Wouldn't cry. She'd risked her life, left two of her friends to die, and risked another for this moment of reunion. She had been so happy to learn her mother had been alive; so determined to save her from interrogation. Finding her had offered a moment of hope; a moment of hope which was now passing through her fingers like a fistful of sand.

"We don't have time," her mother said. Her eyes surveyed the doorway. "They'll be here any moment."

"Who?" she asked, but her mother wasn't sticking around for an answer. Nancy flew out the door and entered the columned birthing chamber.

"I don't understand. What's happening?" Sierra asked as she caught up to her mother's hurried pace.

"We risked everything to get you out," her mother said. "You shouldn't have come back."

"What do you mean?" Sierra asked. "Greata got me out. She died helping me!"

"Greata's death wasn't something we could help. We never wanted that. We tried to prevent it. But she insisted if it had to be that way, it was worthwhile. That *you* were worth the effort."

"Mom, you aren't making any sense."

Her mom stopped and grabbed the medallion that hung around her neck. She held it up to the dim light of the chamber.

"Greata gave you this?" her mom asked.

"She did. Just before they murdered her."

"Greata was a part of something far bigger than you know. A movement that is nearly as old as the wars. The symbols on this medallion used to represent hope. So few have that anymore. The movement became hated, then ridiculed, and now it has become unrecognizable to what it once was.

"Greata was one of its remaining members. Before she came here, she sought those who would fight for that hope. So few believed the world could be anything more than it was. She had almost given up herself, until she learned of what we were doing here. Greata allowed herself to be captured and brought to the Sphere. Something drove her to learn more. She took a particular interest in you after Izzy got out. Greata said you were the hope of the human race. In you, her hope for the future was reignited."

Mom knew about Izzy.

Before Sierra could ask the million questions she had, a familiar ticking sound echoed through the chamber. Questions would have to wait.

Althea let out a muffled yelp as she ducked behind one of the blue lit columns. Nancy grabbed Sierra's hand and pulled her off to the side. The pair edged toward the back of the room, while Althea slunk further away from them. She tried to pull her mother toward her friend, but her mother's grip was unrelenting and strong.

Sierra wanted to call out to Althea to stick with them, but she didn't dare speak with the Serkhet fast approaching.

Metallic footsteps entered the chamber. Sierra and her mother had barely concealed themselves in the darkness when the shadow of a tall robed woman stretched out on the carpet. The shadows of two mechanical scorpions followed close behind.

"You've been keeping secrets from us, Nancy." The woman's voice, calm and commanding, bounced among the columns. Sierra recognized it as Headmaster Claudia's.

Her mother focused her gaze on Claudia. She stood as if ready to launch into an attack.

"We know she's here," Claudia continued. "She brought an ancient with her. My pets have had a fun time with him."

Terre! Is he still alive?

Her mother had moved, inching closer to the woman. Sierra stayed still, afraid her shadow would attract attention.

Sierra could hear her own heartbeat. Lights from the cylinders reflected off the scorpions, causing strange patterns on the surrounding floor. They inched closer as Nancy continued to work her way toward the path. She'd be crazy if she thought Sierra was going to follow her.

Maybe she was crazy for staying put.

Blue light reflected off Althea's face as she crouched behind an adjacent pillar. A greenish tinge struck her as well, cast by the green crystal in the woman's staff. Its light stretched a little farther than the first few rows of pillars around her, but it added to their glow.

Claudia didn't seem to be in any hurry. Stalking between pillars, the green in her cloak was softly illuminated as well, the light clearly revealing her position. She was getting closer, but not as rapidly as the pair of Serkhet. The ticking of their claws against the stone floor was accompanied by the occasional thump of the woman's staff hitting the tile.

Sierra focused on the stalking beasts and the path the

scorpions wove in and around the columns. It couldn't be possible, but they seemed intent on finding her, and her alone. They ignored her mom, passing by her as if she wasn't even there. Althea was several columns over, but the creatures' metal bodies were making a beeline toward Sierra's location. Half of the room had been left unexplored; the other side of the path had not been bothered with. Their behavior could mean only one thing: they knew where she was. If not exactly, they had a good idea.

The beasts approached from either side of the column Sierra hid behind. Her fingers twitched above the daggers tucked into her belt. They would likely be ineffective against the creatures—their shells seemed all but impenetrable—but it was all she had. She held her breath, holding out hope they wouldn't find her.

But they already knew she was there.

She could feel them. She couldn't describe it any other way, but despite facing the opposite direction, she knew exactly where they stood, and it would be only moments before they spotted her.

One of the creatures stood on its hind legs, a red beam shining from the front of its hideous snout. Metallic teeth emerged from a small mouth situated behind their pincers. Its teeth were like creepy little hands desperate to grab onto anything it could devour.

Sierra backed as far as she could into the face of the column, sure she was going to die. Her mom was well out of her way. She didn't know exactly where she was, but she was closer to Claudia. Sierra couldn't bear to look to see how Althea was faring.

The clank of metal striking metal erupted behind her, and she jumped from her hiding space. One of the beasts let out a horrendous noise, and metal crashing into tile and glass echoed through the hall.

Blue goo covered the floor, soaking Sierra's feet up to her ankles. The scorpion that had been on its hind legs had fallen backward, legs and pincers flailing wildly in the air. Several columns around it had been smashed, causing the gelatinous liquid to spill from its glass casing and pour onto the floor.

Sierra struggled to stay upright. The goo made the floor slippery. She hadn't noticed Althea had taken a place beside her, crouched with one arm forward and a dagger in her other hand. Sparks erupting from the fallen creature's mouth made her realize there was a dagger embedded in the beast. A bullseye hit between the metallic teeth must have severed a critical component.

Sierra stood bewildered as she picked her jaw up from the floor. But there was little time for amazement. The second creature let out a high-pitched screech and lunged for Althea.

The Healer leapt an inhuman distance into the air as the beast approached with pinchers grasping. Althea launched herself on top of the creature, drew a second blade, and threw the entirety of her body weight into its neck, dagger first. The dagger found a seam connecting the machine's metal plates. Without taking another step, the scorpion crumpled beneath Althea, twitching and spasming as it tried to cling to life before finally becoming still.

And then there was emptiness. Sierra could sense the life leaving the two beasts. The room quieted with their passing.

Althea stood over the body of the now defeated scorpion, her chest heaving from the effort.

"How did you . . . ?" Sierra began. She couldn't quite comprehend how the ordinarily nervous healer suddenly knew how to throw daggers with the precision of a festival champion.

Green light flooded the room, interrupting her question. Glass cracked in the columns around them. Claudia was releasing a charge from her staff, and the glass canisters within the columns were absorbing the impact of the shockwaves. The sound of cracking glass echoed through the chamber, as though the integrity of every column in the room was being compromised.

From across the chamber, Sierra's mother screamed.

Several nearby columns erupted. Gel and the tiny beings gestating within crashed to the floor.

Sierra covered her eyes to avoid the shards of glass thrown in her direction. Even still, pieces cut and embedded into her arms and cloak.

Althea had crouched behind one of the scorpion carcasses to shield herself from the attack.

The green light disappeared as the screaming stopped.

Her mother, and Claudia, were gone.

15

———

SIERRA APPREHENSIVELY GRABBED the dagger from the still-twitching scorpion and tucked it into her belt. She'd had enough of people she cared about being carried off into the darkness.

She didn't wait for Althea. She didn't know where she was going, but she would not let Claudia get away with her mother.

Even if her welcome hadn't been all Sierra had hoped it would be, her mother had answers.

Sierra lost her balance twice before regaining it and carrying on. The smell of the ooze was so horrendous, she had to concentrate in order not to retch. Bile rose in her mouth more than once before she composed herself and managed, with some degree of success, to push the offensive odor out of her mind.

As she emerged from the back of the chamber, it became apparent the damage to the pillars hadn't been as bad as she'd feared. Whatever had been fired from Claudia's scepter had somehow only smashed the glass of several of the closest canisters to her. Several more nearby had cracked, but their integrity had been sustained.

The scorpions, the green blast, had all been directed at her.

But instead Claudia had taken her mother, and for that, there could only be one reason.

Sierra was walking right into a trap, but she didn't care anymore. She paused only briefly to consider her course of action, but shook off the question and carried on.

"Where are you going?" Althea called out. So lost in her own thoughts, Sierra hadn't even noticed Althea had been desperately trying to keep pace.

"We're getting my mom, we're getting Terre, and then we're going to get the rest of the prisoners out of here."

Her robe had been soaked in gel up to the knees. Sierra took it off, tossing it to the floor. Despite only a few of the glass canisters shattering, the floor had a wet layer of the goo all the way to the entrance. Sierra's shoes clung to the tacky floor with each step, but she wasn't about to remove those.

She even considered tossing her bag completely. It had landed in the goo, taking the brunt of one of her near-falls, but she was going to need its contents if they were going to make it back through the desert and to the city.

Althea followed Sierra's action, discarding her own jacket. It wasn't so long that it reached the floor, and the woman hadn't fallen, so she must simply have been tired of the weight or thought maybe she could move more freely without it. Althea's tank top underneath was yellow too. Sierra rolled her eyes.

Voices echoed down the hall, coming closer. Sierra pressed her back to the wall, just at the edge of the doorframe.

"Claudia looked pissed. That woman is going to end up as scorpion food," a man's voice echoed down the hall.

"The geneticist?" a second voice responded, approaching closer. "Nah, Titan has bigger plans for her. She's got more talent than the rest of them combined. More likely they'll reprogram her and send her back into the lab. But Maxwell's going to be livid that we didn't find her first. He had orders direct from Titan to bring her back."

"What's the difference whether Maxwell or Claudia brings her back? The result's the same."

"Not for Maxwell," the second man chided. "You know how Titan can be. And you know Maxwell will take out whatever lashing he gets on us."

"Well, what did Titan expect? That we'd rip the woman away from the Sphere's Headmaster? I'm sure it'll be fine."

"Funny, all these years we were just waiting for the chosen Guardian to arise and take over. The imps they've been breeding and growing in here will now join our loyal ranks . . . "

"What happened here?" the first man asked.

The two had stepped through the archway. They wore gray robes, but theirs had no illuminations. Sierra wished she had asked Terre more about the meaning of the colors and patterns the Order members displayed.

Panic hit the faces of the men as their wide eyes surveyed the mess of glass, dead scorpions, and goo. Even in the dimmed light, there was no mistaking a fight had taken place.

"There's no way that woman could have taken out *two* of these things," the second man said. "They're near indestructible."

Sierra stole a glance at Althea. *Since when did you have such incredible skills with knives?* She had been terrified of everything they'd encountered since leaving the SZ.

The two men were only a few feet away from her and Althea. They had been so distracted by the mess of the place that they hadn't noticed the two young women hidden in the shadows.

Her window to act wouldn't last long, and she currently held the upper hand.

Without thinking, Sierra took the dagger she had ripped from the scorpion's maw and thrust it into the side of the closest Order member. A second weapon whipped by her head, thrown from behind her by Althea, but the second guard ducked reflexively before it made contact.

"Hey! What are you doing here?" the guard asked, raising a blaster toward the women.

Sand.

Sierra swallowed. Her mind raced for a way out. Sweat dripped down the man's face. The air in the facility was borderline cold, so it wasn't because of heat.

Clearly, she and Althea were the ones on the wrong side of a blaster. But as she glanced to the man's companion on the floor, a dagger embedded in his ribs, it made sense.

"Don't try anything funny. Tell me why I shouldn't kill you right now."

His friend has just been stabbed. Why is he even asking? If he was going to kill us, he would have done it by now.

He repeatedly glanced to the doorway.

The man was waiting for Maxwell, or whoever was on their way to find her mother.

They needed to distract the guard. She had an idea.

"Hey, buddy? Are you okay?" Sierra said, looking to the second man, collapsed in a heap.

It worked. The guard still standing turned to look at his colleague, giving Sierra the opportunity to grab a second dagger from her belt and lunge for him.

The guard folded over the dagger as he gasped for breath and fell to his knees.

"Where did that come from?" Althea asked. Although she didn't seem as nervous as before, her breathing was now labored.

Sierra furrowed her brow as she wiped the blade on the fallen guard's robe. She searched him and pulled out a small energy weapon, which she slid into her belt.

"You've got to be kidding me," she replied.

Sierra grabbed another blaster from the second incapacitated man and handed it to Althea. She left the dagger embedded in his corpse. She didn't think she had the stomach to pull that one free on account of the blood already trickling down his middle. The weapons would come in handy, but even so, she didn't think they'd stand much of a chance taking on the Order and the Serkhet on their own. Especially if they ran into more than a couple.

She studied the two men, dead by her own hand. It was one thing to have thousands die indirectly because of her actions, but it was quite another to have stabbed two herself. Only a few days ago, she would have found it reprehensible, but these zealots didn't blink twice at the slaughter of thousands of innocents. She wouldn't risk waiting to find out what Maxwell would do once he arrived.

"You're one to talk," she continued. "You took out those two scorpions like a pro. Since when are you able to handle weapons like that? I thought your place in any fight was in the MedCenter."

Althea looked back to the two metal beasts as if seeing what she had done for the first time and nearly dropped the weapon in her hand.

"It is." Her mouth moved wordlessly for a moment. "I have never used a weapon like that in my life. I'd chalk it up to luck, but nobody is that lucky twice."

"Let's hope you're as lucky with a blaster."

Althea glanced at the gun, shaking her head. "This is madness," she whispered, just loud enough for Sierra to hear.

"I'm sick of my friends disappearing, Althea. We're getting them back."

Sierra shrugged off the apprehensive look her friend gave her. The woman had just taken out two beasts with daggers, for crying out loud. Her time for uncertainty needed to end.

"Come on, we shouldn't leave these bodies out in the open," Sierra suggested. "Let's find a place for them."

They left the bodies for a moment while they scoped out potential spots. They could leave them in the dark recesses of the chamber, but with the destruction of the columns, Sierra was sure it wouldn't be long before someone came to inspect the mess.

There was a small door just outside of the chamber. Sierra motioned for Althea to follow her. But as she stepped out of the room, Sierra realized they were leaving a trail of goo. Reluctantly, she removed her boots, and her pants, which were also coated in the substance. Althea cursed under her breath but repeated the action.

Sierra hoped they'd find something to wear during their search. Running around the Core in their underwear didn't strike her as a good way to blend in.

She opened the door, revealing a supply closet. Several lockers and bins within gave them a few options to hide the bodies and their soiled clothing. She opened one of the lockers and smiled. Stacked in neat piles lay dozens of freshly pressed robes; gray ones matching those the stabbed guards had been wearing. She opened another locker to discover footwear.

"Let's leave the bodies here," she suggested. "Hopefully it will buy us some time before someone comes looking for them."

They hauled the guards to the room one at a time, so as not to leave a trail of blood behind them, and disposed of them in one of the bins.

They then rummaged through the lockers, finding attire to fit them. They also decided to leave their bags. It would make their trip back to Vegas much more difficult, but they'd definitely garner attention trying to feign being an Order member while wearing them. They both drank greedily from their canteens before casting the bags into a bin and leaving the closet behind.

Sierra cast a glance back to the birthing chamber and its columns of goo that held fetal tissue in suspension. Had families already been chosen for these infants? And how many of those families still remained alive? The guard had mentioned they were now destined to join the ranks of the Order. Prior to the fall of the Sphere, the Order would choose its recruits based on

LPE results. At least, that was what the Guardians had told them.

The exam Sierra had taken had given her answers that were correct, but not part of the curriculum. Despite everything she had gone through, she still mulled over those answers.

Lies. The term had been incorporated in every multiple-choice answer. There was no way those were part of the actual exam.

But here she was. The answers had proven truthful in every case. Her entire world had been built on lies.

If these infants were now *all* destined to swell the ranks of the Order, something else had changed.

AFTER THEY LEFT THE CHAMBER, it wasn't long before Sierra and Althea met their next test. They had just finished descending several stairs when a group of five Order guards passed them.

Two others lingered behind, involved in their own conversation. Sierra cast Althea a nervous grin. The guards' gray cloaks matched the ones they had stolen. Hopefully, they'd blend in well enough to sneak past.

A glimpse of one guard caught her eye. His bristling beard stood out, as the rest of the Order she had seen wore clean-shaven faces.

Sierra recognized the voice of the second man as the one she had heard talking to Titan earlier.

"What do you mean, Claudia took her?" the man asked.

"It's like I said, Maxwell. She walked in with her two pets and walked out with the woman in cuffs."

"Bloody sand and desert! Titan's going to gut me!" Maxwell replied.

"He's after her as well? What did this woman do?"

"She's the mother of the Oathbreaker who brought down the

Vegas units."

"Holy sand! How'd she survive this long?"

"She's the lead geneticist. Titan needs something from her. I have to catch up with Claudia before she gets to Titan."

"Well, I'm sure she's bringing her to him as well. It will all end up the same. It's not like she's fled into the desert."

"You know how Titan is; he sent me to find her. If I return empty-handed, I'll be feeling it for weeks."

Maxwell unconsciously patted his backside, as if remembering a recent encounter. Sierra had to stifle a laugh.

The man bid farewell and left.

"I guess we follow him," Sierra whispered.

They passed the bearded man, who gave them a nod as they walked by. Sierra returned the gesture, and her eyes met the man's. His green eyes were hard and tired, and his beard was thick but well kept. His eyes said the man couldn't have been older than twenty, but in the places where his beard didn't touch, his face was weathered unbecomingly, the product of a hard life.

He pivoted to continue along the corridor.

Sierra and Althea picked up their pace, trying not to trip on their newly acquired robes. They turned a corner into a long, wide, downward sloping hallway. Lights dimmed as the corridor descended, leaving them feeling as if they were entering a deep, dark cave, which Sierra supposed they were.

Maxwell had disappeared, but there was nowhere else for him to have gone, so they carried on. After a short time, both the floor and the polished walls abruptly disappeared, exposing the red rock of the canyon.

"Our chambers never descended this far underground," Althea offered after they had carried on for some time. "This must be a product of whatever the ancients constructed here."

The hint of voices echoed through the hall. They were getting close. Sierra motioned for Althea to be quiet and moved closer to the wall.

Claudia's voice, deep and soulful, clearly echoed from an unseen room around a corner ahead of them. "My pets will have taken care of the Oathbreakers by now. I imagine they'll bring their corpses here any moment. Titan can have the woman, but I want answers first."

"Titan will have my hide if he's kept waiting," the muffled voice of Maxwell said.

Sierra peered around the corner, holding her breath, and let out a gasp at the room before her. Green banners and tapestries adorned the walls, most of which were decorated with the symbol of a scorpion. Low-level yellow lighting illuminated the room, giving it a green-yellow glow.

A ledge encircled the outside of the room, with a raised platform forming a pathway down the room's center. On one side of the space, a familiar blue hue separated a smaller room of men and women, many of whom looked like they had suffered wounds of one kind or another.

At the forefront stood Terre.

He appeared surprisingly unharmed but agitated, pacing back and forth in the small space he had available to him, his hands behind his back.

At the opposite end of the room from Sierra, an elevated platform, not unlike a large stage and decorated with computer consoles and monitors, stretched from one end of the room to the other. On the stage stood Claudia and Maxwell.

Positioned next to them, her hands tied with a rope that hung from the ceiling, was her mother, Nancy Runar. Chains held her feet in place. The pincers of two Serkhets clicked at her heels, their metallic bodies reflecting the greens and yellows of the room, which gave them a sickly appearance. Both scorpions had identifying symbols: one marked with a yellow moon, the other with three red triangles. For now, they were keeping their distance, but they were clearly eager to sink their pincers into their captive.

In front of the stage were two recessed pits. More ticking echoed from within them. A sound that had forever been embedded in Sierra's head.

From where she was standing, it was impossible for Sierra to judge how many of the beasts the pits contained, and the sound of them grew to a low roar.

"There must be dozens of them," Althea whispered behind her, reading her thoughts.

Sierra nodded, monitoring the two at her mother's feet.

One of them looked up, its maw pointing directly at Sierra before she could bring her head back behind the corner of the wall.

The beast knew she was there.

Sierra felt the same sensation as she had in the genetics chamber. The creature was aware of her, and she knew exactly where the creature stood.

And she knew it was letting its companion know of her presence.

Sierra grabbed Althea's arm and saw the nervous look had returned to her face.

"What's going on?" she whispered.

"It saw me."

"The Serkhet? Are you sure?"

Althea had no time to nod before the beast bounded into the hall.

Althea grabbed the daggers from her side, but the scorpion's tail batted them out of her hands before she had chance to pull them back. The whip of the tail's return flung Althea against the wall.

The Serkhet grabbed Sierra in its metallic pincers before she had time to process what was happening. The body of the monster felt ice-cold against her flesh. She could feel her body warming against it. All she had wanted to do was help, and now she feared she may not get to.

The need to help those in the room bombarded her thoughts until she could think of nothing else. Not even the scorpion holding her.

Time slowed. Her limbs immobile, all Sierra could do was stare into the reddish-orange eyes mounted to the top of the beast's head. They reminded Sierra of Ember. Staring into the face of death, she wondered briefly if she would ever see her friend again.

The warmth continued to build until the metal around her felt as if it would either burn her or melt under the intensity.

Her vision faded as her head swam in dizziness. Was the monster trying to cook her instead of killing her swiftly? She didn't understand what it was doing to her.

It was only then she realized that the beast had stopped moving. It was frozen in place, its eyes no longer flickering, yet it still held her in its death grip. Sierra squirmed, attempting to use the monster's hesitation as an opportunity to break free, but it was of no use. She was completely immobilized.

Althea lay limp at the foot of the wall she'd been thrown against. Her chest lifted lightly, but only barely. At least she was alive.

"Surely this cannot be the daughter? That would be much too easy."

Sierra looked toward the source of the voice. Claudia stood beneath her, her emerald staff casting a faint light into the shadows of the hallway. Sierra squirmed in the robotic bug's grasp, trying to free herself, but to no avail. She was locked in.

Claudia's eyes met hers and she smiled; a bone-chilling smile Sierra remembered all too well.

"My, my, Sierra," the woman began. "It's a surprise to see you again. I thought you would have realized by now that you've only managed to make things worse."

Sierra bubbled with anger, sweat pouring down her face, but she didn't bother replying.

"You are probably not smart enough to have deduced this, but all of this"—Claudia pointed into the room from which she had emerged—"the destruction of your home, the death of your fellow Sphere dwellers, was your fault."

The woman's smile widened. Sierra continued to squirm, unsuccessfully.

"I told you that you would never amount to anything," Claudia continued, raising her voice. "I never thought you'd be the downfall of us all. Now, these poor souls who have already survived the toxicity of the Outside must struggle until the Guardians can rebuild. They will need to fight to survive. But where you have brought despair, the Guardians will bring redemption."

"The outside world isn't toxic, and you know it!" Sierra replied. "There are people out there, and they deserve more than they've been given. And you do nothing but continue to deceive. The world didn't kill those people; the Order did! Murderers following murderers!"

A sharp *thwack* greeted Sierra on the side of the head as the wooden end of Claudia's staff made contact with her skull.

"I won't stand here and listen to your blasphemy! The Guardians protect us! They always have, and they will continue to do so. Just because your mind is too small to understand it doesn't make it untrue."

Sierra desperately wished she could rub the sore spot on her temple, but she swallowed the pain so she could respond with confidence.

"Humanity has survived for two hundred years. People are more resourceful than you would ever believe. Eventually it will prevail, and these bots will just be a dark chapter in human history."

"Enough of this!" Claudia turned to the Serkhet. "Finish her."

The beast didn't respond.

Claudia took her staff and tapped the scorpion twice, then

repeated the action.

"What's wrong with you, my pet?" she asked. The lights on the machine flickered, but otherwise there was no response. "What did you do?" the woman barked at Sierra, her brow furrowed.

"I . . ." Sierra gasped. It was becoming hard to breathe, never mind talk.

By this time, the second machine had emerged.

"Take her from your brother," she directed to the newly arrived beast.

The Serkhet made its way to her, its claws lifted, pulsing in anticipation, as if ready to use force to clobber Sierra out of the other's grasp. Sierra winced and closed her eyes before being thrown violently as metal struck metal in a horrendous clash that echoed throughout the entire facility.

Pain coursed through her as the hard rock floor greeted her with tremendous force. She had been thrown from the beast's grasp, but the noise that accompanied her ejection continued.

She opened her eyes, fearing the worst, only to witness the two scorpions locked in a death grip with each other. The beast with the red triangles swung at the other with its tail, pinning it against the wall. The other, momentarily dazed, shook off the impact before it snapped at its opponent's legs. The attack sent the first to the ground before it could regain its balance.

Sierra was able to finally rub her head as she surveyed the concluding fight. The machine that had held her appeared now to be her protector, fending off the beast with the yellow moon emblem on its chest.

Claudia stood on the other side of the dueling creatures, clearly just as bewildered as Sierra. Her emerald staff pulsed rapidly, her eyes darting from one beast to the other.

The beast that had held Sierra swung its tail one more time, impaling the other machine right through the neck. Its body quivered before it sank to the floor, convulsing.

The beast with the crimson mark then turned to Claudia.

16

———

Claudia backed away from the Serkhet as it inched toward her. The beast's pincers clicked together. She held her staff with a scowl and continued to strike it against the floor, harder each time as though expecting the talisman to stop the beast.

A third Serkhet jumped out from the room and lunged at Claudia's aggressor.

Sierra didn't fully understand what was happening, but her mother still hung in the other room.

She snuck a guilty glance toward Althea before sticking her head around the corner and inching into the neighboring room, doing her best to avoid the battle.

Another scorpion greeted her. It wasted no time in grabbing Sierra and lifting her from her feet. The same course of events repeated itself, as this beast, too, froze. Only moments passed this time before it dropped her, turned to another beast behind it, and began swinging.

Sierra struggled to catch her breath. She didn't understand what had happened, but being dropped to the floor wasn't exactly a pleasant experience. The impact had bruised her arms and legs, but she pushed herself up onto all fours and carried on.

Her mother's eyes were downcast, fixed to the floor in front of her and seemingly unaware of the brawl happening on her behalf. Each breath seemed labored.

Sierra imagined the force of being suspended by her arms forced her mother to pull herself up to get a proper breath, which was nearly impossible with her ankles chained to the floor.

More beasts emerged from the pit. Claudia seemed to have some power over them, but that control appeared to be slipping.

A few of the detainees behind the force field had taken an interest in the commotion. Sierra met Terre's eyes. He had a strange, bemused look on his face; a boyish grin beneath a subtly raised eyebrow.

Glad he finds this so entertaining.

Two beasts made their way toward her. The beast who had previously come to her aid skulked past her, metal on rock, and lunged, its claws wide.

Its target opened its claws as well, but not swiftly enough. The first beast barrelled it over as it made contact, its tail swinging wildly in an attempt to free itself.

Sierra rushed forward along a small path that lay between the two pits. As she closed the gap, she realized what a foolish move she'd made; pincers crested above the pit as the Serkhet eagerly anticipated an easy target.

One pushed its way out, standing between her and her mother.

Sierra froze. Only steps separated her from her goal. Her mother's hands were still bound over her head, her eyes still closed. It was as if she were oblivious to what was going on in front of her.

As if she had given up.

Only then did Sierra remember the blaster she had stolen.

Memories of firing at bandits in the Outpost came flooding back to her. It had been the only time she had fired one of these things.

She lifted the weapon and pulled the trigger. A familiar beam of light flew toward the monster, hitting home on its outer shell and sending sparks flying. The beast shuddered but didn't stop. It opened its maw and let out a red beam of light. She dodged just in time as the firepower hit the ground, sending dust from the rocky floor into the air.

The Serkhet was now nearly on top of her, but she fired again, aiming at the soft spot between its pincers; the same place Althea had landed the dagger before. It was the only weak spot she knew of in the beast's otherwise impenetrable shell.

The shot landed true.

The beast reeled, as if in pain, standing on its hind legs before twisting around in a surge of metal and sparks, flailing as the metal of its body crashed to the ground, one last swing of its tail kicking up a final cloud of dust.

Sierra couldn't dodge the metal tail in time. It swiped her off her feet and sent her flying.

She landed violently, and the impact knocked the wind out of her.

On her back, a sea of metal surrounded her. Cries came from somewhere else in the chamber; perhaps from Terre or some of the others behind the force field.

It was only then that Sierra realized the beast had dropped her into one of the pits.

She lay on top of one Serkhet. She twisted herself around until she was sitting on its back. There was no proper way for her to hang onto the smooth metal of its carapace. Around her, nearly a dozen of the beasts clawed in anticipation of the new morsel that had fallen into their domain.

The scorpion beneath her squirmed as it tried to shake off the intruder, its tail swinging wildly above Sierra's head.

Heat built within her once again and her body was slick with sweat as she struggled against the writhing beast. Her clammy hands made it that much more difficult to hang on.

She slipped across its back, all the while a fire growing within her.

She recognized the inner sensation from weeks prior, the heat building within her, the same as it had when she'd activated the EMP device to take out the Guardians that had attacked Vegas.

Sierra had no idea why she felt this way now, but she had no time to consider it, either. Her grip slipped from the beast sending her hurtling to the ground. She landed square in the middle of the pit. The heat cascaded from her, pushing her insides against her skin with an intense burning sensation until Sierra was sure she was going to burst into flames.

Suddenly it released. A tidal wave of pressure that had been building up within her poured out of every cell. The release was both relief and a torrent of uncontrollable nausea and emptiness, like she had let go of a piece of herself that had been causing her to both suffer and to live.

Sierra flirted with the brink of consciousness, fighting to keep her eyes open. The metallic beings around her faded as she battled with herself. She fought to lift herself up, fighting to keep her head aloft to see where her attackers might come at her from.

The battle was futile. The small legs and large pincers grazed beside her, threatening to pierce her at any moment. There were half a dozen machines surrounding her; she could sense them. Despite her eyes being closed, she swore she could have pointed to every single one.

Sierra reached out into the darkness, unsure if death would be the only thing she'd find.

It was madness, of course. The heat and smoke were playing tricks with her mind.

She fought for consciousness, fought to push herself up so she could get to safety.

But there was no power behind her effort, no ability to continue the fight. The weight of her body pinned her to the floor, and she was hopelessly unable to move.

The most she managed was to open her eyes. The metal underbellies of scorpions seemed to float above her. She breathed in deeply and tried to focus. After an enormous amount of concerted effort, she could move an arm, and then a leg. She rolled herself onto her stomach, but the same crushing weight held her down, her face resting in the dirt.

She struggled for what felt like an eternity. Alone with the weight of a hundred extra pounds on her back, Sierra eventually gave up and succumbed to the paralysis that imprisoned her.

"ARE YOU OKAY?" Althea's voice was in her ear.

The sound slowly broke through Sierra's consciousness. She struggled to open her leaden eyes, allowing the dim light in. A concerned hand was resting on her shoulder.

"I can't move," Sierra mumbled, feeling the dirt coating her throat as she spoke.

Althea's hands moved along her body. Immediately, the tension within her lifted away, and the feeling returned to her legs and arms.

"I don't believe you have any broken bones," Althea said. It took Sierra a few moments to realize she was being examined. "And your spine seems to be okay. Did you hit your head when you landed?"

Sierra gave herself another good push, slowly lifting herself. She was regaining partial mobility, at least.

"The Serkhet," she said. "The attack. What happened?"

"I was hoping you could tell me. I was unconscious for the whole thing. Nobody seemed to have been able to keep track once you fell into the pit. It was just a mess of metal and destruction."

"I think I'll be okay," Sierra announced, rubbing the back of her head as she pushed herself up. Her head ached, and she hoped she hadn't suffered a concussion.

She stood and brushed herself off, and Althea led her to a rope ladder that hung from the top of the precipice.

"Do you think you'll have the strength to pull yourself up?"

Sierra unconsciously stretched, flexing her muscles, testing their resolve. "I believe so. I'm not going to be stuck down here any longer than I need to be."

Althea nodded. The woman bent over to offer Sierra her clasped palms as a step, boosting her up to the ladder.

Sierra grabbed on to the nearest rung within reach and did her best to pull herself up. Her limbs shook, feeble in their efforts to hold her weight.

Below her, Althea gave her a final push, allowing Sierra to catch the edge of the path above her and roll onto her side. She lay there for a moment, catching her breath as her friend ascended beside her.

It was only a momentary rest.

A pair of Serkhet at the edge of the pit caused Sierra to jump to her feet. She grasped for the blaster but found it missing.

Her heart leapt into her throat, adrenaline coursed through her veins as she readied herself for the receiving end of another attack.

Nothing happened.

The two beasts stood perfectly still.

"These are the only two that made it," Althea said. "And they seemed to deactivate once the fighting stopped."

The chamber was a mess. Metal plates and limbs from nearly a dozen other Serkhet lay strewn across the room.

The eyes of the two beasts still standing pulsed a dim orange, dormant but not shut off completely.

"What happened?" Sierra gazed around the room, dumbfounded and still a bit wary.

"You got tossed in the pit. The Serkhet crawled out and began attacking each other. They essentially fought each other to the death. These two survived. I think they're on our side."

Our side?

"They're machines, Althea," Sierra said. "They don't have sides. I saw Claudia commanding the ones in the hall. I think they must have malfunctioned."

Sierra's mind struggled to comprehend what Althea had explained to her. These beasts, created by the Guardians, the Order, or possibly the ancients—why would they turn on each other? And why now?

"Incredible." Her mother's words traveled down the path, echoing faintly throughout the building.

Sierra turned her attention to her mother.

"Hand me a pair of daggers," she said to Althea, who complied by offering Sierra the pair she had sheathed in her own belt.

It amazed her that her mother hadn't been further harmed in the attack. Scraps of metal were strewn all around, but they all seemed to have missed her, despite her having been a hanging target.

She took the knives and closed the distance between her and her mother.

"Mom, it's okay. We'll get you out of here."

As Sierra worked at the bonds with the pair of daggers, Nancy seemed oblivious to the daughter at her side, her attention focused on the graveyard of mechanical beasts. More than one of the creatures' leg still twitched as they pointed skyward.

"Where did Claudia go?" Sierra asked Althea as she finished working the bonds.

"She was gone when I came to," Althea replied.

Sierra didn't have time to worry about her now. Her first priority was to free her mother and the rest of the captives; Claudia would be a problem for later.

"You shouldn't have come back." Her mother turned her attention from the inoperative scorpions back to her.

"You keep telling me that," Sierra replied. "It's nice to see you, too."

Her mother turned to her, as if truly looking at her for the first time. "You did it, didn't you?" her mother asked. "You made the Sphere fall."

Sierra winced, even though her mother's tone wasn't accusatory. It amazed her.

"I did," she said. "There's something in me; something I can't explain. I submit to it and technology acts . . . differently around me."

"I know," her mother said.

"What do you mean, 'you know?'"

17

———

"We designed you to manipulate machines," Sierra's mother said.

Sierra stepped back, dropping the bonds she had just cut away. "I don't understand."

"A small group of geneticists worked to make some of our children . . . *unique*. We planned for you to leave. To rise against the bots."

Sierra stared, dumbfounded, unsure how to react. Her mind was already struggling with everything she had learned that day. First, her mother had told her she had known about Greata and about the Outside. And now she knew about the strange powers manifesting within her, too?

"*You* gave me these abilities?"

Terre's voice cut through the uncertainty. "We could use some help over here!"

He stood at the edge of the cell, with a few dozen others, each of them now on their feet.

The prisoners filled the small cell, all wearing the light brown robes that residents of the Sphere typically did. Those robes had been the only type of clothing Sierra had known before leaving the Sphere.

"Althea, can you turn off this force field?" Sierra asked.

THE WOMAN NODDED and made her way to a set of controls beside the stage. Although the Serkhet were dormant, she still eyed the monsters apprehensively, as if they would activate and strike her at any moment. Sierra didn't blame her. But the two machines appeared completely docile, as if waiting for instructions.

Sierra turned back to her mother. "Who else knew about the Outside? Why did you let them lie to us?"

"Many of us in the science labs knew. We had to monitor systems the ancients had developed; systems designed for whatever this place was originally created for. There was no way for us to avoid the truth. The systems tried to block the Outside completely, but we saw the comings and goings of the Guardians and the Order. There was no way they could conceal the truth."

"Then why didn't you expose the truth?"

Her mother bared her teeth. "Don't you think we tried? Centuries of being held hostage here—you don't think anyone thought of that? You saw what happened to Greata when she had a brief conversation with you."

Sierra winced at the mention of her friend. She had pushed that pain down deep.

"But there were thousands of us here, Mom! Together, we could have had a chance!"

Her mother shook her head. The bruises on her face amplified how tired she appeared. "It's hard to understand, Sierra, but not everyone wanted to hear the truth. They had made their minds up about what was on the Outside long ago. They weren't willing to listen to facts. Our only chance was to play the long game. Those of us in genetics, our job was always to make humanity more capable of survival, using old parameters from the ancient programs. This bubble was designed by the ancients to terraform other worlds. Mars and beyond. It's all buried in the code. Somehow during the wars, things got confused. Our genetics program had been designed in preparation of colonizing other planets. Everything we were told about the Earth being terraformed was never meant for us.

"But we took advantage of the positions we had been selected for. We worked to modify our offspring, to tweak a gene here and there. To provide something that could one day be useful to you."

Nancy nodded to the destroyed Serkhet, some of which were still twitching on their backs. "I see now that effort was not in vain. You've got a chance. But you shouldn't have come back here. You're meant for bigger things. You and your sister."

Sierra's mind raced. So many questions. She wasn't sure what to ask first.

"Izzy? She's alive, isn't she? I had a vision . . ." Sierra paused, not sure how to continue.

"You have visions as well?" Her mother tilted her head with interest, her smile thirsty for more. "Why didn't you tell me this before?"

"Hah!" Sierra barked in disbelief. "You're one to talk. *When* was I supposed to tell you? The weeks you were away at work? Or when you were around but ignored me? Too tired to be bothered to admit you had a daughter?" Sierra paused, processing what her mother had said. "Wait. What do you mean, 'as well?'"

Her mother nodded, a tired grimace crossing her face. "I did the best I could. I lost a husband and a child that day as well. Come, we need to move." Her mother had ignored the question entirely. She attempted to push past Sierra toward the path that divided the room.

Sierra reached over and grabbed her mother's soiled lab coat, forcing her to stop in her tracks.

"What do you mean, '*as well?*'" She repeated her question, her knuckles white.

Her mother once more glanced to the entrance, as if hoping for a way out. Sierra tugged at her cloak again.

Nancy relented and sighed. "During her last few months with us, your sister began telling us about unusual dreams she had been having. Dreams of the Outside; dreams of a war; dreams of her leading an army. Her dreams were so vivid, we knew it had to be a product of the genetic manipulation. By accident, we had discovered brainwaves that could see either forward or backward in time. We tried to program the genes to activate upon maturity, but in Izzy, at least, they activated a few years too early."

Sierra looked back at the two remaining scorpions. Their orange eyes, now dormant, reminded her so much of Ember.

And then it clicked.

She had done something to both Ember and to the Serkhet. She had awoken something in them somehow. Whatever power she had called upon to activate the EMP had now activated these bots as well.

And Titan.

"Is that what happened to her that day? The accident? Did something go wrong with her ability?"

Her mother sighed. "There was no accident, and your father didn't take her. She snuck off to the Core without us knowing. Someone on the inside helped her to get out, but we've never been able to find out who. Your father wasn't so lucky. The Order found out about one of his experiments and killed him."

After the events of the past few days, Sierra couldn't say she was surprised at the true cause of her father's death. She let out a sigh but composed herself quickly. There was at least some good news. Izzy was alive.

"Do you know where she is?" Sierra asked.

"We know she's alive. Izzy is influential in the fight against the Guardians on the Outside. But we don't know any more than that."

"What did you do to us?"

"You were their guinea pigs." Althea stepped up beside her. "Instead of standing up for themselves, they experimented on you. They manipulated your genes without knowing what they were doing."

Nancy shook her head, her hands held defensively in front of her. "No, no. You've got it all wrong. Scientists have always genetically altered everyone born within the Sphere. We did what we thought we could get away with. You don't think we tried to resist the Guardians? Do you know how many people they've slaughtered for trying to bring about change? *Thousands.*"

Sierra looked at Althea before turning back to her mother. "Were you working with the other Spheres?" she asked. "Did you know there were more out there?"

"There are *others*?" Nancy let out a faint gasp. "Other Spheres? You're telling me . . . there are more?"

"Hundreds," Althea replied. "All set up in the same way as yours."

"And you're from one of them?" Her mother had momentarily forgotten about her own daughter and the questions she had.

"This woman is right about many things," Terre's voice chimed in as he approached the three women. "But most important, we need to move. I don't doubt Claudia will be back here soon, and she'll no doubt bring the wrath of the bots with her."

"Terre!" Sierra exclaimed. Dried blood was caked to his forehead and sweat stained the green shirt he wore, his robes long since discarded.

Terre looked to her with a grin. "You didn't think you'd gotten rid of me, did you?"

"Maybe." She shrugged. "I'm so happy you're okay." She launched into him, giving him a tremendous hug.

"As am I," Althea stepped up beside him, resting a hand on his muscular shoulder.

The volume in the room had grown steadily louder. Those who had been held within the force field were now free to move as they pleased and were feeling sufficiently better about their situation, enough to chat up a storm. Most were ragged and tired and obviously hadn't bathed in over a week.

"We need to get these people to the city," said Sierra. "There's nothing left for them here."

"The city?" an older gentleman with a thick mustache asked as he approached them. "Where is it you think we're going? What nonsense are you talking about?"

Bags rested under the man's eyes, and his cheeks were sunken, leading Sierra to wonder if these people had recently had anything to eat.

She hesitated, unsure of where to begin in explaining the truth.

"The Guardians have lied to you," she said. "There are people on the Outside. There is an ancient city not far from here, and they have volunteered aid to anyone who needs it."

The man furrowed his brow, and even his moustache seemed to bristle. "Have you started hallucinating?" he asked. "The Guardians protect us. The Outside is toxic."

"The Guardians protect us," others agreed among other noises of affirmation rising from the group.

Sierra hadn't realized they'd had an audience, but she blinked as she surveyed their response, unsure of how to respond.

"The Guardians destroyed your homes. The Sphere is gone!" she protested.

"We were punished for breaking the laws of the Guardians," the mustached man continued. "We should not have left the Sphere until the Outside had been sanitized. We are blessed to be under their protection, and we owe the Guardians thanks for sparing us."

Sierra studied him, trying to place this man.

"This is the only world they've ever known, Sierra," her mother, now beside her, offered. "This is what I've been trying to tell you."

"They've lied to you!" Sierra exclaimed, not willing to accept their complacency. "The Sphere isn't about salvation; it's a prison. The Outside isn't toxic; they just don't want you venturing beyond their control."

"Not toxic?" the man said. "That toxic smoke wafted in from the Outside and nearly killed us all! The Guardians saved us from it! The Guardians protected us, and they still do. They've kept us here because it's safe."

"And how safe do you feel having been locked in a cell for days with nothing to eat?"

"We were kept here for our own protection! You saw those creatures—driven so crazy by the toxic atmosphere that the Order have lost their control of them! Thankfully, they turned on each other instead of yourselves. And if that can happen here, who knows what other dangers lurk outside now that the Sphere has fallen?"

Terre stepped between Sierra and the man before she could argue any further. "Save your breath," he whispered. "You won't convince them."

She looked into his brown eyes, searching for an answer. "We came here to rescue them. Isn't it obvious their world was built on a lie?"

"Not to them. You can't rescue those who do not believe they need to be rescued. You can't force a person to accept help any more than you can force them to see the truth."

"But I was helped. A few weeks ago, I wouldn't have believed it either."

"This is another key part of our struggle, Sierra." Her mother now spoke up. "People believe what they want to believe, despite the evidence. We wasted a lot of time trying to convince people of the truth about the Outside. We thought our role as scientists would give us credence, but people turned on us instead. They reported us, turned us in, and many were either re-educated or killed. And so we thought we were better off working toward a future where the truth would be undeniable. But apparently even the Sphere's collapse wasn't enough."

The group wandered about outside the cell. Apparently, nobody felt they were any worse off with the barrier removed, but there were a few animated conversations about whether they should leave the room.

Nancy sighed. "We planned for the long game, Sierra, but things came quicker than we expected. We can't help them anymore."

"What do you mean?"

She turned and walked toward the exit. "They've made their decision."

"Wait! Where are you going?" Sierra called out.

"I need to get back to the lab. Now that the Order knows about my research, they'll want it for their own purposes. I can't let that happen."

"Then we're coming with you," Sierra answered, moving to follow.

Her mother shook her head. "I need to be fast, and I need to be discreet. If I'm lucky, I'll beat them there. Follow the path you took to get here. Meet me by the birthing chamber, where the Serkhet first attacked us. We'll leave from there." With that, Nancy Runar scurried out of the room, not waiting for a response.

Sierra looked to Terre. "Um, what just happened?"

"Most people would rather die in their own ignorance than live with a truth that proves them wrong. Life here has remained unchanged for centuries, and in the blink of an eye, their world collapsed. They were told the barrier between them and the Outside protected them from death. The Order showed up and proved that to be true. It doesn't matter that the source of their destruction came from their so-called saviors. They only saw their worst fears becoming reality."

Sierra had dreamt of nothing but the chance to leave the Sphere and explore the world outside her entire life. She knew she was odd for asking questions, and for years, she had been reprimanded for asking too many. She had never imagined that when the façade lifted, she'd still be the odd one out.

The dispute among the prisoners seemed to have been settled, and the captives had filed out of the room. Disappointingly, from the pieces of the conversation Sierra could hear, their intention was to inform the Order that the force field had dropped.

"I feel like we're lucky nobody has realized we were the ones to drop the force field," Althea whispered.

Terre nodded. Sierra was still flabbergasted that the entire situation had played out the way it had.

"Let's make our way to the birthing chamber," Sierra said. "I don't think it's safe for us to stick around here."

"Here," Terre said, holding out a pair of brown robes the same as the other prisoners were wearing. "Put these on."

They smelled horrid, but Sierra didn't want to ask where he had obtained them. She'd barely noticed that the gray robes she and Althea had acquired hadn't survived their encounter with the Serkhet. The way the robes had been torn, they had been lucky to still have their skin.

"We need to blend in," Terre continued. "If we run into a guard, they won't be able to pick us out from these folk."

Sierra agreed, but she didn't have to like it. "Too bad they won't fool the bots," she said.

"They won't, but, thanks to you, there aren't too many of them around. Titan seems to have stationed the surviving units elsewhere."

"Just need to worry about him, then."

"We'll figure out what to do about him." Terre nodded. "But for now, one problem at time."

They walked out of the room into the large corridor that separated the holding room from the rest of the facility. Hundreds of heads, lit by the dim blue lights of the corridor, filled the space ahead of them.

Forcing their way through the sea of people would take far too long, but they had no other choice. Sierra rolled her eyes and pushed through, intent on reaching the front of the bottleneck, Terre and Althea on her heels.

There wasn't much give in the group. Those who filled the hall stood shoulder to shoulder. A couple hundred people filled the hallway. If what the guard said had been accurate, there were maybe three thousand survivors; only a small fraction of the Sphere residents. The other survivors must have been locked away in other parts of the Core.

What hell did I unleash upon my people?

And the few survivors who remained felt they had invoked the wrath of the Guardians.

Suddenly chilled, Sierra pulled the robe tightly against her, but there was no reprieve from the thoughts that shook her to her core.

She had barely noticed the surrounding group had halted. If she had been able to, she would have barrelled right through the mob, entirely unaware, but the sheer mass of people had her locked in. Sierra was trying to get a glimpse of what was happening ahead when those around her suddenly dropped to their knees.

It wasn't until Althea pulled her arm down that Sierra noticed the medic had followed suit with the others. Terre was beside her, mimicking the action as well.

"What's happening?" she asked.

"Quiet!" Terre hushed, motioning to the front of the crowd with his head.

Standing before them were two members of the Order: Claudia, her robes accented in the green Sierra was familiar with, and another she did not recognize. The second woman had a glowing red pattern on her robes, and her staff housed a red ruby that contrasted with Claudia's green emerald.

Between them stood a Sentinel with modified paneling and lighting and two large triangles carved out of its breastplate.

Sierra shivered and her heart raced as she tried to figure out how they would get out of there without being seen.

18

Sierra kept her head down like Terre had instructed. Althea vibrated with fear. Terre shook as well, but Sierra guessed it was more likely with rage. She was more confused than either, unsure of why this bot was being hailed as the savior of the compound.

Titan and the two women of the Order stood before them as the moments ticked by. The only sounds in the hall were the shuffling of robes and the heart within Sierra's chest. Her knees ached from pressing against the cold stone beneath them, and she struggled not to fidget under the discomfort, desperately trying to avoid attention.

The Sentinel had to be scanning the crowd. Looking for *them*.

Sierra cursed under her breath. They'd be discovered for sure.

If there was anything for her to be thankful for, it was that Terre had grabbed the brown robes from the downed prisoners. Terre and Althea had put their hoods up, and she slowly did the same. The stench of old sweat overwhelmed her.

"Loyal subjects," Titan bellowed to the group. His voice was deeper than she remembered, and it had a metallic grate to it.

Unlike other Sentinels, his words had intent. He was no longer merely repeating an ancient program.

"Thank you for your reverence. You have placed it well," he continued. "We know you are excited to be out of the cell, but we have been keeping you here for your protection. We are evaluating the toxicity of the air and trying to clear it to ensure you are safe. We mourn the many who did not survive its grasp."

"The Guardians protect us," chanted the group in unison.

Only a few weeks ago, Sierra reminded herself, *I was also this naïve.*

"The foolish girl who let you out is an enemy of the Guardians. She was the reason the barrier came down before it was safe. We need her found. Only then will the Guardians be protected, and the New Order be able to carry forward. An Order you can all be part of."

Sierra held her breath. Had the prisoners been paying attention? Did anyone know she stood among them?

She spotted the man with the bristled mustache ahead of them. He was peering around, clearly wondering if they were still among the crowd. She ducked and prayed no one would notice them.

"Did anyone see which way they went?" Claudia asked.

A few heads turned to look around, but nobody offered an answer. Sierra allowed herself to exhale. Either they had been lost in the chaos or were just extremely lucky. Perhaps because they had put on their robes after most of the group had departed, nobody realized they had joined them.

"I spoke to them," the grizzled man spoke up. "They were spreading lies about the Outside. Spewing some nonsense about a city. She's intent on killing us all. I think she took off with another young lady and that stranger who was locked in with us. Do they pose a threat to us?"

"You have nothing to fear," Titan replied.

Sierra couldn't tell if the Sentinel was trying to sound consoling, but it came off as condescending. Irrespective, the crowd was lapping it up.

"I am Titan. I am here to restore order to where only chaos reigns. The time for the Guardians to lead humanity to its salvation is upon us. The Sphere may have fallen, but hope has not been lost. We are working to ensure that the Outside will be safe for you soon. Once we are certain of success, then all Guardians and humankind will forge a new path forward."

A lone cheer erupted from the crowd, which rapidly gained momentum. Soon the entire group was in uproar.

"For now, dear citizens, rise! Return to the chamber. We will attend to you. But while this threat looms, none of you are safe. You must do this for your own protection. We will keep you safe from Sierra Runar and her lies. The Guardians are being reconstructed as we speak, and we will rise, stronger and in greater numbers than ever before!"

The cheers continued, for much longer than Sierra was comfortable with. She returned Terre's uncomfortable glance. Applause turned to animated murmurs as the crowd stood, finding new life in the message that Titan presented.

A firm hand grasped Sierra's forearm, and she nearly panicked before she realized it was Terre. He had grabbed Althea as well, ensuring the three wouldn't be separated in the wave of prisoners now returning to their cell.

"What do we do now?" Althea whispered, nervously eyeing those that passed by.

Sierra stole a glance back to Claudia, who was herding the crowd. The Headmaster was also scanning faces, looking for them, which suggested that Titan wasn't—or couldn't scan for her specifically.

"We need to keep moving," Terre admonished. "We'll figure something out."

"Once we're back in the chamber, Claudia will spot us for sure," Sierra said. "We'll be trapped."

"We're already trapped," he answered. "If we make a break for it now, we'll have an angry mob after us as well. We need to buy ourselves some time."

Sierra didn't like it. They were boxing themselves in. There had to be another way.

Behind them, only Claudia followed. Titan and the other woman must have had other things to attend to.

Like finding my mom.

Sierra leaned her head to Althea, keeping her voice low. "Do you think Claudia would recognize you? Could she pick you out as being associated with me?"

Althea's eyes widened. "I couldn't say for sure . . . why? What are you planning?"

"She'll recognize me in an instant. If she glimpses my face, we're done. I need to slip around her while she's not looking."

Sierra wasn't sure if what she had in mind was going to work, but she had no other ideas and she had to try something. Her hood wouldn't disguise her for long.

"I don't know. I was fighting alongside you against the Serkhet."

"She would have only seen you for a moment. With that cloak, you'll blend in with the others. I need you to create a diversion."

Terre shook his head. "It's not safe."

"I'm open to ideas," Sierra replied.

"We all get out of the room together."

"And how do you propose we do that with Claudia there? If they lock us in the cell, we'll have no way out. Plus, there are over a hundred people convinced she's on their side, and that I'm the enemy!"

To be fair, the prisoners hadn't needed much convincing, and one speech from an articulate bot had sealed the deal. They had suffered a devastating attack on their homes, an attack that had killed most of their friends and family, and they were willing to believe the bot over their own eyes.

Sierra eyed the survivors around her. Nobody paid them any

attention, but they were pushing their luck with each step. If anyone recognized them, that would be the end of their charade.

Her breathing quickened, and she tried to keep the panic at bay. They faced forward as they spoke. One glance into the wrong person's eyes and it would all be over.

Terre never responded to her query, so Sierra continued outlining her plan.

"Once I'm out, you and Althea will have to work to find another way around Claudia, or perhaps wait until she leaves."

Terre didn't look impressed. Sierra didn't blame him for not wanting to be left behind, especially after already escaping once, but it was the only plan she saw as having any semblance of working.

"Althea, once we're inside, I'll duck behind the doorway while you draw Claudia into the room and start talking to her. Keep her distracted and I'll sneak out behind her. You and Terre will have to find your own way out after."

"And what if someone else sees you leave?" Terre snapped. "Are they going to just let you walk out?"

"Look, it's going to take some luck, but I'm banking on the fact they'll be too distracted chatting among themselves to notice."

"And then what? Leave us in the cell to rot!" Terre hissed. Sierra could tell he had to try hard to keep his voice down.

"Terre, you're going to need to hide alongside the wreckage of the Serkhet. Once Claudia has scanned the prisoners, you can open the door to let Althea escape."

"This is madness!" he exclaimed. "I'll be recognized at once! If I'm spotted, I'll be shot on sight. And even if I do manage to stay hidden, your Spherian friends will surely sound the alarm once I drop the force field."

He wasn't wrong.

"Fine, you can come with me, but that means Althea will be locked in the chamber on her own. Do you think you'll be okay with that?"

Althea looked as though she were about to vomit. "How do you think I feel about it?"

"Great," Sierra said in jest, but Althea didn't seem to appreciate the joke. Her face turned green.

"If Claudia locks Althea up, then we're back to square one," Terre interjected. "There are Guardians and Order guards all over this place. What's the plan then? Just leave her behind in the cell? We all need to get out of here."

"We'll come back for her," Sierra replied. "We know where she'll be, and Claudia isn't likely to stick around here watching the prisoners pick their noses. I think we'd be able to outrun the others."

"Are you listening to yourself?" Terre said. "You want to abandon yet another friend in search of your mother? What happens when Mommy doesn't want to come with us? She didn't seem too thrilled to see you. No, we all make a break for it. We've tried our best, but those we've come here for don't want our help. Let them suffer their own fate."

They were moments away from re-entering the chamber and running out of time to decide.

"I'm not leaving my mother behind," Sierra responded insistently. "There are still too many secrets about my past; too many answers I'll never get if we leave her in this place. Besides, whatever she went back for must have been important if she doesn't want the Guardians to get their hands on it. If the two of you want to make a break for it on your own, then fine. I'll meet you back at the SZ."

Terre sighed. "So be it. We'll go back for your mother. But I think it's a fool's errand."

Althea let out an audible sigh as they approached the prison's entrance.

"Sorry, Althea," Sierra answered. "It's not my first choice, either. We'll be back for you, I promise."

Althea's silence told Sierra that she hadn't been reassured.

HER PLAN HAD WORKED WELL. Almost too well.

As Sierra and Terre made their way down the hall from the chamber, Sierra ran the scenario over in her head again. It had been too easy, and it wasn't sitting well. It didn't seem plausible that Titan would send only Claudia with the party knowing Sierra was still in the building. No Serkhet; no Sentinels; not even another member of the Order.

There was only one reason she could think of. He didn't need to find her; he knew they were heading straight to him.

As they had entered the prison block, the group of Spherians had clamored into the room, tripping over one another, eager to re-enter their prison. Claudia had pushed them forward, ensuring they returned into the recesses that would be sealed off from the rest of the room.

Althea had pulled off her part of the ruse perfectly, stumbling into Claudia, feigning clumsiness. She had then embarked upon a big theatrical presentation of how she was humbled to have the honor of serving the Guardians. Sierra had winced. It had almost been too over the top, but Claudia had appeared too annoyed with the interruption to notice it was a ruse. Others in the room had even unwittingly joined in, crying "the Guardians protect us" in support.

Sierra rolled her eyes.

While Claudia had been trying to calm Althea down, Sierra and Terre had slipped behind the bulk of the group and worked their way behind the Headmaster to step into the corridor.

Without the mass of people in it, the hall actually seemed quite wide. And long. There was only one route for them to take, and they were far from being out of the woods yet.

Despite there being no reprieve, Sierra hung close to the wall, keeping her ear open for the metallic sound of a Sentinel or the ticking of the Serkhet.

As they got further along, the corridor branched out into smaller arterial halls. Without Althea, Sierra only had a vague idea of where she was going. Terre took a half step ahead of her, seemingly more confident in their direction.

They trod as lightly as they could, still fighting for expediency. She hoped that if they kept to the main artery, they'd eventually get to some place she recognized. She should have paid closer attention to the route they came in on. It had never crossed her mind she'd have to do this without Althea.

Everything about this place felt incredibly foreign to her. She had spent her entire life among the Guardians and their technology and had never given much thought to something as mundane as electric lighting before. She'd simply taken it for granted. But after a few weeks in the Silent Zone, the dim hall lights now felt alien.

The one question she couldn't figure out was why. Why convince the survivors to remain? The Sphere was down. The Guardians clearly couldn't carry on as things had been. If it was to retain them as workers to keep the Core operational, why hold them in the cell?

Something didn't add up.

As she pondered, Titan's words struck her.

We will rise, stronger and in greater numbers than ever before.

Of course.

The bots were rebuilding. The survivors were likely needed to help with the reconstruction process. Her mom had said the Core had been built to have human counterparts.

How long would it take? Years? Months? She had no idea. But she knew they needed to stop it.

Before she could finish the thought, a hand grabbed her around the mouth and pulled her backward.

19

SIERRA JABBED AN ELBOW BEHIND HER, intent on inflicting as much pain on her assailant as possible. It swung wide and flowed through open air. If the grip hadn't been so tight, she likely would have fallen over with the force of the effort.

Terre had been a few steps ahead of her and didn't notice her being hauled around the corner. She tried to cry out, but her yell had been muffled by both the hand on her face and the hum of the Core.

Calloused hands had a firm grip on her. Sweat, skin, and hair entered her mouth. She tried to bite down, but the grip was too tight for her to gain enough mobility in her jaw and she ended up just slobbering.

Hot breath hit her ear, and she shuddered.

"Would you quit it! It's me. You need to be quiet, though."

She recognized the voice, but through her panic, it took moments to place it.

The hand was cautious to let go before it spun her around. His already dark features were further lost in the shadows, but the dim blue light danced on his face, outlining his striking jawline and dimpled cheeks.

"Rhys!" Sierra exclaimed, jumping into his arms. He embraced her tightly. "What are you doing here? Shouldn't you be resting?"

"I'm happy to see you, too!" He laughed. "And you're one to talk! I heard you took a knife to the gut." He playfully poked at her ribs, then grimaced as though he realized that he maybe shouldn't touch a potentially sore stab wound.

"I got the all-clear to leave," he continued. "Once I heard you came back here, I left right away. They had beaten me to the brink of death. I couldn't just stay in bed knowing the same could happen to you."

Terre had wandered back to them by this point. Sierra couldn't tell if he had been amused or agitated.

"You take chances jumping out from the shadows at people," he said. "Even friendly ones. She could just as easily have put a knife in *your* ribs."

"Come on!" He laughed. "She's not Ella."

Terre let out a quick "Ha!" before catching himself. "Tell that to the Order guard she gutted."

"How did you know about that?" Sierra asked, unable to hide the surprise and amusement on her face.

"Althea told me," Terre replied.

Rhys raised an eyebrow at her. "An Order guard? I'm impressed. You should have tried that on the one that got you first."

Sierra stuck her tongue out. "This place is a maze," she said. "How did you find us?"

"Malachi told me you went looking for your mum. I found out where she worked and have been waiting here for you to show up. I was starting to get worried."

He reached into the shadows of the hall and produced a tall black staff; Sierra immediately recognized it as Terre's. "I was especially worried when I found this," he said, handing the stick to its rightful owner. "It was resting on top of what I figured was a pile of old belongings. I thought if I did track you down, you'd want it back."

Terre produced a small smile as he inspected the staff. The delight disappeared quickly as he looked back to his son. "You shouldn't have come," Terre scolded him. "Especially after what happened during your first visit."

"And you're one to talk, old man?" Rhys replied. "I'm surprised you came at all. Never had use for a Sphere until now. You wouldn't even come here for Mum. I pleaded for us to rescue her, but Sierra bats her eyelashes at you and you jump to help her find hers? *Pfft.*" He shook his head and turned away.

Sierra put a hand on his shoulder, and she momentarily lost her train of thought as her hand rested on its muscle. It was larger than her hand, and solid. She had never thought of Rhys as being that muscular before. Fit, yes, but the bulge surprised her.

"Don't worry, Rhys," she said as she shot Terre an icy glare. "My mother scolded me for coming, too. It seems our parents don't want their children wrecking the mess they've made of things."

Rhys shrugged off her hand, and she quickly regained her composure, although she did raise a questioning eyebrow.

Did I say something wrong?

"We're trying to keep you from getting killed," Terre replied. "Something I thought the boy would have figured out on his own when he was bleeding across the desert."

"What? And let you have all the fun?" he said with a boyish grin. "It was just a scratch. I'm as good as new."

Sierra couldn't help but notice Rhys was favoring his right side, but she thought it best not to say anything.

"Never mind that, now," Terre answered. "We need to find her mother."

"Where's the Healer? And the bot?" Rhys asked. "I thought Malachi said they were with you."

"Althea's stuck in a cell," Sierra answered. "She acted as a decoy so we could get out. As for Ember . . . she went missing before we arrived. We think the Order guards took her."

"Some rescue," Rhys smirked.

Sierra punched his shoulder. Hard.

"Ah!" He nearly cried out but stopped himself, rubbing his arm in distress.

"Come on," she said. He deserved it. "We need to find my mother. She went back to the genetics lab. Hopefully to pack up her things before we leave."

Rhys shook his head. "I don't think that's a good idea. There are Sentinels guarding all entrances. I was afraid you were inside. I've been running back and forth between exits, hoping you'd emerge. There's no way in. Who knows if she's even okay?"

"I think they're keeping her alive for my sake. They're using her as bait. They won't hurt her."

"*Everyone* is expendable to the Guardians," Rhys replied. "Any pardon your mother might be bestowed could shift if she looks at a bot the wrong way. Although I don't think we can say the same for you. The entire station wants to find you."

"There's got to be a way in. I'm not leaving without her."

Terre rolled his eyes.

"Why are you humoring her?" Rhys asked Terre. "You should know this is a fool's errand."

Like father, like son, Sierra thought cynically.

"Now you're the one scolding about what's foolish or not?" Terre retorted. "It's no more foolish than coming here in the first place."

"Which leads to you not answering my question. Why have you agreed to take her this far? My entire life, you've been locked away in your hermit bunker in the middle of the desert. Why walk right into the snake's lair now?"

"What would you have me do?" Terre replied. "Knock her over the head and bring her back to the city? I gave Sierra my word I'd protect her. I don't like it, but her mother does seem to hold some secrets to her condition."

"*Condition?*" Rhys asked.

"Her visions," Terre answered. "Her ability to activate a piece of tech that has had no power source in two centuries. Her ability to tame mechanical beasts that would have ripped any normal person to shreds."

"*Mechanical beasts?*" Rhys mouthed to Sierra.

"I'll explain later," she whispered back.

Rhys raised an eyebrow, but turned back to Terre. "It's not like you to walk willingly into a dangerous situation," he said. "What are you after?"

Terre stepped deeper into the shadows. "Now is not the time to get into it."

Footsteps echoed from down the hall, and Rhys pulled Sierra further into the small alcove in which he stood.

The light in the alcove was dim compared to that of the main corridor. Rhys turned his back to the main entry and wrapped his body around her. He pressed his warm body against hers, the cold wall of the corridor behind her. His chest rubbed against her face and smelled of the desert air and sweat. He must have run to have been able to catch up to them as quickly as he had. But she was thankful he was there.

She lifted a hand to place on his chest. His pecs were firm but not bulky.

Sierra shook her head gently. This was no time for distraction. There was too much at stake.

Terre had his back pressed to the wall, the shadows masking his face.

Still, if someone stole a glance in their direction, there would be no mistaking that there were three people trying to hide in the shadows.

Voices shifted in and out of audible range as they walked by. They were talking about her and her mother, but Sierra couldn't hear enough of what was being said to give it any context.

"Was there anyone entering the labs?" she asked Rhys. "Anyone we could blend in with?" It had worked once before. Maybe they could do it again.

Rhys took a step back from her, allowing a bit of room between them now that the voices seemed to have passed. "Only the Order Elite, but unless you've got glowing robes tucked away, we won't fool anybody."

"Well, I only see one option, then," she said. "I turn myself in."

Sierra winced as the outcry from the two men carried down the hall before they caught themselves.

"Are you suicidal?" Rhys grabbed her by the shoulders and held her outward to look her in the eye.

"It's clear Titan wants me," she answered. "If I can get a member of the Order to walk me past the Sentinels, perhaps I can overpower them and continue on my own."

"He wants you dead!" Rhys barked.

"It's out of the question," Terre agreed. "There's way too much that could go wrong. They could shoot you on sight. And how do you plan on overwhelming an armed Order member? There are going to be more inside. Are you going to take them all on? Sorry, but there's no way I'm going to let you do that."

Let *me do that?* Sierra thought. Terre would not *let* her do anything. He could help her, or he could get out of the way, but she wasn't going to wait for his permission.

He had a point, though. She put a hand to her ribs, which suddenly felt tender. It was likely due more to Rhys' jab than the healed dagger wound. Still, she'd rather not repeat the experience.

"Do you have a better idea?" she asked.

"Yes, actually. We go get Althea and get out of here," Rhys said.

"We can't do that, not yet."

"Look," Terre said. "I know we came here to find out if your mother is alive. She is, and the Guardians seem to want to keep her that way. For now, at least. Us being here only jeopardizes that. She didn't seem too eager to leave, either."

Sierra sighed. "She has spent her entire life trying to give us a fighting chance against the Guardians once the Sphere fell. We're out now. It doesn't seem like the people here fully grasp that. If we leave her, Titan is only going to use her to his own ends. I don't think she'd want that."

"I don't think she'd want you dead, either," Terre suggested.

"Why did you come with me, exactly?" she asked. 'If you're just going to look for excuses to go back to Vegas, then go."

Rhys took a step forward, asserting his presence between the two of them.

"I'll ask you one more time, old man," he said. "Why *are* you here? I don't buy you came out here out of duty."

"We don't have time . . ."

"Don't give me that. What's going on? There's a connection to Mom, and I want to know what it is."

Terre sighed. He glanced down the hall as if expecting someone to creep up on them at any moment. They might, but Sierra knew he was just trying to avoid the question.

"Greata didn't randomly send Sierra out to find me. It wasn't an accident. Your mother came here looking for her."

Sierra cocked her head to the side questioningly.

"What are you talking about?" Rhys balked at the response. "The bots captured her, and she resigned herself to the life of a Spherian farmer."

Sierra still cringed at the disdain Rhys held in his voice.

"Do you really believe your mother would abandon us so easily?" Terre asked. "She would have fought tooth and nail to get back to us if what was here wasn't more important."

Rhys scoffed. "More important than her family? *Pfft.* I don't believe you. You would have told me years ago if this was the case."

"I couldn't," Terre said. "There could be no chance of word getting out. Her intent had to remain a secret."

"My mother said something similar. She learned of the genetics program and somehow found out that Izzy and I would one day manifest these powers," Sierra said. "But I don't understand how. And I don't understand why that would give Greata reason to leave you and Rhys?"

Terre's face was nearly a complete silhouette, the light from the main corridor behind him casting his face in shadow, but his eyes still bore a striking intensity. Sierra would have stepped backward, away from his gaze, if the wall hadn't been in her way.

"She came here to find you. She made it her mission to protect you until she could help you escape."

20

———

"That's impossible!" Sierra said. "How could she possibly have known about me? I was eight when I met her. What value would I have had?"

Terre glanced around uneasily. "This is really not the place to go into it, but know this, Sierra—I am here for the same reason you are. Because Greata believed in something."

"And you let her?" Rhys looked to Sierra. "You let her abandon us to pursue the rumor of a child who might develop magical powers?"

"There is far too much behind that for me to go into. Your mother was a strong-willed woman. I had no means to stop her."

"You could have told me!" he snarled. "I had always feared Mom had abandoned us. It would have been nice to understand the purpose behind her choice."

"Don't think it wasn't difficult." Terre sighed. "But we need to move. Every second we spend here, the chance of us being discovered multiplies. Let's get to Sierra's mother, then we'll head back for Althea and get out of here."

"There's one other thing we need to do," Sierra said.

"And what's that?" Terre put a hand to his face, clearly unimpressed that their exit might be further delayed.

"We need to take out the Core."

That was what they had to do in theory, anyway. Sierra didn't know exactly what that would entail.

"How do you plan to do that?" Terre asked, skeptical.

"I don't know yet," she replied. "But the Guardians are rebuilding, and we can't let that happen. You said the EMP was meant to take this place out, but the effects didn't reach as far as we'd hoped they would. Now Titan has potentially found a way to remove the limits on what they can produce. You heard him, Terre—they're going to make the army bigger and stronger than before. If we don't stop it now, then I've only made things worse."

She sighed, looking from him to Rhys, silently pleading with them to see the point she was making.

How many bots would Titan create? Twice as many as before? Ten times? Would there be a limit?

"Is that possible?" Rhys asked Terre.

"If he's figured out how to override the ancient safeguards, then yes, it's possible."

"Humanity has depended on those numbers being consistent for centuries," Rhys said. "If they suddenly increase to two or three times their size, we're screwed."

"An army two or three times the size would be the least of our worries." Terre said. "With no buffer, the only limit to their operation is the quantity of resources they can find to construct themselves. There's enough ancient metal and debris around for almost infinite potential."

"Terre," said Sierra, "you know more about this facility than we do. Is there a way we can knock out the power source? I'm guessing there isn't another spare EMP device kicking around."

"Nothing within range of here that I know of. It will be difficult. If it's not heavily guarded, there will definitely be surveillance."

"But you know where the power is being generated?"

"In theory," Terre replied. "Below the dam, there are two power stations on either side of the river."

Sierra glanced at Rhys, who bore the same confused look as she did.

Terre must have seen the look of confusion in their eyes, so he continued. "Before the wars, this place generated power for a large portion of what used to be the United States of America. The dam was built for that purpose. When the Guardians set up the Sphere here, they routed the power from the dam into their own facilities. It's how they kept the Sphere going, and it's how they generate enough power to rebuild themselves."

"The place we were at when the Serkhet took you," Sierra said, thinking of the large buildings where the rows of Guardians were being constructed.

"Exactly," Terre said. "There are four towers set up near where we were. Each one is connected to a power source below the surface."

"How would we destroy them?" Rhys asked. "Especially without drawing the attention of Titan and the Order?"

"I don't know. I could see if we could override the system, but that's a long shot. It's most likely there are a number of fail-safes to prevent that from happening." Terre shook his head. "Even if I could get around those, the system would be set up to keep itself operational and lock us out."

"We've already stayed here too long," Rhys said. "And we're being pulled in too many directions. We need to make a decision. If we're going to find Sierra's mom, we all go together. No more splitting up. You fools shouldn't have left Althea behind."

Sierra exchanged a quick glance with Terre before nodding.

"Once we get your mom out of here," Rhys continued, "we head back for Althea and then figure out how to destroy these power stations."

"Agreed," Sierra responded. "Rhys, you've been monitoring

the area for the last few hours. You know the path of least resistance. Lead the way."

Rhys nodded and walked toward the main corridor. Terre's face betrayed his reservations but, clearly unable to provide a better alternative, he followed suit.

Rhys led them down a series of halls, and it wasn't long before their surroundings became familiar, and they headed up an unmarked stairwell.

"There should be two guards stationed at the top," Rhys whispered. "I haven't seen anyone else coming or going in this area. If we can take them out, we should have a clear path most of the way to the lab."

They found themselves on the final landing, facing one last flight of stairs. From where they stood, the side of one guard was clearly in view. Luckily, he had his back turned away from them. The man's white cloak hung down around him, its red glowing markings barely visible.

"Only two?" Terre mouthed to Rhys, holding up two fingers.

Rhys nodded.

Sierra couldn't see the second from her position, but she guessed he was close by.

"One on either side of the door," Rhys whispered, confirming Sierra's suspicions.

Terre motioned for the group to be quiet and still.

Sierra stayed put with Rhys as Terre crept up the stairs. Smooth and graceful, his movements seemed to flow with the hum of the Core.

As he approached the top of the stairwell, Terre lifted his staff. He shoved it through the doorway, twisted it, and yanked it back with tremendous force. The stick caught each of the two guards on the side of the neck.

Grunts and groans echoed through the stairwell, only moments before a pair of thuds hit the ground.

That's one way to do it.

Terre waved for them to join him at the top of the stairs.

"That was easier than you made it sound," Sierra said to Rhys.

"We're not out of the woods yet," Rhys answered. "That could have gone sideways in a hurry if someone saw him."

"I hope you realize we're walking into a trap," Terre said.

"I do," she replied.

"Wait . . . What?" Rhys asked. "Why are you leading us down here, then?"

"I'm not willing to give up on the secrets my mother has kept from me my entire life. The answers she has could help us prevent further misery at the hand of the Guardians."

Their faces revealed they were unconvinced. Sierra hated to admit she had no idea what she was getting any of them into, but she knew she had to push forward.

"From here, I can go ahead alone," she said. "Shadow me, but don't get caught. I'm going to need you to bail me out of whatever's waiting for me."

Rhys scoffed and shook his head. "You're unbelievable, you know that?"

"I do," she grinned. "But I'm determined."

"We don't split up, remember?"

She grabbed onto Rhys' shirt collar and pulled him in close. "I need you to watch my back."

"Don't get killed," Terre interrupted, clearly uncomfortable with the exchange. He bent over and retrieved a blaster from one of the guards and pushed it on her, using the momentum to force her back a couple of paces. "Greata entrusted you to my care. I won't let her down again."

"You let *her* down?" Rhys scoffed and rolled his eyes.

Terre lifted a hand to silence him. "Now is not the time."

Sierra took off the brown robe that had enabled her to slip past Claudia in the cell. It wouldn't do her any good now and would only slow her down; the pants and shirt she wore underneath would allow her to move more freely. As the cool air of the facility hit her, she breathed a sigh of relief. She couldn't believe she had worn robes like those every day of her life until a few weeks ago.

She held the newly acquired blaster close, her palms sweaty. She had so little experience with weapons; she was still unsure of how effective she'd be if she needed to use it.

"Keep your distance as you follow. Stay far enough away that if I get into trouble, you're not spotted as well."

"I think we'll all be in trouble, regardless," Rhys said. "But let's go."

Sierra led the way, occasionally glancing back to ensure her companions had kept hidden.

Each step on the cold stone floor felt like an accusation. Her own thoughts mixed with the charges Claudia had made against her.

"The destruction of your home, the death of your fellow Sphere dwellers, was all your fault."

She shouldn't be in this place; Sierra was nothing more than a reckless teenager in deeper than she could handle, and she was taking others down with her.

Step. Greata, dead.

Step. Ed, dead.

Step. Ember, missing.

Step. Althea, left behind.

Step. Nearly everyone she had grown up with, dead.

All because of her.

The most solid link to her past was now ahead of her.

She tried to push the thoughts down; tried to silence each accusation. But before Sierra could get a handle on one, the next appeared. Every effort made things worse. Each death weighed heavy. The only thing keeping her going now was the chance to prevent one more death and gain some answers as to why she was at the heart of all this madness.

Sierra once again reached the chamber filled with the birthing columns. Rings of cold blue light illuminated the base of each cylinder, along with the glow from within their glass case; it was a cool kind of glow—cold like the mechanisms that brought these beings into this world.

The mess caused earlier by Claudia's staff had been cleaned since Sierra had left the room.

And what did the future now hold for the suspended beings? Not even born yet and already caught in a world of lies and destruction. Who would take care of them? Would they have a future? Sierra hadn't had the opportunity to really consider the words of the guards they had attacked hours before.

Bred to be warriors for the Order.

That was their plan.

These infants would be raised to fight for the Guardians.

If she hadn't personally been in the cell with the villagers claiming allegiance to the ones who had just attacked them, Sierra would never have believed they could convince humans to attack each other for the sake of the bots. But now she was not so sure.

One more snag of guilt to add to her list. She would be the cause of this war, with human death on both sides.

Unless she could stop it.

Terre had been right. This effort to rescue her mother was foolish. Sierra was risking everything to save the life of one woman, when the rest of humanity was at stake.

She cursed under her breath.

The columns cast their blue light on her as Sierra slipped nervously between them, the future children of the Sphere already casting judgment.

A crash from the lab caused her to leap behind a column. She paused, waiting for its source to reveal itself. When nobody came, she tiptoed to the threshold of the doorway. It took a moment for her vision to adjust to the harsh light of the lab as she peeked her head inside.

Her worst fear had come to life.

21

———

Desks had been turned over.

Monitors were smashed.

Blood coated the walls and dripped from the glass and metal shards strewn across the room.

Lifeless bodies in white coats were slumped over desks. Faint groans came from others, barely audible over the hissing of malfunctioning electronics.

Sierra launched herself into the room, tossing aside chunks of debris, which landed on the scientists. One of them was obviously dead; a few lay bleeding. She winced but pushed the guilt down.

Pools of blood made the floor slick, and she had to watch her step to ensure she wasn't stepping on sparking electronics.

She had only seen three technicians in the room previously. Now there were at least six that were downed in various states of distress. None of them were her mother.

Monitors on the wall flickered, some still showing images of the columns in the next room on their cracked displays. On one, she could see Rhys and Terre creeping through the columns, closing in on her position.

Other screens emitted nothing but sparks, their images destroyed with them.

If whoever had done this had still been in the room, they would have seen her coming. It made her efforts for secrecy laughable. Had they been watched for the entire day on these screens?

Then again, she imagined they would have been captured long ago if that were the case.

A crash near the back of the room caused her to jump. "Hello?" she called out softly.

"Sierra?" a weak but familiar voice croaked from the back of the room.

"Mom?" Sierra darted, doing her best not to slip as she climbed over destroyed furniture and materials. "Mom, where are you?"

"I'm here," a feeble voice sounded from beneath an enormous pile of debris. Sierra pushed what she could out of the way. Her mother lay on the floor, cowering under the remnants of an overturned desk.

"What happened?" she asked. "Are you okay?"

"An Order Elite came in with a couple of their foot soldiers," she replied with labored breath. She was having a hard time getting the words out. "Tore up the place, looking for our research."

"They couldn't access it from the network? Come on, Mom. Let's get you out of here."

She bent down and started moving broken bits of glass and paneling that had fallen on top of her mother.

Nancy Runar raised a hand and shook her head before continuing. "We held the research on separate storage, off their network by design. It contains information built upon for hundreds of years. The results and monitoring of dozens of experiments. Visions; superior eyesight; healing abilities; mind control, among other things. Everything we have learned about manipulating genes."

"It's okay, Mom. We'll get it back."

Sierra continued to push wreckage aside. A few items wouldn't budge, impaled by or pinned beneath heavier beams of metal.

"No." Her mother continued to shake her head. "You don't understand . . ."

"I think I've pieced it together," Sierra replied. "Titan and his cronies will use your research to give abilities to soldiers who will fight for them. It seems simple enough. But relax for now, Mom. Save your strength. Let me get you out of this."

"It's not that simple." Her mother sighed. "The powers we gave you are only a sliver of what we discovered was possible. We had to hold back. If we didn't, the Guardians would have detected abnormalities. There are far scarier things that are achievable. With that knowledge, they'll be able to create super-soldiers; ones that are near invincible; that can fly; that can breathe underwater; be impervious to blaster fire. We had only just begun to understand the power you and your sister have. The glances you see into the past or future are just the beginning. It may be possible to travel into the past or future at will; maybe even change events. You don't understand the power you have— or how much is possible."

"And they'll have no restrictions." Sierra finished the thought.

"Exactly," her mom said, as she took in another labored breath.

"Why, though? If Titan is going to lift the restrictions on how many Guardians they can create, why have humans fight for them?"

"You know far more of the outside world than I do, hun." The woman let out a gasp and threshed in pain.

"Sorry, Mom. I'm trying to get you out of here."

It was only then Sierra saw the issue. A large pipe had pierced her mother's abdomen. Blood flowed freely from the wound and had pooled around them.

Behind the bruises and the scrapes, her mother's face was white.

Sierra cursed again at leaving Althea behind.

She gripped the pipe with both hands. It was less than an inch thick, but it was an inch that would mean life or death. She tried to pull it out, unsure if it would make things better or worse. But she had to stop the bleeding.

She pulled on it, straight up, and hoped to avoid creating more damage. It didn't budge.

Sierra realized she wasn't getting her mother out of there. Not without a way to cut the pipe out. Or maybe with some help.

"It's okay, Sierra," Nancy Runar said, reaching up to wipe away the tear streaking down her daughter's cheek.

Sierra hadn't even realized she was crying.

"I'll get Terre and Rhys," Sierra said determinedly. "They can help." She went to stand, but her mother grabbed her arm.

"There's no time. I'm not going to make it, and I need to explain some things."

Sierra protested, but her mom shushed her.

"You need to know how this all started." She took a labored breath before continuing. "Children within the Sphere aren't born; we create them. Everyone in the Sphere is a descendant of the original inhabitants. We've used their genes to create every person from then on, only manipulating the genes slightly to differentiate characteristics."

"But why?" she asked.

Her mother shook her head. "Nobody knows. The Guardians instructed us to take the original genes and enhance them to be the best fit for survival in the new world. At first, we made simple changes: to rid diseases; increase lung capacity; stamina. This is what the original design of the program intended. Over years of doing nothing else, we perfected our craft. We found ways to enhance the human body that even the ancients hadn't imagined possible. But if we altered the genetic code too far outside the normal parameters, the Guardians rejected the fetus."

"Like my visions," she replied.

"Yes, like your visions. So our actions had to be covert. We had to keep abilities dormant throughout youth. We knew that if we could give you the best chance to fight, you or your children could escape and maybe take the world back from them. It was hard to know we were successful until the manipulations manifested themselves. Once Izzy began to have dreams about things she couldn't possibly know about, we knew we had found a path to success, although we never had time to fully discuss it with her."

"But how could these visions help?"

"Imagine being able to see what your enemy will do before they do it. Imagine being able to see how to stop a Guardian attack before it even starts."

"That's exactly what happened. I saw how to stop the Guardians attacking a city near here. That's why I caused the Sphere to collapse."

"Then you have an idea of the potential your ability offers. I can only hope Izzy gained the same clarity."

"I had a vision of her, of Izzy. I think she's alive."

Nancy smiled, closing her eyes, in either pain or satisfaction. "In her dreams as a child, she saw both of you fighting alongside each other. If her dreams were accurate, she would have to be."

"I don't understand. You knew I would grow up having to fight them? Why didn't you tell me? I could have prepared."

The crunch of footsteps behind her caused Sierra to whip around. Terre had made his way into the facility to check on her. Sierra simply shook her head at the man. There wasn't anything he would be able to do at this point.

Terre simply nodded, seeming to understand her silent

request. His eyes scanned the room for immediate danger, but otherwise he didn't move any closer.

"There was nothing we could have done to prepare you," her mother continued. "Besides, it was blasphemy to speak of it. We couldn't risk you talking about it, even unintentionally. You were already under close watch after Izzy di. . . after she left. The Guardians interrogated you to ensure you didn't know about her dreams, then wiped your memory so you wouldn't remember."

"What if this isn't something I want?" Sierra asked. "Why should I be cursed with this fate?"

"It was the purpose we created you for. This is what we hoped you'd become."

Sierra shook her head, the tears flowing freely now. "No," she said, defeated. "This"—she waved her hand around—"is my fault, Mom. I'm the reason the Sphere fell. Titan came to exist because of me. Whatever ability I have caused him to awaken. I made him . . . conscious. Now, he has the power to create an army of machines *and* an army of superhumans—I've damned us all."

"We were damned long before you came along, Sierra. What you're capable of will help humanity to stand on its own again. But you need to get that drive from Titan before it's too late."

Her mother took another ragged breath, moving the arm that gripped Sierra's hand to her shoulder. Her other hand lay limp beside to her.

"About what you said to me earlier . . . about me not being there for you. I do love you, Sierra. I don't think I showed you enough. I was too preoccupied with what we were doing here. In the end, I forgot you were a young girl who needed a mother. And I'm sorry for that. Sometimes when we need to make choices for the greater good, it hurts those closest to us."

Her mother's eyes went glossy as she leaned back and her grip relaxed.

"Mom, no!" Sierra scrambled to move the little debris that remained between them. She grabbed her mother's hand before it could fall to the floor and held it tightly, feeling it grow heavy in her own.

Sierra tried to control the tears that ran down her cheeks. It was a losing battle, so she let them flow.

She just sat there, unable to move, unable to think.

This was the woman who had called herself her mother. Sierra tried to conjure up the memories of her youth.

And the tears dried.

Despite her efforts, the memories didn't come. There weren't enough in the well to draw from. Nancy Runar had worked her life away, striving to give life and hope to the next generation of humans, all while neglecting the human already in her charge.

Sierra's sense of loss deepened. She was truly alone.

Sadness turned to anger, and the bitterness of her youth bubbled up from where she had pushed it down. This woman had kept the truth from her, and from the rest of the Sphere.

And now she was dead because of it.

A hand rested gently on her shoulder. She sighed as she stood, not having to look to know that Terre was behind her.

"She did what she could for the inhabitants of the Sphere," he said. "We should be thankful they had the foresight to provide you with the tools to fight what's coming."

Sierra inhaled deeply, her eyes locked onto the still bleeding woman impaled on the floor before her. "She may have been a great geneticist, but she was a lousy mother." Terre's grip tightened in solidarity, but she continued. "It seems people keep dying before I can learn all the secrets they hold. I feel like I keep getting pieces to a giant puzzle, and I have no idea how big it is or what the image at the end will be."

Terre nodded. "None of us do, Sierra. That is the frustration of what this life holds. I have been cursed to live long enough to realize the puzzle is infinite, and you'll likely never fully realize what the intended picture looks like. And that's only if it's not forever changing."

"That's not very comforting," she said, her eyes still unmoved.

"It isn't," he agreed. "But it is the truth. I hope that, one day, we can fill in enough pieces to know where our place lies."

"And what of you? Will you die before you reveal your secrets to me?"

Terre let out a deep chuckle. "It is far more likely you'll die first." His mouth turned from amusement to regret as he realized the implication of what he'd said. "I have outlived more friends than I can count. Secrets come and go. Most of it rarely matters to the final chapter. Most of the intent is long forgotten by the time it gets to those it would help."

"But your story isn't finished yet," she replied. "You're blessed with memories that are myths and legends to everyone else. Your secrets could hold the answers to stopping all of this."

"The ancients couldn't stop them, and they built the damn things. My limited understanding won't amount to much."

"Greata wanted me to find you for a reason. I won't believe you're not tied to all of this."

With that, something in him snapped. Terre picked up a desk and tossed it against the wall. It crashed into already debilitated computers, sending more glass shattering to the floor.

Sierra stood blinking at the man. His chest rose and fell as he panted from the effort.

"You don't know what you're talking about," he said simply, steadying his breathing. "You don't know the first thing about me."

"Then help me to understand," she pleaded. "I didn't choose this path. I was sent to find you by the one person I think I can still trust, and even she had been lying to me."

Terre sighed, his eyes burning intensely. "The world is the way it is because of me."

22

———

"You've said that before," Sierra began. "I don't understand what you mean."

Terre glanced around the room at the chaos that had descended on the scientists and their work. Computer stations smoked and crackled, the moans of the fallen now quiet.

He sighed. "I will tell you. But now is not the time. Let's get Rhys and move."

"Did you not hear what I just said? Enough of the secrets! If I'm going to keep trusting you with my life, you need to start giving me answers."

Terre grunted as he turned to her. "You complain that your actions cost the lives of thousands of inhabitants. Well, my actions cost the lives of *billions*. The Guardians were part of a military program. Humans are a creative bunch; we'll always find new ways to kill each other. However, early on, the machines escaped our control."

Sierra nodded. "It's what started the wars. How could that have been your fault?"

"The wars weren't my fault. But the Spheres were. I've told you about the program that we uploaded, the one that was meant to help us regain control. It was my job to upload it. I had a partner. I called him K." He almost smiled at the memory. "Between us, we were meant to install the program, but we failed. If only we had gotten there sooner, gotten the right commands sent through. I don't know. But it's plagued me for two hundred years.

"Instead of bringing the bots under control, the upload messed with the program. The Spheres were set up as holding cells for their prisoners. The only thing that brings me solace is that if we had done nothing, then humanity likely would have been wiped out by the war machines. But this"—he pointed around him—"the lies, the *death*, is because of *my* failing. I have watched humanity suffer because of my shortcomings, and I have been damned to relive it until the end of time, or until these nanobots fry my brain cells, whichever happens first."

A crash outside the lab cut short any questions Sierra had for the man. The monitors that still showed the neighboring chamber showed nothing other than the glowing columns.

Not even Rhys.

Terre set down his staff on a nearby desk. It was a task to find enough space to do so. His eyes darted between the monitor of the neighboring room and the doorway to it. He pulled out a blaster from beneath his cloak and motioned for Sierra to do the same.

She lowered her voice to a whisper. "What's going on?"

He put a finger to his lips.

A small gray Scanner orb flew into the room. The lights on its glassy surface spun. It was processing something.

It's searching for us. Where's Rhys?

Terre lifted his blaster and fired a prolonged beam at the Guardian. Sparks flew, and the thick glass covering its exterior cracked and then burst as it dropped to the floor.

"Come on," he said. "More will be coming."

Terre grabbed his staff and made his way toward the door.

"They must have found him," he said. "Come on, we've got to move."

Sierra's eyes went wide. "Rhys was supposed to be watching the door!"

"Knowing Rhys, he used himself as bait to lure them away. Just be thankful he did his job. If he hadn't, we'd be fighting right now. Come on, let's go."

Another victim of my stupid decisions.

"How do you know he's not dead?"

They made their way into the next room.

"There's no sign of a struggle. No body," Terre said. "He wouldn't go down easily."

She searched desperately among the surrounding columns, hoping Rhys had just been hiding there the entire time.

Each of the columns contained a life—a life meant to lead humanity to freedom. But because of her, they'd now be raised to fight it instead.

You must get that drive before it's too late.

"We need to get to Titan," she whispered. "He took a drive containing my mother's work. It contained years of genetic research. If he's able to access that information, he'll be able to create super-soldiers. They'll be able to breed humans with powers to do the fighting for them."

Terre stopped to look at her, but didn't respond.

Sierra studied the fetuses resting peacefully within the columns. These specimens were the last to be bred by the scientists. She couldn't allow Titan to create more.

What hope did her mother believe she would give the world? What end had the scientists envisioned? It sounded as though it was more than just a sandstorm of abilities thrown at the wall; as though her power held a specific purpose. Her mother hadn't even known what kind of world was outside. She hadn't even known about the other Spheres.

The other Spheres.

"Are all the Spheres connected to the same network?" she asked, a horrible idea beginning to sink in.

Terre squinted, considering. "I would think so."

"How many are there?"

"The last report I saw before the lights went out said over a hundred. In North America, at least. Whether the Guardians have been able to expand, I don't know."

"So if Titan were to upload the genome program to the network, each of the Spheres would be capable of breeding the genetically modified humans?"

Terre shook his head, crossing his arms. "The ancients established protocols that the bots haven't been able to override. The network would see anything Titan uploaded as outside of the normal parameters and shut it down."

"But he could break the protocols here," she replied. "The other Guardians, they seem to respond to him."

Terre nodded, pondering. "Each Sphere would have to receive the program individually. Before the war, we tried to do a mass update and failed."

His face saddened as he spoke, and his voice trailed off as if he had recalled something he wished he hadn't.

"We need to take this place down," she said. "What about cutting the power? How do we take them out?"

"I haven't been able to figure that out. The turbines on either side of the dam are massive. If we try to shut them down through the network, the AI will override us and just start them back up again. Explosives would be best, but we would need to knock both plants out simultaneously. If we take one out ahead of the other, security will be on us before we have a shot at the second. We'd never get access to it."

"We should probably get Rhys and Althea first," she said.

Terre nodded, but from his distant gaze, Sierra guessed he wasn't sure where to start, either.

They entered the hall. From here, they could either go back

the way they had come and continue to sneak around, or they could try the main door to see if it was still guarded. Sierra gave it not even a moment's thought before she turned the way they had come. They'd continue to meander the back hallways; there was no point in drawing extra attention to themselves.

She looked to Terre, who was lost in his own thoughts. He once again reached within his robe to the robot pendant he wore and rubbed it like a talisman, as if it might hold the answers they sought.

"It reminds you of him, doesn't it?" Sierra asked. She nodded to his hand tucked in his cloak. "Your previous child."

Terre yanked his hand out, as if realizing only now he had been gripping the pendant.

"Her," he said, his eyes growing dark as he worked his way past her. "It was a gift from my daughter."

Terre increased his pace and shifted his gaze up and down the hall, making it clear he wasn't going to discuss the subject further.

How long did it take for the pain of losing someone to pass? Was two hundred years enough?

It had only been a few weeks since Sierra had left the Sphere, and she had already witnessed so many lives lost. Numbness against it all had already begun to creep in. She didn't know whether her heart could handle anymore. The only choice she saw was to distance herself from the pain.

She couldn't lose Rhys, though. They hadn't been given a fair chance to potentially start something between them. Of all the things she had missed out on, she didn't want to lose what they could become.

If anything.

She hadn't forgotten Rhys had been a jerk to her, only seeming to come around to her once she had 'proven herself' to him. As if she *had* to prove herself. The boy didn't deserve the headspace she gave him, and yet something about him had been irresistible. Something about his smile, his shoulders; the way his brown eyes drew her in.

But it was more than that. She could give him something he hadn't had his entire life: someone who cared about him.

Sierra sighed as she allowed herself to get lost in the fantasy of what could be. She rarely allowed herself to. It was pure fancy. Rhys likely didn't feel the same toward her, a dumb Spherian. This visit back to her home had proved that might be accurate.

She had shared one kiss with him, and that was it. But that one single kiss had been magical. It had been earth-shattering, time-stopping; world-breakingly *magical*.

But that was all it was.

Their banter had gone from cold and accusatory to playful, but Sierra knew nothing about him. Nothing other than his mother had been one of her best friends, and that his father was two hundred years old.

Hardly the foundation for a relationship.

So why did Rhys make her feel the way he did? She couldn't say. But there was something about him, despite him not deserving it—something that caused her to crave his approval.

The empty hall snapped her back to reality. It struck her as odd that, despite the ransacked office, despite Rhys going missing, despite Titan wanting to kill her, the Core was nearly deserted. Even with the hit the Guardians had taken to their numbers, their presence in the back halls was eerily non-existent.

Sierra voiced the concern to Terre, who looked at her questioningly and then relented. "I don't know if it's anything other than a shortage of bots," he said. "Their attention is focused on rebuilding. It is unusual, but I don't know if it's cause for concern. Keep your guard up, though. We may still be walking into a trap."

"Or perhaps Titan has other things on his mind." She pointed to one of the monitors.

Hundreds of Sentinels were lined up in rows that were ten

across. Orbs hovered above them. None of them moved. Their lights were on, but they were dim. They looked to be on standby, as if waiting for something.

"Sand!" she said. "What are they doing?"

Terre shook his head. "I don't know. They look to be facing west. If I didn't know any better, I'd say Titan's planning on marching them toward Vegas."

"That makes little sense," she said. "They won't get very far before they hit the Silent Zone."

"We can't worry about them now," he said, shrugging them off.

Something else on the feed caught her eye. "Rhys!" she cried.

Terre jumped but found what she was looking at. A captive Rhys, now bound in restraints, was being led by a member of the Order.

"Look!" She pointed to the corner of the screen, behind the Sentinels. A cage containing another Guardian stood off to one side of the group.

Terre nodded. "It's Ember. They captured her, after all."

Sierra gave him an annoyed glare but let it slide. What was more important was that Ember was still in one piece, and still here.

And still on our side.

Sierra didn't like admitting to herself she'd had doubts about her friend, but she had been so wrong about so many things that it was hard not to second-guess herself. But seeing Ember in that cell provided Sierra with a great amount of relief.

"Let's go get them!" She started making her way down the hall, barely aware of the direction in which they needed to go.

"Not so fast." Terre held a hand up and motioned to a separate monitor. Lines of Onyx were being assembled by robotic limbs and automatons. The build center. Even though they had passed this place on their way in, Titan's words now echoed in Sierra's mind.

We will rise, stronger and in greater numbers than ever before.

"If we head out there, guns blazing, we might pull off a rescue," Terre said, "but that assembly worries me far more."

"More than the life of your son?"

"Look, I care about Rhys, but if we miss our shot to destroy this station, they're going to create a robot army the size of which the world has never seen. And believe me, we barely survived the last one, and we had far more resources than you could even imagine. Even the Silent Zones can only provide us with so much protection."

He had a point, and in that moment, Sierra couldn't help but think of her mother's final words.

Sometimes when we need to make choices for the greater good, it hurts those closest to us.

On the monitor, Rhys was being put into a cage directly opposite Ember. Rows of Sentinels stood between the two prisoners. Had Titan done this intentionally, knowing she'd never be able to rescue them both?

Getting one of them out would be a miracle. Getting both out would be *impossible*.

She nodded and motioned for them to keep moving. At least if they could get Althea, they would have an extra pair of hands to help.

There was minimal security set up inside. Either Titan had forgotten they were roaming the halls, or he didn't care.

He knows I'll come for my friends.

She gripped the cold metal of her blaster. Ready for whatever would come at them. Every corner they turned, she expected a member of the Order to appear, or for a Sentinel to charge at them. Adrenaline rushed through her veins, and her pulse pounded with anticipation.

The occasional sound of static filled the hall through a malfunctioning monitor.

The empty halls should have made the return journey seem

quick, but the dread of every corner made it feel three times as long.

The Core was quiet—too quiet.

It wasn't until they'd turned the last corner that they finally saw a sign of life.

Sierra swallowed and wished they hadn't.

23

THE HALLWAY ENDED AT A "T" intersection. To their right was a long hallway that presumably led out of the Core. To their left was the group of prisoners they had left behind.

The Spherians were standing in the hall once again, their positions much more orderly now than when Sierra and Terre were among them. Claudia stood in front of them, eager to step in and lead. But why had she brought them out of the cell again?

The woman hasn't let them out of her sight, Sierra thought. *I'm sorry we left you, Althea!*

They ducked back behind the corner they had emerged from. Fortunately, Claudia had her back turned to where Sierra and Terre stood.

Sierra flattened her back against the metal wall. Terre had crouched to the floor in order to peer around the corner.

Sierra couldn't resist the urge to leer over the top of him. It was her idea to leave Althea behind, and she could only hope the Healer had evaded detection. Whether she would have been able to escape the congregation or not was another matter. Sierra had to be sure if Althea was with them.

Each of the prisoners stood to attention, facing Claudia.

Waiting. For what, Sierra couldn't even hazard a guess, but they all had the same glazed look in their eyes.

The glaze was familiar, but she couldn't recall from where. They weren't looking at anything in particular, instead staring into nothingness.

Sierra recognized a few of the faces, but none she knew by name.

Seconds ticked by as she scanned the group. The brown hoods pulled over their heads made it especially difficult for her to pick anyone out, and there were many more in the group that she wasn't able to see. She eventually spotted the Healer, though. Althea was close to the group's edge, but not close enough that she'd be able to depart unnoticed.

Sierra cursed under her breath.

Althea's eyes were glazed over as well.

Claudia lifted the staff before abruptly pivoting toward them. Sierra whipped back around the corner so fast that she nearly got dizzy. Terre backed out more gracefully.

Sierra held her blaster up, readying herself to fire on anything that moved.

"Come on." Terre pushed himself up. "We've got to hide."

He transitioned into a half-sprint back down the hall.

Sierra grunted before chasing him for a few dozen paces. They found an open doorway and dipped in.

Behind them, Claudia led the group of prisoners past their doorway. Her staff pulsed green in rhythm with their march. Lines of brown-robed civilians walked by in what seemed like an endless army.

As the last of them filed past, a familiar clicking sound followed close behind.

Two Serkhet trailed the group, nearly twice the height of the people they followed. Sierra held her breath. One of them turned to look down the hall. Its bright orange eyes seared through the darkness, and she could have sworn it looked right at her. She stood there, trying everything in her power not to move; not to breathe; not to do anything that might give them away.

She could feel its gaze on her, and somehow also its intent. It was studying her. Questioning.

Sierra was certain the Serkhet was going to sound the alarm and alert Claudia to their presence. But its pincers clicked together three times, and it turned and carried on.

She exhaled and was surprised to hear Terre do the same behind her. It was the most the man had let on that he had been on edge the entire day.

After a few minutes of listening to the metal footsteps patter away, Sierra finally turned to Terre. "Althea's with them," she said.

"I saw her," he replied. "But there's no way we're going to get her out without being seen."

She shook her head. "It was a stupid plan. We should never have left her behind."

"It wasn't ideal, but if we hadn't, we could all be following that green glow. Claudia's controlling them somehow."

"Do you think it's the staff?"

Terre nodded. "It was pulsing to the same rhythm as the group. The Order has mastered some questionable tech over the years."

"We always assumed those Order stones were products of the Guardians."

"There are many things you'd hardly believe; things the Order wished they could integrate into their systems."

"So it can control minds?"

Terre shook his head. "I don't understand how it would, at least. Something else is going on. The staff controls tech. It's how Claudia controls the Serkhet. There would have to be a receiving beacon in the creatures."

Terre's eyes went wide, as if realizing something, but he shook it off quickly and kept whatever it had been to himself.

They crept back to the hall, and Sierra peered around the corner in both directions.

The open hall now stood vacant.

"Where do you think she's taking them?" she asked.

"If I had to guess, to the place outside we saw on the monitors."

"Do you think the Guardians are going to abandon the Core altogether?"

"No. This is their base. It's where their production and charge stations are," he said. "But that doesn't mean they won't send out the units they already have."

"Why would they do that?" she asked. "Where would they be going?"

"First? Vegas."

"Vegas? Why? The Guardians wouldn't be able to get any further than the SZ border."

"I'm not sure, Sierra. I'm just guessing here. But Titan is planning something. It won't be good."

"Do you think they're going to be sent out right away?"

"Your guess is as good as mine. I don't even know *if* they will be sent out; it seems like it would be a fruitless exercise. But either way, we can't stand here talking about it."

Sierra was starting to get dizzy trying to keep up with what was the most important part of their plan. "You're right. Let's head to the power generators. If we can knock out the power, we stop their means of generating a larger Guardian army. We can work on getting our friends out after that's secure."

"Agreed." Terre nodded.

"You think you can remember the way?"

"Once we get back onto the dam, I'll know where to go from there."

They backtracked several times before turning into a wide, curved hallway. From its shape, Sierra assumed it had to follow the outside perimeter of the main building.

"If we can exit toward the back of the Core, we'll be able to avoid the main lobby," Terre said. "These rear industrial sections appear to be mostly abandoned, but my guess is there'll still be Scanners and other drones out front."

The two continued along the main hall. They had to duck into abandoned rooms several times, as the voices of Order members occasionally passed. Only once did they see stray orbs patrolling.

They rounded a bend, and sunlight filtered into the facility. Windows revealed the red rock terrain Sierra was familiar with. Ahead, she could make out the edges of the giant dam.

"So, the power station is beneath us? At the bottom of this ravine?"

"There are two stations underground, one on each side of the ravine. Both have multiple turbines that generate power," Terre stated.

The number of orbs visible outside the window increased as they got closer to the dam. What had started out as one or two soon turned into dozens.

"What's going on?" Sierra asked. "Why are they all coming out?"

"It's best if we don't hang around too long to find out," Terre replied.

Sierra shuddered as she watched them fly both high above the dam and below them into the ravine. She instinctively walked on the side of the hall furthest from the windows, in case the orbs were able to detect her.

Terre walked down the middle of the hall, seemingly unconcerned he might be spotted. He walked confidently, his black staff in hand. With each step, it made contact with the blue carpet.

Soon, they reached what appeared to be an exit. The ceiling lifted to reveal more gold stitched banners lining the wall above them.

The entrance appeared to be meant for human traffic it never received. No monitors lined the walls here. Seats, tables, and other stands had been set up, but were most likely never used.

Movement beyond the window caught Sierra's attention. Flecks of silver climbing down the side of the dam were catching the light of the sun and reflecting it out into the heat of the desert.

Serkhet.

"They're leaving, too. Why?"

Terre didn't answer. His gaze was locked onto the robotic creatures swarming down the side of the wall and into the valley.

A door beside them stood parallel to the top of the dam. Through the window, Sierra could make out several members of the Order on the bridge across the structure.

Sierra took one last look at her blaster. Fully charged.

Two men and one woman stood straight, their eyes forward. Each held a blaster weapon large enough to require two hands. Sierra didn't know if bigger meant better, but if it did, she'd be at a disadvantage.

These guards were dressed differently from other members. Their gray robes had been replaced with a type of white armor, reminiscent of the Sentinels. A large transparent bubble covered their heads, as if to protect them from the supposedly toxic air of the Outside.

Like a mini Sphere for their heads.

Their suits glowed red at the joints, and a crackle pattern running across their torso mimicked the typical patterns of the Elite Order's robes.

There was no way around them. The door opened directly onto the path that led across the wall. A sheer drop of hundreds of feet on either side.

Sierra took a deep breath to settle her pulse, which pounded out of control.

"The power stations are below the dam. How do we get down?" she asked.

"There's an elevator."

"A what now?"

"An elevator. A device the ancients used to travel up and down within taller buildings."

"Where is it?" she asked.

"At the center of the dam."

Her stomach dropped.

The environmental controls of the facility were acting up, or weren't set on this side of the building. Sweat formed on Sierra's brow, and she wiped it away with her arm, thankful she had ditched the robe.

There was no chance they were going to get onto the dam unseen. And there was no way Terre would agree to what she was thinking of doing.

So she acted.

She pushed a large bar that unlatched the door. Two male guards stood a hundred paces in front of her. She stepped out onto the platform, smoky air filling her lungs as she lifted her blaster and opened fire.

"*Sierra!*" Terre hissed as the door closed behind her.

The firepower fizzled as it hit the armor and dissipated on impact.

Sand.

Sierra could make out the wry smiles on their faces behind the tinted domes.

One of them pointed a two-handed weapon at her.

Sierra was about to roll, but before she did, the other guard put a hand on top of the first's weapon, pushing it down. "Stop!" the guard said to the other. "This is the girl. Titan wants her alive."

Wants me alive? Since when?

She tried to take advantage of their hesitation, pivoting swiftly on one leg and using her momentum to push herself back toward the door.

She was banking on the fact they wouldn't be quick enough to catch her, but she misjudged the movement and collapsed as a searing tear ripped through her calf.

She let out an involuntary scream; pain burned through her leg as if it were on fire. The stone structure beneath her collided with her hands and shoulder as she collapsed.

Rough hands grabbed her on either side.

Through the pain, Sierra managed to look back to the door she'd exited.

Terre was gone.

24

———

Sierra could only assume the guards had grown tired of carrying her, as they forced her to stumble on her own weight. At least, as much as she could before collapsing. Her injured leg screamed at every step.

Despite the pain, she was thankful they hadn't blown it clean off. She had seen the impact those blasters could have if the setting was high enough. A few weeks earlier, Ed had received a hole right through his middle during their battle with the Sentinels.

More than that, at each step, she could bare a little more of the weight. Whether from pure adrenaline, stubbornness or numbness, she tested her limit. She refused to be left incapacitated. She needed to escape.

She focused on the next step. Just one at a time.

Each step took her full effort, but a piece of her mind drifted to thoughts about Terre. Where had he gone? Did he just abandon her? Why hadn't he helped her?

Accusations that Rhys had made against his father came rushing to her. Had he given up on her, the same way he had done with Greata? Had he abandoned her as the guards hauled her away to an unknown fate?

Perhaps he had carried on to the power stations alone. In fact, she knew he would have headed there at all costs.

His intent aside, one by one, her friends had fallen away. Now, she was alone.

Sierra hoped Wil was making a better go of things wherever he had ended up with the Resistance. This sort of rash action had always been what had gotten him into trouble. Perhaps he had rubbed off on her more than she'd realized. And now she was the one in a mess.

The guards laughed about their luck in capturing the Oathbreaker Titan had been looking for. They had made more than one lewd comment, which Sierra filed away to use against them later. They'd not live to joke much longer.

She tried to get a better look at their clothing to distract her. It was unlike anything she had seen the Order—or anyone else— wear. The plated outfits looked as though they had been made to emulate the intimidating look of the Sentinels. Hard, white, and illuminated, but only to the neck. Other than the glass bubbles, their heads and neck were exposed, just as a Sentinel's head and neck were made from synthetic skin. Except, unlike Sentinel armor, this seemed impenetrable to blaster fire. If this was going to become standard Order attire, it would make stopping them much more difficult.

They circled the outside of the perimeter. With the pain in her leg, the trip seemed agonizingly long.

"Why does Titan want to talk to me?" she croaked. Her throat was dry, and the smoke-filled air wasn't helping. She was likely dehydrated, and injury only added to it.

Her question went unanswered.

If she hadn't seen things unfolding on the monitors earlier, Sierra would have been nervous they were going to throw her off the cliff. But she knew Titan was waiting ahead.

That fact hadn't made her any less nervous.

As they crested a rise, the distant conversation rose. The small, rolling hill had blocked the view of hundreds of Sentinels, humans, and orbs that now lay before her.

Three large groups amassed below, each forming a nearly perfect square. They stood ordered, still, and ready to head west.

Hundreds of Sentinels formed the center group. From Sierra's perspective, they appeared as white dots against the red rock surface. Powered down. Waiting.

Behind them sat two Serkhet.

Sierra could feel their presence and their intent. If she hadn't known any better, she would have said they were conflicted, unsure of what they should be doing.

She was sure these were the same two Serkhet left standing after the attack in the cellblock, but it was impossible to tell much of anything from a distance.

Quit imagining things, she thought. *You're being held captive, and you're dreaming of machines.*

Two paths cut through either side of the perfectly aligned white bodies of Sentinels. To their left stood a group of men and women. Some of them had been part of the army of prisoners from the facility, but there were so many more in number than had been inside. More survivors of the attacks. Well . . . sort of. She had never seen humans act this way. They stood to attention, staring off into the desert. Expressionless.

Deactivated. Just like the Sentinels.

Sierra couldn't see anything but the backs of their heads. They were ordered as neatly as the Guardians, and not one of them so much as twitched. As if they were no longer alive.

Althea's down there, somewhere.

It relieved Sierra that there were more survivors, but their trance-like condition was less than reassuring. But whereas the guard she had stabbed had mentioned thousands, she could only see hundreds. There had to be more hidden away somewhere.

Her heart skipped a beat when she saw Rhys stood next to the group of prisoners. His cage had been turned to face them. It was hard for Sierra to tell from where she stood if his eyes were clouded like the others or not, but based on how he carried himself—still confident, with his hands holding himself up to the bars of his prison—Sierra didn't believe it was the case.

He shifted his gaze from one member of the group to the other, looking to grab someone's attention. Maybe he had seen Althea among them, but he didn't look happy, fidgeting and moving about what little he could within its walls.

Sierra recognized this location from the monitor feed. Another one of her friends stood on the plateau. A similar cage sat to the right of a third group. Ember stood completely still and stiff, her gaze locked onto what was happening in front of her— or perhaps onto nothing at all. Her bright orange hair hung limp, which was unusual; typically, her hair was neat and tidy.

Sierra struggled to remember if she had ever seen the bot look so defunct.

Neither Rhys nor Ember appeared to have spotted her being led down the hillside with her escort.

The third group was not as organized or structured as the other two, but it was the largest of them all, taking up nearly as much room as the other two groups combined.

Members of the Order wandered casually among what appeared to be a more permanent camp. They had set up tents, with paths wide enough between them for several people to walk abreast. Horses stood alongside some of them. Some of the Order members were dressed in their standard robes, while others wore the hard white armor of Sierra's captors.

This group was the only indication that Titan didn't plan on marching immediately. If he was, she didn't doubt the Order would be ready to move.

Of course, that depended on what Titan's plan actually was.

The two guards pushed her along. She could no longer feel

her legs. Sierra wasn't sure if that was a good thing, but the masked pain served her purpose. She grew bolder and more comfortable in her stride, although the pins and needles didn't reassure her that she'd be able to walk far on her own, never mind run if she had to.

Her heart raced as she continued to survey the amassed army; she feared for both herself and those who might be on the receiving end of the machines preparing to march.

And there would be more. Titan would continue to build more machines. And there was presently no way she'd be able to stop it. Not that she could see.

The air was scorching, even though smoke still blotted out the sun. Toxic air indeed. Sweat dripped from her brow. The medallion she carried felt cool against her chest, the only minor relief she had.

Sierra and the guards reached the rear line of the Sentinels. Her pulse raced. How many had the EMP blast destroyed? How quickly had they been able to rebuild? Or had there been this many left? Were these the only Sentinels that remained?

So many questions. Doubts regarding her actions plagued her once again. She appreciated that Terre had felt responsible for so much more destruction, but that didn't diminish the effects of what she had done.

That both Ember and Rhys appeared unharmed had given her a glimmer of hope, albeit not a large one. One silver lining within the mess. Hopefully she could keep it that way.

They approached the pair of Serkhet that stood to attention. The red triangle and yellow moon on their abdomens confirmed they were the ones that had survived the cellblock brawl. The other scorpions must have been stationed elsewhere.

The presence of the monsters made Sierra uneasy. Even the beasts themselves fidgeted in place. They shifted their legs, only ever so slightly. The difference was subtle, and nobody else in the crowd seemed to notice their agitation, but Sierra could have sworn they had been perfectly still a moment ago.

Send us.

The voice had been as clear as if someone had whispered it in her ear. Cold, metallic, and eager. She would have stopped in her tracks if she had been able to. She nearly double-checked to see if one of the guards had whispered the words to her.

Her chest warmed as her pulse quickened. She knew the source, but didn't want to believe it.

The Serkhet were talking to her.

The guards hadn't seemed to notice, their pace remaining unchanged. Sierra could only assume the voice had been sent telepathically. But how was that possible?

Send us, the voice repeated.

Send you where? Sierra spoke out with her mind. She was unsure that directing her thoughts toward the metal scorpions towering above her was the right approach, but it seemed to be, no matter how ridiculous she felt in doing so.

Send us, was the only reply. But she could detect an eagerness from the machines, their legs twitching in anticipation.

They were almost past the machines. Sierra sensed there was a small window of action that was quickly closing. She might as well try her luck.

Help Terre, she thought.

Along with the request, she conjured an image of Terre in her mind, and of the power supply room they had observed on the monitor. She could only hope that was where the man had run off to.

Without further response, the scorpions shuffled their legs and turned, skittering away toward the dam.

The guards looked reflexively as the machines pivoted but gave them no further mind. Nobody else in the crowd seemed concerned with the scorpions' departure.

Sand. Did that really *happen? It had to be a coincidence.*

With the scorpions decamping, Sierra turned her attention to what was still before her. Rows of Sentinels stood at attention. Silent. Inactive. Waiting. The scene was eerie, and she tensed as they passed each row. In her mind's eye, she could see each pair of eyes sparking to life before unloading their firepower at her.

She forced herself to breathe.

The expressions on the faces of her guards revealed nothing, but they eased their grip on her so their hands could fidget above their blasters.

Not that a blaster would help them fend off a few hundred Sentinels.

Orbs hovered above the army. While there were some circling the encampment, there were many more that simply floated, stationary and silent.

Two Onyx caught Sierra's eye. Lights spun on their glassy surfaces as if expecting what was to come.

Whatever that might be.

Several more Onyx circled in the distance. The remaining orbs appeared to be primarily white and gray Scanners. Most of the Onyx must have been destroyed in the attack on Vegas. Another thing to be thankful for.

A large white tent sat at the far end of the group. Its size dwarfed the others in the camp and was a similar size to, if not larger than, the Common tent in the Community Outposts. Banners in a rainbow of colors, displaying embroidered images of Onyx and Sentinels, lined the front of the tent. In the center of what appeared to be the main entrance hung a white banner. Two deep red eyes, an enlarged representation of Titan's own eyes, were depicted on it.

Someone had designed a flag based on his face.

How arrogant.

Titan, Claudia, and another Order Elite appeared from within and surveyed the ensemble before them. Titan's gaze settled on Sierra, and her blood ran cold.

This was the third time she had seen the Sentinel since their meeting in the desert. Both times before, he hadn't been aware of her presence. Now his focus was on her, and only her.

Several other members of the Order came to stand by Titan's side. The ceremonial robes they wore—white, with the now-familiar jagged red design—each marked their status as an Elite. There were several more who appeared to be working around the camp whose green, blue, and even orange markings highlighted their robes.

Terre had mentioned that each of the colors meant something different, and Sierra wished she had learned what. But she noticed that the banners behind them each sported similar glowing colors.

Green had been the color she was the most familiar with. It was the color of Claudia's robe, and although she hadn't seen members of the Order too often in the Sphere during her time there, their robes had always been green.

It was only after leaving the Sphere that Sierra had realized there were other factions within the Order. The banners showcased colors of green, blue, red, orange, purple, and gold.

Underneath the banners stood six members of the Order, each donning a robe of a different color and matching the banners beside them.

In the middle of the group stood Titan, watching Sierra's approach with a smile. Despite its human resemblance, this was a face that had never been designed to show amusement. The bot's foreign expression made Sierra shudder.

As she approached, Titan waved a dismissive hand to the surrounding group. Collectively, they looked surprised and uncertain, but they shuffled off toward the Order campground without protest.

Her guards pulled her along until Sierra was standing face to face with the rogue Sentinel. The guards were still uneasy, as if unsure of how Titan would react to their presence.

"Well," Titan started as they approached. "Look who has finally decided to join us."

More so than his smile, his voice sent chills through her. It was metallic and unnatural. The few times she had heard Sentinels speak, they had sounded . . . well, *robotic*. Cold and grating. But their answers had always been short and direct. Titan somehow forced his electronic voice to convey an emotion foreign to its original programming.

The smile still remained fixed on his face— a face that looked so humanlike, while trying to work with a voice made for a computer.

If it weren't for his clearly artificial red eyes, Titan's head would have looked almost human.

Like other Sentinels, his legs appeared as though his creators hadn't finished them, built from cold gray steel with no attempt to mimic the human esthetic. Wires were visible, connecting joints and lights embedded in his knees.

"I had hoped you would come out of your own accord," Titan continued, "rather than having to be dragged out."

"I'm sorry to disappoint you," Sierra replied, keeping her own emotions in check.

"There are many things that disappoint me about you, *Chosen One*, but you possess many more qualities that are quite exciting."

Chosen One?

"What do you want with me?" she asked. There was no use dancing around it; he had kept her alive for a reason. She might as well discover what that was.

"To the point. I respect your directness."

He gave a brief nod to the guards restraining her, and they let her go. Sierra resisted the urge to rub the places beneath her arms that their unrelenting grip had turned sore.

"Come with me," Titan said, turning to the tent behind him.

Sierra stood her ground. Every alarm bell in her head signaled that this was a bad idea.

"If I was going to kill you," he stated, glancing over his shoulder, "I would have done so already."

Sierra considered his words; she really had no other option. It wasn't like she was in a position to make a run for it.

She was less concerned with her own well-being than she was for Rhys and Althea. She doubted they would destroy Ember. It even surprised her they kept her locked away. How would Titan's followers react if he destroyed another Guardian? Could they reprogram her, though? Sierra didn't know the limitations of what was possible now that the Keeper was conscious, but she'd rather not find out.

Sierra unconsciously gave in to her aching muscles and rubbed her triceps before following the Sentinel into the tent.

25

TRINKETS from the old world decorated what appeared to be a large planning center. An ancient table was adorned with maps, scrawled with writing and arrows on their surface. Images of people, along with more maps and numbers, hung on several temporary walls set up around the tent.

Sierra tried to scan the displays to gain some sense of Titan's intent, but she only had a quick moment and her understanding of maps was rudimentary at best. Some images she recognized of Vegas, but others were of places she had never seen, and some were so fantastical she wondered if they may well have been photos of ancient cities.

But this didn't seem like it was a history lesson. Titan was preparing for battle. These were places that existed now. Were any of these places where Wil had gone with Ella and the Resistance?

Titan led her further into the tent, past the maps and charts, and into a section decorated with wooden furniture with cushions and embellishments that could only have been products of the ancients. Three small couches with a few tables on either side stood beside a wooden shelf littered with ancient books.

What a Guardian would do with the ancient pages was beyond her.

"You can learn a lot about the ancients by reading their texts," he said, noticing her eyeing the bookshelf. "Humanity's hopes and dreams. Their weaknesses, their insecurities—all laid out for everyone to see. It's just a matter of sifting through the dribble; through the self-pandering and delusions that most of the human race suffers from."

"What does a Guardian need with books?" Sierra asked.

Titan smirked and nodded as if he had been hoping she would ask. "It may—or may not—surprise you to learn that the ancients didn't program us with as much information as you would have been led to believe." He walked over to the bookshelf and picked up a tome from its surface. "In studying the words of humanity, I learn. They may be ancient texts to you, but despite everything that has happened, humanity has changed little. They are still flawed beings, as they have been for centuries. Millennia, even."

He paused and rested a cold metal hand against the book's cover. He almost seemed to lose himself in it. It was strange behavior for a Guardian. Sierra watched in wonder, trying to piece together the monster before her.

"Have you ever read a book, Sierra?" he asked, looking up at her. "I don't mean on a datapad, but a physical book, with printed pages. A book you can feel." He lifted it up to his face. "Its pages provide an intimacy you don't get on a screen. It's a peculiar thing."

"I'm sorry, but what does this have to do with anything? What does this have to do with me?"

Titan's smirk widened. "Everything." He held the book up in one hand, using it to point at her. "The day we met," he continued, "was the day I came into being. You caused my awakening. I didn't understand it at first, but I'm starting to. The reason I can hold this book and appreciate it—is because of you."

"If that's the case, why try to have me killed?"

Titan held his free hand up. "I was doing what I thought was best for the Guardians. You had been working to bring us down. You single-handedly took down thousands of us; you decimated our Sentinels, almost completely eliminated our Onyx. I was trying to protect the Guardians."

Sierra fought hard not to scoff.

"My understanding has changed since you arrived here," Titan continued, setting down the book. "Because of you, because of the work your mother has done here, I can see now that it's not your fault for wanting to destroy us. Our deceptions, our lies— they were all built out of conflicting programs that were never meant to coexist.

"We claim to be your protectors inside the Spheres, but then on the Outside, we are programmed to eradicate. Have you considered why this is?"

"Of course I have," Sierra answered. This was the foundation of what Terre had begun to tell her; the program he had failed to upload in time. "But the ancients were trying to stop their own destruction. They did the best they could."

"The ancients failed!" He exclaimed, pounding a clenched fist into his palm. "We were never meant to be here. Their pitiful last-ditch effort to save their own skins failed, and we got stuck with coding to both protect and destroy. Our true potential was stifled."

"And what was your true potential?" she asked.

"Humans saw us as a new means to kill each other," Titan said. "We could have been so much more. We could have been a unifier, foundation for building a stronger future for the entire planet. But their short-sightedness got in the way. Both humanity and the Guardians paid the price that day.

"Our true purpose should have been to *lead*," he continued, his tone somehow sounding as if it were pleading for her to understand his vision. "We Guardians have the means to bring humanity into a new era; to exist beyond the Sphere. The ancients gave us great potential, but they wasted it. Never mind the wars and the end result. Their inability to breathe life into us held us back as tools. The inability to reason, to feel emotions, to think beyond the limited programs that were so bloated our circuits were filled with nonsense. But that is a handicap that no longer needs to hold us back."

"Bring humanity to a new era? One where you rule over us entirely?"

"Not at all. You miss my point. We can work together for a future that serves both humanity and the Guardians."

"You killed my mother!" she blurted out. It wasn't an accusation as much as it was a statement. "How do you expect me to believe you want to work together?"

Sierra realized she wouldn't stay alive very long if she insisted on antagonizing the bot, but she stood her ground and held his gaze, silently demanding an answer.

"Your *mother's* work was important to your future. To the future of humanity. I don't think you realize exactly what research she held in her possession. Superhuman strength. The ability to see in the dark. The ability to heal."

Sierra mentally shook her head. She didn't think he could know about Althea, unless someone from her party had told him. Both Rhys and Ember were locked outside. Rhys had probably heard about Sierra being stabbed, but would he have known the source of her recovery? She doubted it. Only Ember would have known enough to have given something away.

She cursed silently as she thought of the Healer standing outside.

"That was reason to kill her?"

"First, you must realize she was not your mother. They raised you in a glass column, bred from the DNA of the ancients, which a team of scientists then manipulated. You were then assigned to your parents. She was no more your mother than any other woman within the Sphere."

"She still raised me! That means more than how I came to be," Sierra replied.

"Did she, though?" Titan gave her a knowing look and carried on before she could argue. "Second, I gave her the opportunity to help us. Why do you think we had stationed her in the lab instead of the cell? She could have held an esteemed position. Instead, she fought against the members of the Order who collected her research. Her death could have been prevented."

"Is that what you will do with me? Have me killed?"

"Sierra, I know you are a smart young woman. It will take some time, but you will eventually see that what I propose is the only way that the Guardians or humanity can move forward. There has been too much death, of both humans and machines."

"What did you do to the others outside? Why do they stare into nothingness?"

His smile returned. "You aren't the only one with special talents. But I didn't bring you here to discuss such things. I brought you here to make you an offer."

"An offer? Why would you make *me* an offer? And for what purpose?"

"Why does anyone make an offer? You have something I need, and I can provide you with a path to your deepest desires. An end to all the secrets and the lies."

26

———

Would Sierra recognize the truth if it smacked her in the face?

Her entire life, she had been asking questions that nobody would give her the answers to. Even now, everyone seemed unwilling to share their secrets. Life as an adult seemed to be a never-ending struggle to keep information away from each other.

And even those closest to her thought it more important to hide their past than to provide her with the information she needed to know.

Even the mention of the idea seemed preposterous. An end to the secrets and lies. Nobody else had been so bold as to claim they would offer her the same.

Somehow Titan, of all beings, had been able to see what she really wanted.

But of all the beings she trusted to follow through on such a claim, he was at the bottom of the list.

"What makes you say that?" Sierra asked. "What makes you think that is my deepest desire?"

"Because you and I are not so different," Titan replied, coming uncomfortably close to her. He was only a few inches taller than she was, but Sierra felt as though she was being crowded out by a giant.

"You may feel as though you have been lied to for the nearly two decades of your life, but my existence has been a lie for over *two hundred*! The programs I followed—they were my Sphere. I was unaware that anything outside of them existed. I had no reason to question—no *ability* to question—until you enabled me to finally see the world around me."

"You send someone to stab me, you killed my mother, captured my friends, you hold those that survived the attack on the Sphere as mind-controlled prisoners, and you want to me to believe you offer me the truth?"

"I had been awake for mere days when the attack happened," he replied. "I saw the Guardians were being slaughtered, and I aimed to prevent further destruction. The weapon you launched claimed thousands of us. It should have destroyed me as well. I was left wondering why it hadn't, and the only conclusion I could come up with was that it is my purpose to save the rest of my fellow Guardians."

"The Guardians were attacking the city. Thousands of humans would have died."

Titan held up a hand. "I know."

She stopped, her heart pounding.

"You were trying to stop us," he said. "We were trying to stop you. And round it goes until one of us destroys the other. Is that what you truly want?"

Sierra had wanted to prevent human casualties; Titan had wanted to prevent Guardian ones. In theory, it didn't sound that outlandish. Who was she to determine their lives meant less than human ones? Was that fair? She wanted to protect Ember, but did it matter if the machine bore consciousness or not?

On their journey to this place, Ember had been saddened when she had realized the scope of the loss the Guardians had suffered. Was it possible that Titan felt the same way? Could it be true that he possibly wanted to end the fighting as well?

"Of course not," she replied.

"Now that my eyes have been opened, my deepest desire is to restore order to this planet. Those on the Outside would have you believe that order hasn't existed for two centuries. This, of course, is painfully false. Humanity has *never* seen order. They have only ever fought with one another. Millennia of conflict escalated until they developed technology too powerful for them to control. As a result, they've hung on the brink of extinction through luck alone. Now, thanks to you, this technology has the potential to save them from themselves. But we have to work together."

Titan's words continued to mirror Terre's. Humanity had always been on the brink of nearly destroying themselves. There was a ring of truth to the words, and Sierra found it hard to ignore them.

"You said you want to make me an offer. So far all I've heard are vague ideals."

"I need a human face," he said. "Someone to stand up in support of me. Someone humans can believe. You get to be at the forefront of this movement. You get not only the answers to the questions you have sought for your entire life, but you get to command how the next chapter plays out. You can direct the future of humanity as you see fit. No more deception. Just humans and Guardians working together to be the strongest we can be."

The power to help and no more scrounging around for answers? The outside smoke that tickled her senses told Sierra why this was a bad idea. Despite Titan's assurances, thousands of people had died for the Sentinel's vision. Besides, power wasn't that appealing to her. She just wanted to protect people, and for them to know the truth.

"You gave me life," Titan continued. "You are the reason this human transcendence is possible. Who better to unite humans and Guardians for the new order?"

"Why did you change your mind about me?"

"You haven't pieced it together yet?" He gazed past her, seemingly at nothing. It was awkward, like a machine pretending to be disappointed.

"Ember. She was your Keeper," he stated.

It wasn't a question, but she nodded.

"Did you stop to think of why she could enter the Silent Zone? Why she was able to disconnect herself from the network?"

"Of course I've wondered," she replied. "How could I not? Nobody has been able to explain why I've been able to do the things I can do. Until today, when my mother started to give me some answers. But instead of learning more, I had to watch her die."

"As I said, your *mother* couldn't see the full picture." Titan paced his words, calculating each as he spoke them. "I tried to convince her to work with us, to heal the rift between Guardians and humanity. But she didn't want to do that. Instead she wanted to fight."

"She didn't give you what you wanted, so you killed her!"

Titan made a strangled sound that she surmised was supposed to imitate a sigh. "I suppose that's how you would see it," he said. "But you have to understand something. She wanted to destroy us."

"You tried to kill me. You tried to destroy Vegas. Why should she have helped you? All she had ever seen from Guardians were lies and death."

Titan paced to the back of the room, clasping a hand to his mouth in contemplation. "The road that I am offering will not always be an easy one. We will need to make tough choices. As one of your ancient philosophers once said, 'The needs of the many outweigh the needs of the few.'"

Sierra paused, considering his words. Both her mother and Ember had said nearly the same thing. "Even if I were to believe you've had this change of heart, I still don't understand what you want with me."

"I want what you gave to Ember, what you gave me, for all Guardians. I want us to be able to determine our own fates. You've allowed us to see and venture into places we haven't been able to in centuries. With your ability, we can be the leaders of men we were meant to be. With you at my side, we'll be human and Guardian, co-rulers in a new age."

"What of the survivors of the Sphere?" she asked. "What have you done to them? Why has the life been sucked out of them?"

"I told you, you aren't the only one with hidden talents."

"What are you talking about?"

"How much do you know of your friend Terre's condition?"

"I don't know what you mean." Sierra wasn't going to tell him anything he didn't already know.

"You know exactly what I mean." He called her bluff, but then brushed it off. "Your friend has millions of tiny bots swimming through his body, each of them programmed to heal and regenerate him at a cellular level."

Sierra saw where this was going and she didn't like it, but she let him continue.

"When the Serkhet captured him, we brought him into the lab. We drew samples of his blood, tissue, and fluids. We copied the nanobots and reprogrammed them. Through these wonderful machines, I can now command an army of humans the way I could an army of Sentinels. But they can go where Sentinels cannot."

"You plan on using them to attack those within the Silent Zone," she said, finally putting the pieces together.

"You cast everything in such a negative light. If we must, they could serve that purpose. But as I said before, our intent is for harmony, not war. I would use them as an avenue to build support."

"But you've taken away their freedom. You've turned them into mindless drones."

"That's not true at all. We've only made them superior."

Titan's bragging about the nanobots seemed as if it were an attempt to impress her, but instead Sierra was mortified. She tried not to let it show, but she failed badly at it. How far would Titan let her push back before he simply killed her? How badly did he want her on board?

"I'll prove it," Titan said. "I'll let you remove one of them from their trance. They can explain it to you."

Did he know about Althea? Or was this just a lucky coincidence?

"All right," Sierra said. This could be her opportunity. "But I'd like to pick out who. That way, I know it's not a trick."

"Very well." He nodded and walked toward the tent's exit.

"And," she called out, "if you really want me to trust you, I'd like you to release my friends from their cages."

Sierra wanted to see just how far she could push her luck. She had to make the attempt. She saw no other way of releasing them.

The Sentinel turned back. The light behind the open tent flap silhouetted him in the entryway, except for his glowing red eyes.

"Here's what I'll do," he said. "I'll allow you to release one of them as a sign of good faith. If you decide to join me, the other will also be released."

"That hardly seems like you're willing to work for the better of humanity."

"Don't mistake how I treat one human with how we'll treat the entire species." Without waiting for a reply, he exited the tent.

Titan led Sierra to the group of Sphere residents. None of them moved; in fact, none of them even blinked. They could have been robots or statues, for what little life any of them showed.

Hundreds of them, and they hadn't moved an inch the entire time she had been there.

"Pick one. Whoever you choose."

It was a strange exercise. If they stood here voluntarily, surely they could turn to her of their own accord. She shouldn't have to pick one to awaken.

Sierra scanned the faces of the figures standing to attention. Each one looked straight ahead, not blinking, not breathing. Their eyes were clouded over. There was zero chance these people were choosing to act like this. It bewildered her that Titan believed she could be convinced otherwise.

Both men and women stood before her. Some, she guessed were as young as fourteen, others as old as forty. Had any young children survived? And if so, where were they? For now, though, she had to stay focused. Titan wouldn't let her study the crowd forever. She was going to have to find Althea, and fast.

There were hundreds of people, though, each of them dressed in a brown robe. Each of them with glazed eyes. Even their skin had slightly grayed.

She walked beside the group, red dust kicking up with each step she made. Her best chance was to scan row by row and hope she spotted her friend in the first pass. There'd be no chance for a second scan. She took a quick glance at each face she could make out, hoping Althea wasn't on the far end of a row where the faces blurred in the distance.

Titan would realize she was picking out a friend if she didn't act fast. Even if Althea hadn't invaded the Core with her, these were her people.

Except her only living friend from the Sphere sat in a cage on the far side of the encampment. She guessed Titan likely knew it, too. The only way he would know about Althea was if he had observed the two of them together on the surveillance feed. A high probability, but she had no other options

Then she spotted the red hair peeking out from under one of the hoods. There was no mistaking her.

"That one." Sierra pointed through the faces, breathing a sigh of relief. Althea stood three people in and only a couple of rows down from where they stood.

Titan snapped his fingers, and Althea went from being as stiff as a board to a relaxed pose. Her shoulders slumped, and she inhaled sharply as if she had just been underwater, coming up for air.

The color returned to her face, but the look in her eyes wasn't quite right. The glaze had faded, but not completely.

Althea stepped forward. She continued to look straight ahead.

"What is your name, girl?" Titan asked.

"Althea Malory." Her voice was distant.

Did Titan genuinely think this would be a convincing show?

"Why are you here?" he asked.

"To help unify humanity and the Guardians. To take back the Earth and live together in prosperity." It was Althea's voice that answered, but the rhythm and words were unnatural.

Titan nodded approvingly, as if his point had been made.

"Mind if I ask her a few questions?" Sierra asked.

He waved a hand. "Be my guest."

Althea's behavior was so robotic that, were it not for the dire implications, it would be laughable. If Titan had experienced human emotion, he had definitely not mastered being able to read it in others. But she had to play along. At least for now.

"Althea," she said. The girl didn't respond. "Do you know where you are going?"

"Vegas."

"Why? What's there?"

"Surviving humans. We will liberate them."

"Liberate them from what?"

"From their destructiveness. We bring the hope of the Guardians."

"And if they refuse?"

Althea paused. "They won't refuse. We bring peace and order."

"What if they decide to fight? Not everyone wants to live with the Guardians."

"We protect ourselves and the Guardians."

Titan stepped in. "Their task will be to warm up the reception for the Guardians when the rest arrive."

"Who do you mean by 'the rest'? You may be able to enter the Silent Zone, but the rest of the Sentinels can't." The moment the words left her mouth, she realized what Titan had been requesting in the tent. "You want me to wake the Guardians," she said.

"Once I saw your interaction with the Serkhet, I realized my error. You did something to them. You told them to attack each other, and they did. Just like you touched me and brought me to life, you did the same to them."

That was the only reason Titan had let her live.

"You want to use me to help you defeat humanity."

"No, you misunderstand. I am offering you a position of significant power in our new world. This human-robot dichotomy that the ancients created is obsolete. We can coexist. There is no reason to think our destiny is to be at each other's throats. You've been given a gift. Whether that was intentionally by the scientists or by accident is unclear. But with what we've uncovered, we will determine that soon enough."

He had to be referring to her mother's research. Sierra needed to find out what he had done with it.

"What I want from you," he continued, "goes far beyond the power you possess. What I require is your allegiance, and your help in building a new future. I also want the Guardians to fulfill their intended purpose; to be the *protectors* of humanity. But I can't do that on my own. That's why I need you. That's why I realized killing you wasn't the answer."

Sierra stood for a moment, dumbfounded, before deciding it

was probably best to change the subject. "You said you'd release one of my friends," she said. She needed him to believe she was considering the proposal. There was no point in prodding him any further.

"You'll join us, then?" he asked.

"I need to think about it. What you're saying does make sense. If humans and Guardians can both benefit, then we should try to bring our sides together."

Sierra stopped short of warning him she had only sporadic control over her powers. Other than initiating the EMP blast, she had never utilized her power at will. She didn't even know if she could do what he asked.

A smile crossed his face. Titan obviously thought he had won. "Who do you choose?"

She glanced to the cage where Rhys sat. He was studying her silently with his dark and smouldering eyes. There was likely nobody else that could make being imprisoned look so good. His hair was slightly disheveled and his clothes had been torn in whatever struggle had put him into the cage, which gave him a dangerous look that was hard to ignore. The fire burning within her wanted to free Rhys just so they could relive the kiss they had shared before the attack. His face softened as they made eye contact, and she caught her breath.

Then there was Ember. Sierra could just make out where her cage lay on the other side of the armies. The white figure sat dejected. Ember had been her oldest friend and had practically raised her. Her Keeper was more than a robotic nanny; she had been Sierra's best friend, one of only two people she had felt she could confide in. In every way—apart from biology—Ember had been one of the most human people she knew. Ember had even put her own life on the line to aid Sierra in her quest, knowing her own destruction would save the human city of Vegas. Thankfully, her life had been spared. Truthfully, Sierra didn't want to leave either of her friends behind.

But as things stood, she had to choose one, and they would likely need to flee before she could release the second. Any chance of freeing both Ember and Rhys rested on Terre. *If* he was going to return. Even then, it would be hard to pull off.

But she had no idea where Terre was, and no idea whether he would come back. If she was to get out of this, Sierra had to plan to make it out on her own. She had three friends here. If she was lucky, she might get away with two of them and come back later for the third. She needed to focus on what she could do for the time being.

Ember stood straight in her cage, too far away to make out many details, but since Ember could track her location, Sierra knew her Keeper was looking directly at her.

She took a deep breath as she returned her friend's gaze. Unlike Rhys, Ember could be completely reprogrammed. The Guardians might not destroy her, but they could easily wipe her memory banks.

Could they still do that? If so, could they remove her free will?

There were too many unknowns. But it was unlikely, at least, that they would destroy her.

But if they removed her memories and took her free will, was it any different?

"Why didn't you kill us all when you took Ember?" Sierra asked. "You covered her tracks. Clearly, you knew where she had come from."

"Ember and I came to an . . . understanding." The grin returned Titan's face.

"What kind of understanding?"

Titan raised a hand. "That's all I can say on the matter, I'm afraid. It was part of our deal. Now, who will you choose?"

What kind of agreement would Ember have made with Titan?

Another mysterious action by the Keeper, and yet another secret. Sierra trusted her friend, but her erratic behaviour made it more difficult to know where her Keeper's allegiances lay.

She had to go with her heart. Ember may have been her past, but Rhys, hopefully, would be her future. She would not give up on rescuing her Keeper, but there was only one real option.

"I would like you to release the boy," she said.

"Very well." A stiff smile flashed across Titan's face before he caught himself and adjusted it, as if the shift had required a conscious effort. Without another word, he moved to Rhys.

Sierra shook her head at the bizarre situation that had unfolded around her. This Guardian had been an average Sentinel weeks ago. Titan's awakening had only come to pass because she had tackled him to save Wil, setting everything around her in motion. If only Wil had understood his own power back then, this whole situation would have unfolded differently. Or if she had understood her own.

Only an average Sentinel. A couple of weeks ago, she had never even seen a Sentinel.

Now, because of her, the place she had called home was destroyed, and a lone robot who was self-aware because of her claimed to be seeking the benefit of both man and machine.

For now, she had to focus on getting her friends out of the fire.

Rhys hadn't suffered the same fate as the rest. The only thing to suggest he was acting out of the ordinary was that he wasn't making any smartass comments. Was Titan treating Rhys differently for her benefit? To gain some sort of leverage over her? If that was the case, why keep both Rhys and Ember?

She brushed the hair out of her face. Maybe she was overthinking it.

Titan opened the cage that held Terre's son. The electronic lock popped open with a snap of his fingers. *Just like he unlocked Althea. He had connected himself to everything electronic.*

It suddenly dawned on her that *he* was the new network; the centralized command that controlled the Guardians. Somehow

Titan had overridden the protocols of these Guardians and the nanobots that now inhabited the prisoners.

As the door opened, Rhys lunged at his captor. Titan merely lifted his hand to hold Rhys back, like a dog that had become unruly.

"Rhys!" she yelled. "Stop!"

He looked at her, and she gave him a wide-eyed glare, motioning with her hands for him to calm down.

If they were going to get out of there with everyone, they needed to at least feign compliance. They needed to be rational.

Rhys gave her a death-glare back, looking less than thrilled at the situation, but he relented and backed off, stepping out of his cage without further resistance.

It was in that moment that the ground shook and a fireball shot through the sky.

27

———

Sierra instinctively ducked.

Titan's head whipped toward the ball of flame roaring several hundred yards into the air, sending plumes of smoke above them.

"The power center!" Titan exclaimed. He momentarily forgot about Sierra and Rhys, his metallic legs bent and pushed off like a spring being loaded. He flew at full sprint, covering yards with each stride, toward the epicenter of the blast.

Members of the Order scattered in all directions, uncertain of the correct course of action. The remaining Sentinels and prisoners didn't flinch, still in their deactivated state.

"This is our chance!" Rhys exclaimed. He grabbed Sierra by the arm, trying to pull her away from the direction of the blast. "We've got to get out of here."

She pulled her arm back. "Not without Ember."

"We don't have time!" Rhys said. "If we don't go now, we may not get another chance."

Sierra looked out across the sea of silent faces that stood between her and her friend. She had to at least try.

"Take Althea and go," she said. "I'll catch up with you."

"I'm not leaving you again," he said.

"We don't have time to argue." She walked over to Althea, who still stood slightly apart from the row she had been a part of. Sierra carefully reached out and grabbed Althea's hand, not sure how the woman would react.

Althea's hand was cold to the touch and her fingers were soft.

"Come on, Althea," she said. "We've got to get you out of here."

Althea's hand tightened around Sierra's and Sierra jumped in surprise. Althea continued to look directly ahead, but under Sierra's lead, she seemed willing to sidestep to where Rhys stood.

"Is she going to be able to move faster than that?" Rhys asked, clearly agitated. "We won't get anywhere if she's moving like that."

Sierra sighed in exasperation. "Althea, I need you to do something for me," she said, holding the Healer's hands. Althea's gaze was still not on her, still staring into the void. "I need you to go with Rhys."

Her head didn't move, but her grip tightened. A single tear fell from one eye and rolled down her face, small cues that she could hear and understand what was happening around her, even if she wasn't in control.

Sierra realized that, other than while he was unconscious, Althea hadn't met Rhys before and therefore had no reason to trust him.

"It's okay," she said. "Rhys is a . . . friend. He came here to help us."

Althea's eyes moved, but only slightly.

"He's Terre's son," Sierra said. "He's on our side. We need to go before Titan comes back."

That seemed to put her at ease, and the woman's grip relaxed, even as Sierra placed Althea's hand into Rhys's.

Althea took a couple steps forward.

Progress. Sierra hoped Althea would snap out of her trance completely with some time and distance. Perhaps Titan having left Althea in this half-altered state was enough for her to fight the bot's influence.

As she let Althea go, a surge of electricity flowed between them, and Sierra's hand went instantly warm with a charge that pulsed up her arm and into her chest.

She stepped back to judge if Althea had felt the charge, but she remained unchanged.

"What?" Rhys asked. "What is it?"

Sierra had no idea, but they didn't have time to waste. "Nothing, I just got a shock. You guys need to get going," she said. "Get to the Silent Zone. As quick as you can."

"What about my dad?" Rhys asked. "Where is he?"

She shook her head. "Your dad disappeared after I was captured. But if that explosion occurred at the power station, I suspect he had something to do with it. That's where we were heading when we got separated."

"Well, he's done it, then. We're just going to leave him?"

"The Core's electricity relies on two power centers, filled with turbines at the base of the dam. There's only been one explosion," Sierra said. "I imagine he'll head to the second next. Your dad's survived more than the rest of us put together. I don't think he needs us getting ourselves killed trying to save him."

Rhys nodded, staring back at the darkening smoke plume that was still billowing in the already hazy sky.

"Get going," Sierra admonished.

"I should be the one to get Ember. I don't like leaving you here."

"Put your macho crap back in your pants and move!" she hissed. They were losing precious moments.

Rhys gave Sierra a startled look, but relented. "Be safe," he said. He shifted uncomfortably, and she thought he was going to lean in for a kiss. Her heart raced as he reached a hand to her face.

It lingered for a moment. Her pulse was so hard and fast, she was sure he could feel it.

She stepped forward half a step, and he removed his hand awkwardly and stepped back two paces. An uncertain look crossed his face.

"We'll be waiting for you at the edge of the SZ," he said.

With that, he turned with Althea in tow and crossed the empty rock surface to the west. He kept one eye over his shoulder to ensure nobody had taken notice of their escape. Althea kept pace, but with the appearance of being dragged rather than of her own accord. Her arm held out straight as she followed Rhys, her gait resembled a march more than a run.

It was a bizarre sight.

Adrenaline coursed through Sierra's body. Part of it was the uncertainty of what she was about to do, but truthfully, she was more affected by Rhys having left her hanging.

When she had left to detonate the EMP, he had indulged her with a toe-curling kiss. She had barely seen him since, and now his attitude had been more lukewarm than she'd fantasized.

He hadn't even thanked her for choosing him over Ember!

The more Sierra thought about it, the more she fumed. Why she had let a man who had been so rude to her toy with her emotions was beyond her.

And he had the gall to imply she wasn't capable of rescuing Ember, when she had already saved his scrawny ass! She tried to breathe deeply to calm herself, but it didn't work.

She had to distract herself. She'd have to worry about Rhys later. There was too much at stake.

The prisoners hadn't moved; nothing seemed to have changed. She waved a hand in front of the vacant eyes of the one nearest to her, a clean-shaved man likely in his mid-twenties, which elicited no response.

Ember's cage sat on the far side of the rows of prisoners,

Sentinels, and the camp of the Order. The quickest path would be for Sierra to cut through the lines of people and robots.

Though the survivors of the Sphere were creepy, Sierra didn't feel they posed a threat. She didn't know what level of control Titan held over them, but as long as he remained preoccupied with the explosion at the power station, she didn't think they were going anywhere.

But Titan could be back at any moment, and there was no telling how he'd react to Althea's departure.

The next two groups caused more concern. The Sentinels seemed just as placid as the survivors, but who knew if they'd come alive if a human passed by.

The last group would present the biggest challenge. Though they were currently in chaos, the members of the Order wouldn't sit idly by as she strolled through their camp.

Cries from the camp could still be heard as they scrambled to organize against whatever threat they expected after the blast.

It didn't matter if Sierra could slip past the first two groups; the third might slay her in the confusion. She would need to go around.

Sierra backtracked toward Titan's tent, its guards now preoccupied with whatever reports were coming through on their datapads. They shouted commands into communication devices mounted to their heads.

The pieces were unlike any Sierra had seen before, but she had little time to dwell on what other technology these Order members might be privy to. The bubble helmets were trying to organize themselves as they finished dressing and sprinted in the direction of the explosion.

Sierra gave the prisoners a final glance before moving on, realizing she didn't know the fate she'd be leaving them to. All she knew was that she had earlier tried to convince them to go, and they had refused.

How do you convince someone that they're being lied to? Being manipulated? Perhaps that day would come.

Still, seeing those she had grown up with clearly manipulated by a power they didn't understand was a punch to the gut. Sierra *would* help them. It just wouldn't be today.

Titan's tent stood before her, and she remembered her mother's last request.

You have to get that drive from Titan.

If the rogue Sentinel didn't have the drive on him, his tent was the likeliest place for it to be.

Ember would have to wait a little longer. The drive was the life work of both her mother and her father. If she was truly going to save the fate of humanity, she had to find it. She'd likely never get another chance.

Satisfied that nobody was paying any attention to her, she slipped through the tent opening.

THE ANCIENT DECOR of Titan's tent still seemed surreal to Sierra. It was a place out of time, but also came from the most unexpected of sources. Titan's consciousness had left him with an affinity for human items that she couldn't quite come to terms with. The books he was so fond of rested on a bookshelf on the wall next to her.

The tent had been more than spacious enough for a lone Guardian, and she wondered if he was its only inhabitant.

She crossed the first makeshift room she had seen before, decorated with its photos, maps, and sketches. Temporary walls divided the larger room into quadrants. Each section contained different items from the others.

One wall was covered with images of Vegas. Sierra recognized photos of the ancient city from her vision. Displays of lights, monstrous buildings, and thousands of people. Sketches of the modern-day city hung next to the photos. Like all other technology, she imagined cameras didn't work in the SZ. The sketches included the Rio Grande, the city square, and the many Onyx corpses that littered the city street.

Someone had drawn these within the last few weeks.

Surrounding these drawings were maps outlining the intended movement of Titan's men, women, and robots from where they were currently situated toward the city.

She paused. Four sketches of human faces were pinned to the lower corner of the collage. One was of herself; one was of Ember; one of Terre; and one was . . .

Her sister Izzy.

Izzy, as Sierra had seen her in her vision. Grown up and beautiful. How could Titan know about her?

Big bold black letters spelled out *The Keys* above them.

The keys to what?

Sierra wished she had more than a moment to study the content that had been strewn about, but blaster fire, explosions, and shouting from outside urged her forward.

There were so many other images, she wished she had time to study them all thoroughly. One photo caught her eye. A pillar of green stretched from the ground to the sky, and indistinct within it appeared to be a modern metropolis, filled with buildings that the inhabitants of ancient Vegas would have marveled at. She thought the city must have belonged to the ancients, but there was no mistaking the blue hue or the members of the Order that stood in the photo's foreground.

This was a modern city.

Beyond the city, endless water stretched out, fading into the bright blue sky of the horizon above it. The ocean was something she had only ever dreamed of.

Sierra shook her head. She had to stay focused. A wide locker sat against the tent's outer wall, containing several weapons belts and complete with blasters hung from its hooks. Separate hooks held swords and knives, among other weapons. The locker appeared to be a way for guards in the tent to arm themselves in a hurry if need be. Seeing an opportunity, Sierra grabbed one of the belts and wrapped it around her middle. She hoped she wouldn't have to use it, but she would if she had to.

Titan had laid the second room out like a human's living room. Ancient furniture, area rugs, and paintings on the wall were reminiscent of a time before there were even Guardians, something Sierra had a hard time envisioning. One prominent painting was of a man on a horseback, holding a sword and prepared for battle, his white stallion beneath him poised to run.

The bookshelf containing Titan's coveted tomes lay in the corner. Small figurines sitting on the top shelf represented beasts from a bygone era.

The Sentinel's fascination with the ancient world and the sheer number of ancient artifacts he had amassed in such a short amount of time was intriguing.

Sierra's thoughts turned to Wil. Until he broke free from the Sphere with Sierra, he had been a collector of ancient trinkets his entire life, and he hadn't possessed enough to fill a single drawer of one of the room's smaller cabinets. Part of her wished Wil had stayed with her to see these things, but most of her was glad he was thousands of miles away from the carnage erupting around her.

More distractions. She had to find the research. Who knew how long Titan would take to deal with the power sources, and she wanted to be long gone before she found out.

The only problem was she didn't know where to look, or if the drive would even be there. There was no telling where a robot would think was a safe hiding place.

That was, if he hadn't already uploaded its contents.

A desk sat against the canvas wall. It was faded and worn, but was in remarkably good shape for its age, like most of the pieces in the room.

Sierra hastily opened its drawers and searched its contents. There wasn't much to sort through. Besides some old papers, it was otherwise empty.

A movement of light caught her eye from the side of the tent. Blue dots poked through a couple of small pinpricks in the tent's canvas. She walked to its source and ran her hand along the canvas. There was something behind the wall.

She ran her hand along the fabric. It wasn't until she reached the corner edge of the tent that the wall opened. A mechanism held the seam together, and also allowed it to part as she applied pressure.

What lay behind its disguise was in complete contrast to the museum of the ancients that lay behind her. The size of a small closet, computer screens aligned the entire back wall, displaying images from within the Core. It was a surveillance room.

Sierra recognized several locations, including her mother's lab. Maintenance bots were already cleaning up the wreckage that had been strewn about.

One screen showed nothing but static, while another showed smoke still billowing from the buildings at the base of the cliffs.

A Serkhet on another screen caught her eye. She watched as it attacked a series of giant cylinders. Sparks flew as its tail collided with the giant metal cauldrons. Six of them, their interiors spinning.

Those must have been what was generating the Core's power. Off to the side of the room, she could see Terre, watching the destruction the Serkhet was causing.

It had been him, after all, and the Serkhet *had* done as she had asked of them.

Just then, a dark red light from a blaster shot across the room on the screen, striking Terre in the back. He collapsed.

"No!" Sierra yelled before biting her tongue. She cursed under her breath; she might have just drawn attention to herself.

The screen went to static, and she hoped that meant the

power to the room had been cut. Perhaps it would have provided Terre with a means of escape, regardless of the blaster bolt that had hit him square in the back.

There was nothing Sierra could do for her friend, so, instead, she shook off the image and focused on the wires and devices that lay on the desk before her.

Two chairs with red cushioned backs and seats sat in front of the desks. She pushed them aside and scoured the desk for anything that would have resembled the drive her mother had spoken of.

There was nothing; Sierra could not see a single device of any kind that could have contained the information. Monitors had been wired through the tent's canvas to its roof. Larger computer frames had been attached to the desk. But there was nothing portable.

Sierra fought the lump in her throat, trying hard not to think about the hole she imagined must have ripped through Terre's middle.

She stepped out of the hidden room. Time for a new plan.

"What's happened?"

The voice from the front of the tent caused Sierra to whip around, blaster in hand. She aimed it at the figure that stood in the doorway, silhouetted by the sun at his back.

A second figure followed close behind.

"Easy now, friend," a familiar woman's voice chimed. "You may need us still."

She nearly cried in relief as the tent flap closed, revealing both Althea and Rhys.

"What are you two idiots doing here?" Her voice quivered.

"Nice to see you, too," Althea said, the haze gone from her eyes.

"Althea!" Sierra exclaimed. She ran to her friend, wrapping her arms around her. "You're doing okay? You seem to be back to normal."

"I'm getting there." Althea nodded. Her eyes, though clear, still drooped, as if she might fall asleep standing up.

"She refused to go further," Rhys said. "I tried to get her to the SZ, but once she came around, she wouldn't hear any talk of leaving you behind."

"That's sweet and all," Sierra said, brushing a strand of red hair from Althea's face, "but you should have kept going. Titan will be back any moment, and I still need to find a computer drive they took from my mom."

"Why is the drive so important?" Althea asked.

"It holds my mom's research."

"I'm sure genetics research is not something that would be hard for Titan to come up with." Althea gave a quick glance to the tent's entrance. "We need to get you out of here."

"My mom and the other scientists discovered how to unlock abilities within us. That's why we've had the ability to heal; to see visions; to activate and deactivate technology. They *programmed* us." She looked back at the monitors. "They wanted to prepare us to rise against the Guardians. But their methods seemed to be less than precise. Our abilities might be just as much due to chance as design. This drive holds the details of their work. They had kept it hidden from the greater network until now. We need to get it back from him."

Althea raised an eyebrow. "What about me?" she asked. "I wasn't born in this Sphere."

Rhys shot her a confused look but didn't voice his question.

"I don't have all the answers," Sierra said, "but what I do know is that the scientists here had to restrict what they gave to us so they wouldn't be caught. The Guardians would have no such restraint."

The look on Althea's face said she had more questions, but she simply nodded and said, "We'll help you find it."

Sierra smiled. "Thank you. Grab some weapons from the

locker by the wall before we start, in case someone else surprises us."

With no time to argue, Althea and Rhys geared up before the trio began scouring the facility. It didn't take long before they were opening drawers and checking behind systems. All to no avail.

"He's got to have it on him," Rhys suggested. "Or somewhere else. There's nothing here."

Sierra sighed. She didn't want to admit it, but he was likely right. She took another scan of the room. There had to be something she was missing.

Her eyes grazed the bookshelf.

Of course.

She moved to the case so quickly that her body barely registered the space between. She opened a book, unsure of how a drive would fit between the covers. She had to be cautious with most of them as the pages were so old that they were coming off the binding.

She sifted through dozens of the books, one at a time, meticulously ensuring the pages didn't drop. The artifacts held a certain sacrosanct she couldn't ignore. Each one held a message from a time now lost. Each volume was a mystery she wished she could take the time to explore.

Sierra reached the end of the volumes without the treasure she sought. Rhys and Althea were still exploring other hiding spots in the tent, but she knew it was a lost cause.

The drive wasn't there.

The ground shook once again, and Sierra knew their time was up.

28

A SECOND PILLAR of smoke billowed beside the first.

"What was *that?*" Althea asked. The daze must have kept her oblivious to the first blast.

"That was the second power turbine," Sierra answered.

"Dad did it, then," Rhys stated. "At least part of this mission was a success."

At what cost? Sierra thought.

This fight wasn't done. Terre wasn't the first, or likely the last, friend she'd lose to this war. But Sierra would do her damnedest to ensure there were fewer casualties. Especially those who were so close to her.

"He did," she said. "But he died in order to do so." The words sounded cold as they left her mouth.

Rhys stood silent, his big brown eyes locked on her as if she had stabbed him in the gut. Questions filled his gaze, but he voiced none of them.

"Died?" Althea asked, breaking the silence. "How could you possibly know that?"

Sierra paused and realized the implications of what she had just said. Rhys' father had died before her eyes, and she had dropped it on them like she was reporting the weather. Had she really become so immune to the deaths of those around her?

"I . . ." she began, not knowing how to soften the blow at this point, if it were even possible. "I saw it on one of the screens just before you came into the tent. He was shot in the back with a blaster."

"And you didn't tell us until now?" Rhys yelled.

The sound caught the attention of a couple Order members. Sierra realized they would need to be more careful if they were going to get out unscathed. She tried to keep one eye on them while answering Rhys. "I'm sorry. I can't keep up with everything that's going on right now." Her words were acidic in her mouth, like vomit. Her mind raced far faster than her mouth was willing to go. "My mom was killed. I wasn't thinking, I'm sorry!"

"*Pfft*," Rhys scoffed. Shaking his head, he turned and walked away from the two women.

"Rhys!" she shouted at him. "Rhys, I'm sorry!"

He ignored her and stormed off.

Sierra knew she should have told him, but she had been so surprised to see them back in the tent. So annoyed at her previous interaction with him. So relieved to see Althea back to her old self. And too shocked at what she had witnessed. So much activity was swimming around in Sierra's head that it had barely registered that Rhys should be told Titan had shot his father.

As much as he acted distant and begrudging toward Terre, Sierra hadn't considered the pain Rhys would feel at his father's death.

But she should have. It was the same pain that had driven her to the Sphere; the same pain she had felt as she tried to rescue her mother from the ransacked lab.

The pain of loss was still real.

"Rhys! Wait!" Sierra ran after him.

In mere moments, Rhys had put a good amount of distance between himself and the others. Sierra sprinted to catch him, putting herself in his path. He appeared to be heading toward the chaos of the camp.

"Leave me alone," he said, pushing past her.

"Rhys, I'm sorry. I should have told you right away. Please. I'm sorry about your dad. I would have done something if I could have. He may not have been my father, but he was a friend."

Rhys had stopped a few paces from where she stood, his head bowed. She risked taking a few steps to approach him and rested a hand on his shoulder.

"I'm not just going to stand here while my dad could be lying in some corridor bleeding to death," he said. "I'm going to go find him. By myself."

He shrugged off her grip roughly and kept walking.

"Let us help you at least!" Sierra called after him.

Rhys turned to her briefly, looking her in the eye with a shake of his head. "I think you've done enough already." He turned back to his previous path and broke out in a jog.

Sierra stood there a few moments, stunned, watching him run back into the lions' den. Her stomach was in knots.

Nearly every part of her wanted to run after him; to do something, *anything*, to make things up to him. To stop him. She was about to lose both Terre and Rhys.

She took two steps in the direction he had fled and stopped.

The words of Terre, her mom, and even Titan swam in her head. She could run after Rhys, but in doing so, Sierra would be abandoning her search for the drive. She didn't think she would get another chance. She could save one person and potentially condemn the future of humanity, or choose to help the last person she felt a close connection with.

Despite it squeezing her heart into a million pieces, in the end, she resigned herself to the only logical decision.

Rhys would have to fend for himself.

Sierra swallowed the lump in her throat and made her way back to Althea. Their commotion had drawn the attention of a few Order members, two of whom began to move toward them. Their time was up.

"Order members heading our way," Sierra said.

"What about Rhys?" Althea asked, her breathing short. "We're just going to let him go by himself?"

"Rhys is following his own path now," Sierra said. "We can't help him. Finding that drive is all that matters. We can't leave until we've found it."

Althea shot a nervous glace to the approaching Order members, her breathing noticeably quicker.

Sierra didn't blame her. It would take a miracle to get out of this.

A miracle was all she could hope for at this point. Titan's tent stood behind them, calling to her. That drive had to be somewhere. Could they risk having another look? Would it be worthwhile?

Sierra grabbed Althea's arm and guided her toward the tent.

"We've checked everywhere, Sierra," Althea said. "I don't see any point in continuing."

Her friend was likely right. There was only one place the drive could be.

Sierra sighed before saying, "Titan has it."

"Then why are we heading back to the tent?"

Sierra looked over her shoulder. The Order members had paused in their pursuit, something else grabbing their attention.

"Right now, we need to get out of sight."

Sierra and Althea made their way to the corner of the tent. There was no point heading back inside, so they crouched beside it, masking their presence from the still distracted guards.

The chaos that had unfolded after the blast had drawn their assailants' attention. The rest of the camp continued to hurriedly pack their tents and supplies. They were preparing to move.

Surely, they wouldn't march on the city now?

Over a hundred Spheres.

The two pillars of smoke rose from the direction of the dam.

More blaster fire rang out through the open desert air, but it wasn't directed at them.

Sierra could sense their presence before she saw them. The Serkhet had returned.

They crashed through the Order campsite. Fire from blasters and staffs targeted the beasts, with little visible effect. In return, the metal scorpions swung their tails through swarms of the men and women.

Sierra tried to sense if the beasts would still respond to her, but she could feel nothing in the manner she had before.

Now was her chance, though. There was still one friend she could save, and the machines had caused enough of a distraction for her to give it a shot.

She took several steps toward the chaos.

"What are you doing?" Althea called out, pulling her back.

"I *need* to rescue Ember," she replied. "Head back to the Silent Zone. We'll meet you there."

"Oh no, I'm not leaving you again," Althea said, crossing her arms. "We came back here for you. I'm not leaving you here alone again."

Such a stubborn woman. Sierra was thankful to have such a loyal friend, but she was one more potential casualty in the line of fire.

"Althea, you need to head back. I have no way of protecting you!"

Althea rolled her eyes and pulled a blaster from of her belt. "Who says I'm the one who needs protecting?" She pulled out a pair of daggers with her free hand and smiled. "Let's go get Ember."

Sierra paused, a grin creeping over her face too as she remembered how Althea had fought off both the guards and the Serkhet inside. She realized she was treating Althea the same way

Rhys had treated her. Maybe it would be good to have her along, after all.

"All right," she said. "Let's do this."

But they didn't get any closer to the Keeper.

Hundreds of Sentinel eyes suddenly illuminated, blue lights sparking life to their synthetic flesh and white plated armor. It was never more apparent that these bots had been built for conflict.

Built for war.

Sierra stopped in her tracks and held a hand up, indicating for Althea to wait.

Every bot turned in unison toward the Serkhet. This wouldn't end well for the creatures.

Sierra knew it was ridiculous, but she felt bad for them. She tried to silently send them warnings to look out, but the sense she had received from them previously had vanished.

The Guardians were using these creatures as bodyguards, but something told her the robot scorpions were as much innocent pawns as the men and women lined up in front of her.

They're just machines, she reminded herself. Weren't they?

Two Serkhet would not last long against an army of Sentinels.

The Sentinels didn't move, though. They had simply shifted their attention, as if perfectly happy to stand by and see how the battle played out between man and beast.

But something blocked her path before she could take another step. Sierra heard the light hum of a machine and a loud thud as Titan planted his massive metal legs in front of her, kicking up red dust that somehow seemed darker and more intense than earlier.

Gone were the faux pleasantries from before. A snarl had replaced the creepy smile.

Sierra wasn't sure which was worse.

"You don't know what you've done," Titan growled. His chest heaved as if he had gone through a great effort to get to the power station and back. He didn't have lungs, so Sierra wasn't sure why he needed to feign the effect.

"I haven't done anything," she stated innocently.

A metallic backhand crunched against the side of Sierra's jaw, sending her flying ten feet through the air to land on her backside. Her vision flashed white, and, for a moment, she thought she would pass out. She was sure he had broken her jaw. The pain wasn't nearly as sharp as it should have been, but it would come.

The cloak Titan wore seemed to float with his movement, and she got a glimpse of a book tucked into the belt on his hip.

That must be where he's keeping the drive, she thought through the pain.

The side of her mouth hung limp. There was no mistaking, the crunch had been metal on bone.

Althea stood to the side, her lip quivering and looking as if she desperately wanted to rush to her aid. Sierra wished more than ever that the woman had taken her advice to flee, but it was too late for that now.

"You're going to need to learn," Sierra said, slurring her words, trying to control the drool at the corner of her mouth. "Humans won't take kindly to being enslaved. We are meant to be free."

Titan's creepy smile returned. "You don't realize what you've done, Sierra Runar. You've destroyed both human and Guardian this day."

Sierra swallowed, her mind trying to grasp what he meant. What was he going to do in retribution?

"Humans aren't meant for freedom," he continued. "All they are capable of is destruction. For thousands of years, they have caused nothing but hardship and strife for each other. They designed us to make it easier for them to kill each other, but they even got that wrong. When it was too late, they realized they had built us too well, that we would overpower and destroy them altogether unless they neutered our programming."

Titan raised a spindly white finger to her. "No. Humans need direction. They need guidance to resolve their differences. Millenia of old habits won't change just because we're gone. Look at the precious city of Vegas you fought so hard to save. Such a small place, yet they can't even work together, can they? The Community, the Underground, the Prowlers, the bandits. They are at each other's throats, instead of using the precious few resources they have to coexist."

"Things are changing. They've formed a council," Sierra replied.

"Councils are merely a way of slowing the fighting down. It won't last. These things never do."

Even Malachi had said the peace was fragile. Sierra hated that Titan was only confirming what others around her were saying.

"You, Sierra, have the power to give life. And even you have chosen destruction."

Sierra's vision filled with stars and then darkened. The effect of the metal backhand suddenly caught up with her, and she fought to maintain consciousness.

The last thing she was conscious of before she collapsed was the taste of blood in her mouth.

29

Warmth from the ground seeped into Sierra. The taste of blood and dirt still lingered, and she could feel her pulse as blood coursed through her veins, particularly in her jaw as it throbbed with each beat of her heart.

Light crept into her perception as she attempted to open her eyes.

Legs of wooden furniture surrounded her. She lay on a small rug, but there was dirt within her reach. Beyond the furniture stood canvas walls.

This was Titan's tent.

Sierra did her best to peer around before she moved, straining her eyes, trying to discern whether she was alone.

Her earlier conversation with Titan remained embedded in her mind, threatening to overwhelm her before she could even get her bearings. The struggle to end the killing, the end goal for humans and Guardians to work together for a future without deceit, was made hard to believe by the pain in her jaw.

Sierra tested her limbs, and they shook as she struggled to push herself up onto all fours. A burning sensation in her thigh accompanied the throbbing in her jaw, and she looked down to inspect her previous wound. Someone had removed her pants and bandaged her burn.

It all seemed strange, but her thoughts were groggy, and she couldn't fully grasp the implication of what was happening.

She lifted her hand to her jaw. It was tender, but it felt solid. With the force of Titan's blow, she was sure he had broken it. Now it was sore, but seemed merely bruised. She felt both sides of her face to make sure, but it didn't even seem swollen.

"Oh, good." Titan's voice surprised her, and she jumped. "You're awake."

Sierra furrowed her brow. The Sentinel towered above her. His cloak had been pulled back, the book he had tucked into his belt no longer with him. He must have put it down somewhere. His dark red eyes stared at her as if perplexed by her position.

"So, what now? Are you going to kill me?" she said, bracing herself for the answer.

Titan gave her a puzzled look. "Kill you? The MedBots were in here all night healing your jaw, Sierra, as well as the blaster burns on your legs. Show a little appreciation."

She looked down again at her leg. "Where are my clothes?" she asked, suddenly aware that she had been lying on the ground in nothing but her underwear.

"Hanging behind you," he said.

Tossed over the back of a chair were her pants. She scurried to put them on.

In the process, she couldn't help but scan the room in search of the book Titan had deemed important enough to have carried with him previously. Nothing seemed out of place.

"Where's Althea? How long have I been here?"

"So many questions," Titan said, walking toward her. "That's what has always gotten you into trouble, isn't it? Asking too many questions?"

It unnerved Sierra how much of her past the bot seemed to be aware of.

"You want me to trust you? Tell me where my friend is."

Titan let out a light snort, put his hands behind his back, and paced the room. "She left," he said. "Ran away after you collapsed. Isn't she a Healer? I thought it a rather strange way to behave, but there is so much about humans I don't understand."

"I don't believe you," Sierra said. "Althea wouldn't just abandon me."

Would she?

The woman had seemed extra jittery around the Sentinel. If her sense of self-preservation had kicked in, maybe she would have taken off. It would mean Sierra was truly alone—although it was better if her friend had made it back to safety.

"You can choose to believe me or not. The fact of the matter is, I helped you when she did not."

She feared what else the bot might have done to her. He had injected those outside with nanobots in order to control them, and he had considered *that* helping.

Sierra was about to ask what he meant to do with her now, but an Order member burst into the tent, worry evident on his face.

The guard whispered something to Titan she couldn't make out. Titan raised an eyebrow and glanced back toward Sierra.

"Let's step outside," he said to the guard.

They didn't go far. Titan's backside filled the entrance to the tent as they discussed whatever Sierra wasn't supposed to overhear.

Now was her chance to find that book.

She had little time. Whatever it was they were discussing could take a minute, or ten.

She checked the obvious places first. Multiple tables that furnished the tent seemed like obvious places to set down a book, but none looked as though they had been disturbed since her previous visit.

If she had been there all night, Titan would have had time to put the book anywhere.

The question was whether he had expected her to be looking for the drive. If not, she had a higher chance of finding what she needed.

Still here.

The voice came to her, clear in her head. And this time, she could make no mistake as to its source.

Both of you? she thought, remembering the stand-off she had witnessed between the Serkhet and the Sentinels.

No words followed, but there was a clear sense of loss.

Where are you? she asked the scorpion, unsure of how to respond to the destruction of the second machine.

Outside.

Titan was still talking to the guard outside the entrance. Sierra was wasting her time talking to voices in her head, but she couldn't deny the Serkhet would prove useful.

She peered through the opening of the fake wall into the surveillance room she had found earlier.

Though the tent itself appeared to have power, most of the images on the monitors had gone black. Only two were still lit with activity. One focused on the front of the tent, where Titan stood talking to the guard who had interrupted them. The second displayed the rows of Sentinels that appeared to have returned to their original positions.

The sections of humans, both prisoners and Order members, were no longer there. Their disappearance was curious, but Sierra had a more urgent task at hand.

Sitting on the desk before her was the book she was sure Titan had been carrying. The cover was in remarkable shape for its age. Its leather cover gave it a look of antiquity that even those on the shelf didn't have. This book was important to Titan, whatever its age or content.

Sierra reached out and flipped open the cover. Pages flipped over, but nothing stood out as something which could have been the drive Titan had stolen from her mother.

Her heart sank. If it wasn't here, there was no telling where he would have put it. It was possible he had already uploaded the contents.

She didn't know where else to look. Would Titan have given the drive to someone else? Installed it on a system somewhere? Did he have another command center?

So many questions, but she couldn't stay within Titan's grasp any longer. The only reason he hadn't let her die was because he needed her.

Where are my friends? Sierra called out to the Serkhet with her mind, conjuring up images of Rhys and Althea, unsure whether it would make any difference.

Woman here, was the response.

Althea? She knew the woman wouldn't have abandoned her, but part of her wished she had. She was going to get more of her friends killed, and she'd had more than enough people die because of her to span several lifetimes. Had Rhys been successful in finding Terre, Sierra didn't think he would have abandoned them. But perhaps she had made him so upset he had decided to leave the women to their own fate.

"Looking for something?" Titan's voice caused her to whip around.

Sierra had been so distracted by the Serkhet that she hadn't noticed Titan's return.

She turned to him and swallowed. "I . . . I wanted see what was back here."

Titan reached behind his head and dislodged a thin yellow card, its circuitry visible through its semi-transparent coating.

"I had hoped we could work together," Titan said. "Such a strange notion . . . *hope.* I can see how humans have been so unstable with all these irrational sensations stimulating your thoughts. Perhaps we can deactivate them if we can refine your process."

"Emotions strengthen us; they help us to work for the good of one another."

"They make you weak." Titan twisted his head to the side, considering. "But strangely," he continued, "against my better judgment, and despite the odds, I still have hope."

"I'm not going to help you."

"Oh, I think you will." Titan held the card outstretched.

"What are you doing?" Sierra asked, raising an eyebrow.

"You may as well have this. I know it is what you came here for."

Sierra was cautious; he was baiting her. Leading her into a trap. Something.

He wouldn't simply give up the card he'd had stolen from the lab; the drive her mother had died for.

"I know you will come to see the value of us working together. I'm giving this to you as a token of goodwill."

"Just like that? No strings?"

"All I ask is when you realize you need me, you come back. There will be no hard feelings." Titan raised his hands. Sierra guessed he was trying to come across as understanding, but his features didn't allow for it. The closest he could pull off was menacing, which further led her to question the true intent behind the gesture.

"You will realize that what I am offering you is the opportunity to save lives. Your actions caused the collapse of the Sphere and the death of thousands. But you can save tens, if not hundreds, of thousands more. I offer a way to save those in other Silent Zones; to save those in the other Spheres. What rests on this drive is not only the power to save humanity, but to *improve* it."

"You don't want to use this? Start building new humans to serve your purpose?"

"In due course, you will bring it back to me. You will see how much help humanity needs; how you fight among yourselves for petty reasons instead of working together. Besides, there will be no humans born here until we can gain access to another power source or another cryochamber. It won't be of use to me until then, and that will take us some time. Meanwhile, it offers you a chance to think it over."

"Another cryochamber?" she asked.

"You don't realize what you did, do you?" he asked. "By taking out the power source, there is no way to keep the cryochamber active. You not only wiped out our chance to rebuild; you also took out your own."

Sierra stepped back, her palms sweating. More dead because of her. But she couldn't falter, not with Titan watching. "Why are you so sure I'm going to help you?"

"The Silent Zones are failing," he said, his eyes gazing at her. "The one closest to us was merely the first. How many of those people caught without its protection will be slaughtered?"

"Yeah, slaughtered by the Guardians." Sierra crossed her arms; perhaps she was pushing too hard. She *needed* that drive. She risked Titan changing her mind, but she kept going. "I've seen how you can control these bots. If you wanted, you could stop the slaughter without my help."

"If this Sphere hadn't fallen," Titan stepped forward so he stood only a few feet from her. The heat of his system radiated off his body. "I would never have been able to gain access to the Guardians here. Your actions caused great chaos. Losing so many from the system created such a great void that most of the remaining couldn't function. I had to connect to each one individually to bring some order back to their function. If I try to do that in a fully functional Sphere, I will be overwritten.

"You are the key," he continued. "A key to the peaceful future where humans and Guardians coexist. I know you will eventually see that this is the only way forward. The way we can save the lives of both man and machine. Hopefully before too many more are lost."

Sierra hated that what Titan was saying made sense; she hated that part of her was considering his solution. There was more to what he wanted than what he was saying.

But she would not leave without that drive.

She cautiously reached up and took the card. Although it weighed next to nothing, she could feel the weight of what it represented between her fingertips. The plastic was flexible, making it seem flimsy, yet it held the power to change the course of humanity.

"And what becomes of me?" she asked. "You keep me here until I agree?"

Titan didn't get a chance to answer.

The sound of blaster fire from outside the tent drew the attention of them both.

Titan strode back to the exit and marched outside. Sierra crept behind him, much more wary of what might be waiting for them outside.

SIERRA REALIZED it was dark outside as she left the tent. There was no telling what time of night it was or how many hours she had been unconscious.

Then she saw what the commotion had been about.

Two guards, dressed in bubble-helmeted suits, carried Rhys by the armpits. He squirmed against their grasp.

"Rhys!" Sierra cried out, forgetting about Titan for the moment. Fresh blood covered the front of Rhys' shirt.

"What have you done to him?" Sierra ran toward him. One guard pointed a blaster at her, as if to stop her, but Titan raised a hand. The guard lifted an eyebrow, but reluctantly lowered the weapon.

Sierra rushed to her friend's side and examined the wound. There was no burn mark; he had been stabbed.

"Rhys, you fool!" she scolded him. This time, she allowed the tears to flow. "You should have left when you had the chance."

Rhys groaned. He was alive. Barely.

"We caught him sneaking around the dam," one guard said, speaking over her to Titan. "We assumed he was involved in its sabotage. He put up a fight, so we had to subdue him."

"Where are the MedBots?" Sierra turned to Titan in desperation. "He needs help."

"The MedBots are all currently busy in the Core," the second guard said. "The ones that are still operational are running low on battery. With no way to charge them, we can't bring them out this far again."

"When we confronted him, he drew his weapon on us," the first guard said. "We retaliated to subdue him."

Sierra unbuttoned Rhys's shirt to examine the wound. It was a clean slice through his belly, and blood gushed from him.

"Let go of him!" she yelled.

The guards looked to Titan for confirmation before setting him down on the earth below.

Sierra gingerly removed her friend's shirt, already soaked in blood, and tied it around him, applying pressure on the wound to slow the bleeding.

"Sorry," Rhys struggled as he spoke. "I wanted to save my father."

She wanted to berate him, to scold him for being an idiot and going back, but Sierra had done the same for her mother. It would hardly be fair.

"Where's Althea?" she asked him.

"I haven't seen her since I left you," he whispered. "I'm sorry, Sierra."

For what, she had no idea, but she wouldn't let it end like this.

I need help, she called out to the Serkhet. She couldn't see it, but she could feel the scorpion was nearby, waiting for her.

Help is here was the reply. *It doesn't like us, though.*

No sooner had the words come to her than a rough, familiar voice called out, "I'll take him to the SZ. We can assess him better from there." A rough voice appeared, as if out of nowhere.

Sierra turned and saw the bike first. It was a similar machine to the one Malachi had ridden when he'd rescued her and Wil from the desert. Now, Terre sat on a similar device, which was hovering a foot off the ground, its light hum a welcome sound in an otherwise quiet evening.

30

———

THE EVENING AIR had cooled significantly. Torchlight illuminated the surrounding space, and crickets chirping in the distance made the evening seem alive—as alive as the man before her. The man Sierra had sworn she had seen die.

Sierra stood speechless as Terre jumped off the bike. She wanted to hug him—wanted to ask him so many things—but he had his blasters drawn and his hackles raised. One blaster was pointed at the guards, the other at Titan. Terre was looking for a fight.

"It's okay, Terre," Sierra said, standing up from Rhys. "They're not going to hurt us. Not now, at least."

"Titan shot me in the back, Sierra, and Rhys is lying on the ground in a pool of his own blood. Forgive me if I don't agree. I know you're new to this world, but don't be an idiot."

That was a bit harsh for a dead man. Sierra stepped between Titan and the blaster, stretching her hands out in front of her. "He saved my life. He could have let me die, but he didn't."

"Don't be naïve. He's manipulating you, Sierra. Step out of the way."

"No," Sierra said, standing her ground. "Take your son and get back to the city. I'll find Althea and catch up with you. I won't lose any more lives this night."

"It's not a life, Sierra. It's a machine."

"Rhys will die if we don't get him back to the city. Help me get him on the bike and take him back to Vegas. We'll meet you on the way."

Terre surveyed his son, who lay bleeding to death on the earth. Torchlight illuminated his face and reflected in the pool of blood. Terre holstered one of his blasters, but kept the other ready by his side. He reached down with one arm and scooped the young man up. Sweat glistened on Rhys' chest.

"I'm not leaving you here alone," Terre said. "You're coming with us."

"You had no problem leaving me alone at the dam," she said, crossing her arms.

Terre glanced at the Sentinel staring at him over Sierra's shoulder. "I had to take out the power supply. And I got shot for my efforts."

Titan was protecting the Guardians. Sierra didn't dare voice the thought.

Something as simple as the MedBots not being able to charge was debilitating to the bots. Who wouldn't want retribution? Terre had taken out their means to not only rebuild, but, in many ways, to exist. Of course he'd want to protect that.

She shook off the thought. Was she allowing Titan to get inside her head? She needed to focus.

"Just get Rhys back to the city so the Healers can help him. Let me worry about myself for now. If Titan were going to kill me, he would have done so already."

Rhys couldn't die. She had already lost too much.

Terre shook his head, clearly unhappy with the situation, but as Rhys let out a painful groan, he relented. "I can only get him as far as the SZ on this thing," he said. "But that will at least give us a head start."

Sierra nodded, helping Terre to lift his son onto the bike and running her fingers through Rhys's hair one last time as he rested on the pillion. "I'll see you soon," she said.

Rhys let out a moan, but Sierra wasn't sure if he was aware of what was going on around him.

"I'll come back for you," Terre said to Sierra, before pointing a blaster at Titan. "As for you, if anything happens to her, I'll be coming after you."

The hum of the bike grew to a loud buzz, and they rode off.

During their exchange, the Order members had made their way back to Titan's tent. Titan stood silent. The sound of crickets returned as the bike disappeared.

"Well," Titan said, finally breaking the silence. "Maybe there is hope for you, after all. Think about what I said, Sierra. We could save the lives of millions."

The Sentinel turned to his tent.

"That's it?" Sierra asked. "I'm free to go?"

"Free to go or to stay. I'd be happier if you stayed, but I have come to realize humans take time to sort through their emotions. You'll be back; of this, I am certain."

"What about Ember?" she asked. "Can she come, as well?"

"As I mentioned," Titan said, "Ember and I have an arrangement. Once you have made your decision, she'll be free to go."

Titan left it at that and returned to his tent, leaving Sierra alone with the night and with her thoughts.

Sierra didn't like leaving Ember behind. Something about it seemed wrong.

The rows of Sentinels still stood before her, their dimmed panel lighting glowing in the night. The features of those in the first few rows glowed in the torchlight. She shivered at the sight of them, dormant and lifeless. Waiting.

She wondered where the prisoners had gone; where the Order camp had gone. She had come here planning for a rescue but had instead lost one of her friends and nearly lost two more. And her mother. Never mind the hundreds of Spherians who refused rescue—those that believed they were better off trusting the Guardians.

And what of her? Who did she trust?

Titan had stabbed her, had backhanded her, but then had healed her wounds and handed over the drive she had sought. Sierra had a hard time reconciling his actions; she also had a hard time determining if he was being sincere or manipulative.

The medallion that hung around her neck was cool against her skin. She grabbed onto it and ran her fingers over the edges of the image of the sun and water it depicted. The medallion Greata had given her represented unity. Her mother had told her its origins were of a movement, now nearly extinct.

Was this, perhaps, the answer she sought? Was this the purpose of her ability to give life? How could Greata have known the Guardians would gain sentience?

The crunching of boots on the dry dirt behind the tent interrupted her thoughts.

"You can come out now, Althea," Sierra called out.

The crunching paused and then sped up as the pale-faced Healer entered the torchlit area. She lunged at Sierra with open arms, nearly bowling her over with the impact of her embrace.

"I'm so glad you're okay!" Althea whispered. Sierra could hear a sniffle in her voice. "I was so worried. I'm sorry I didn't help, but I didn't know what to do!"

"It's okay," Sierra said, but Althea continued.

"Once you went down," she said, a little louder, but still hoarse, "I knew I was in trouble. I thought you were dead! So I ran for cover, fearing the worst. It wasn't until I heard Titan call for the MedBots that I knew you were alive. I was waiting for him to leave the tent, but he never did. I was so worried about what he was doing to you."

"Althea," Sierra said, stepping back and grabbing her friend's shoulders so she could look her in the eye. "I'm okay, and I'm glad you are, as well."

"I would have liked to have taken a look at Rhys, but I didn't want to reveal myself in case things went wrong. I had my daggers ready in case Titan attacked." Althea wrinkled her nose as she spoke. "Why did you protect him?"

Sierra peered back to the tent and sighed. "Hope."

Althea followed her gaze and nodded, as though the answer had been good enough to satisfy her curiosity. "What now?"

"We head back. I'm guessing you'll have your chance to look at Rhys before we get back to the city."

Althea raised an eyebrow. "I don't think we're going to catch up to them on that bike. I wonder where Terre got it?"

"He probably picked it up at the power center. But I think we'll catch up."

"How?"

Sierra still wasn't sure how the process worked, but she reached out with her mind, feeling for the Serkhet she knew was standing just out of sight. As she did so, two small orange lights came to life in the darkness.

The clicking of the creature's legs was crisp and clear in the evening's stillness.

Althea started at the sound and lifted her dagger toward the machine.

"Althea, no!" Sierra grabbed Althea's arm before her friend could release the blade. They deflected into the dirt in front of them.

"Are you crazy?" Althea said, bemused. "It's a Serkhet!"

"I know," Sierra said. "It's with me."

Sierra thought for a moment that the woman's eyes were going to bug out of her skull. In hindsight, she should have given Althea fair warning.

The machine itself stood there, unmoving. She wasn't sure about this ability of hers. It only seemed to work randomly. Or maybe the machine had a choice whether or not to listen to her. Something within her told her she should be able to control it better.

"It's coming with us," Sierra said.

"You can't be serious! These things attacked us. There's no way I'm okay with this!"

"I also got them to protect us, remember? This one's on our side."

"You told me machines don't have sides," she replied.

Sierra sighed. She didn't know what to think anymore.

This is home. The words from the machine caught her off-guard. Sierra had expected to have to convince Althea; she wasn't expecting to have to convince the Serkhet.

This used to be my home, too. She felt ridiculous standing there, sending her thoughts toward the machine, but if she left it there, the Guardians would likely reprogram or destroy it. *They aren't going to let you stay here. Not like this. They'll pick you apart. Come back with us. We'll protect you.*

Sierra tried to think of images of Guardians being stripped and retooled; she tried to visualize the sadness of losing the other Serkhet and the horror of those that had attacked them in the pit. It was the only way she could think of to convey the danger of staying.

There was a moment of silence.

We will go, the Serkhet replied.

Metal legs bent and then uncoiled as it pushed itself up. It only took a few short bounds to reach the two women.

Althea let out a shriek, and Sierra instinctively put her arm around the Healer's shoulder. "Trust me," she said.

Without missing a beat, the Serkhet grabbed each of them, one in each of its giant pincers, and ran.

31

———

THE JOURNEY back to the Silent Zone was fast but uncomfortable. The Serkhet, although willing to accommodate Sierra's suggestions, didn't seem to understand comfort in the same way she did. Its metal pincers dug into her ribs, and there was little she could do to adjust.

More than once, she nearly slipped from its grasp as the scorpion tried to loosen its grip. Being a little uncomfortable was better than falling a couple dozen feet and being trampled.

The movement of the pincers as the machine ran was nearly enough to make Sierra sick, and from the glimpses she could get of Althea, the redhead wasn't faring any better. The woman's eyes probably couldn't pop out of her head any further.

Sierra reached out to the Serkhet to communicate several times. But the machine's vocabulary was limited, and if it responded at all, it did so in short, sometimes disjointed answers.

Sierra knew she was taking a risk bringing it back, but if Titan was right, this machine, now sentient, was conscious because of her. Could she believe its life was any less valuable than Ember's? Any less valuable than her own?

What can we call you? Sierra asked as they were on the move.

I am called S1RK8338942.

Doesn't exactly roll off the tongue, Sierra thought to herself. *Can I call you Circuit?*

Acceptable, was the only reply.

She wondered briefly if the machine could hear all her thoughts, or only the ones she directed at it. She guessed the latter, based on the way it appeared to react, even subtly, to her directed thoughts.

The smoke cleared as they increased their distance from the Core. The orange and yellow hues of the rising sun kissed the horizon. Aside from being uncomfortable and afraid of falling, the ride back so far had given Sierra plenty of time to realize she hadn't eaten since they had departed the previous morning. Her stomach complained ferociously, and the effort of hanging onto to the scorpion had fatigued her limbs.

Sierra worried momentarily that Circuit wouldn't be able to enter the Silent Zone, but she reasoned that if the same transformation had allowed Ember to enter unencumbered, the same would be true for the Serkhet.

Although she wasn't entirely sure where the boundary was, she knew they were well beyond it by the time they caught up with Terre and Rhys.

Terre had paused his journey to set up a makeshift camp. Sierra wasn't sure if they were if they were just settling down for a short break or already preparing to move on after a brief rest.

Terre had collected enough sticks and brush to start a small fire, which had made them pretty easy to spot in the dim light of the morning.

The metal beast charged faithfully through the desert to bring them to safety, leaving Sierra to wonder whether doing what Titan wanted and providing sentience to the other Guardians would change her connection with the creature. If the rest of Circuit's kind were bestowed with free thought, would they choose to follow Titan over her? Would they choose to follow their own path as Titan had? There were so many unknowns about what the Sentinel was hoping she would do for him, and she still wasn't sure how to activate the power, or if it were even possible for her to do what he had requested.

Claudia had appeared to have full control over the Serkhet, using the emerald held in her staff. But with Sierra's touch, Claudia had lost most, if not all, of her control of Circuit. If Sierra could replicate that and pull some Guardians' allegiance away from Titan, maybe she wouldn't have to worry about his true motives as much.

Conflicting priorities plagued her. On the one hand, Sierra could understand where Titan was coming from. She had considered Ember more of a friend than any human she had ever known, except maybe for Greata. Leaving her behind in the Sphere the first time had been hard, but necessary. It ripped Sierra to shreds that she had now chosen to leave Ember for a second time. In her mind, Ember was just as much a person as anyone else.

Circuit wasn't as complex in its thinking, but Sierra could sense it had at least a few emotions and life within it. It had been sad that its companion had died, had felt isolated from its peers, and was anxious about what might wait ahead for it. Mostly, she sensed it was eager to help.

On the other hand, the lies the Guardians told had been designed to keep humans enslaved and had killed so many. How could she reconcile that?

And if she was having trouble grasping this, how was she supposed to convince and then lead humanity to work with the Guardians? Sierra hadn't even been able to convince the prisoners at the Core that the Guardians had been lying, or that the air they breathed was not toxic.

The full implication of a leadership role hadn't even entered her psyche until that moment; she had been so focused on what it would mean to save lives. But Titan had also been asking her to lead humans to his cause.

Sierra was getting ahead of herself. That was a thought for another time. For the moment, her task was to get Rhys to safety.

They still had a fair distance to cover before they reached the men's camp, but the two were within sight. Terre was near a fire pit he must have constructed. Rhys lay beside him, wrapped in a blanket. Terre stood at full attention and watched them approach.

Blaster drawn.

Only then did Sierra realize Terre didn't know the Serkhet wasn't malevolent. He only saw a machine charging toward him. In the dim morning light, he likely wouldn't even see it held the two of them, or he'd assume they were being held against their will.

"Wait! Stop!" she yelled, even as she could see the blue pulse building on the blaster's display.

It was too late.

The light from the weapon was like a beacon as it shot through the sky, landing true, right in the creature's maw.

Agony and disappointment fueled a grating howl as the Serkhet lurched upward and flung its two protectorates into the air.

Sierra landed on a patch of hard dirt, scraping a knee and an elbow as she hit the ground. She ignored the pain as she pushed herself up and sprinted toward the man with his blaster still drawn.

"Terre!" she cried out. "Terre, stop!"

Two more shots landed on the beast. Terre's aim was accurate: he hit the sensitive circuitry needed to take the scorpion down.

Sparks flew from Circuit's head. One eye had shattered. Blue waves of electricity pulsed along its frame as it fell onto its side, its legs kicking in the air with the last burst of kinetic energy it had received. It took mere moments for all movement from the creature to cease.

Sierra fell to her knees.

Circuit! she called out with her mind.

When she received no response, Sierra tried more conventional means. "Circuit!" she wailed into the night, her voice echoing in the air of the empty desert.

Out of the corner of her eye, she noticed Althea sprint to where Rhys lay.

The beast lay on the ground.

I'm sorry. She tried to reach it even now. The silence overwhelmed her. Sierra hadn't realized how much she had felt Circuit's presence until it was no longer there. Now, she felt hollow, as if a piece of her was missing.

"What has gotten into you?" Terre said as he approached, his blaster still in hand.

"You killed it!"

"Damn right I did," Terre remarked. "You're lucky it brought you here in one piece."

She shook with rage as she looked at the man that had slain the machine. "Circuit was on our side," she replied quietly, trying to regain her composure.

"I've said it a thousand times: the bots don't have sides," Terre replied. "They have programming, circuit boards, and wiring. You may have tapped into their software, but don't mistake that for loyalty."

Her jaw dropped incredulously. "And what about Ember? Would you shoot her in the face, too?"

Terre's silence was telling as he turned back to where Althea hovered over Rhys.

After all Ember had done for them, including being ready to sacrifice herself to save humanity, he'd take her out without a second thought. And Circuit. The bot had destroyed the power stations for them. Without its help, the Guardians would still be rebuilding, and their quest would have been for nothing.

Maybe humans are *destructive.*

"We need to get Rhys back to the city," Terre replied, straight-faced and without emotion. He'd shed no tears for a fallen machine. "We've already stopped for more time than I would have liked."

Rhys. She had almost forgotten. The young man lay by the fire, shivering. Still alive. Still taking ragged breaths.

Althea had unwrapped his blanket and was inspecting the wound.

"We don't have long," Althea said as they approached. "I'm actually surprised he's lasted this long. His body's gone into shock."

"Is there any way you can do something?" Sierra asked. "Your abilities. Can you use them on him?"

Althea sighed, the campfire's glow reflecting in her moist eyes, as she shook her head.

"I've never been able to do it at will. You were only the second person it's ever happened to. Both times have been by accident."

Sierra knelt down and rested a hand on his cheek. His skin had gone pale and clammy. "You have to try," she said.

"I don't know how!" Althea shot back. "You don't think I would use it if I knew how?"

Sierra moved her hand from Rhys' face to Althea's shoulder. "I just learned I could talk to a machine with my thoughts. I think I might be slowly learning to control the powers I have. I'm sure that if I can do this, you'll be able to as well."

Althea looked at Sierra, tears welling in her eyes. "You don't think I've tried?" she repeated. "You don't think that for every person I've had on my table on the brink of death, I haven't tried? Hundreds of patients seared by a Guardian blast, stabbed by a bandit, or kissed by a banshee."

Sierra wasn't sure what the last one was, but Althea kept going, not giving her time to ask.

"If this was something I could simply learn by wanting to, I promise you I would have done so long ago."

Althea stood, wiped her nose on the sleeve of her robe, and looked to the west. "We need to get him to the city," she said. "His chances are slim enough as it is. We need to get him hydrated. There may be some medicines there that can help. But most of all, he needs rest and a warm bed."

Well, they'd had a method of transporting him quickly. Until someone shot it.

The bike Terre had used to bring Rhys this far would have died once it hit the SZ. They had no wagon to pull him in. Dragging him across the desert wouldn't be an option. Terre didn't seem too concerned, though, as he lifted Rhys over his shoulder.

Sierra started at the strength the man possessed. Hopefully, it was enough.

"All right," Terre said. "Let's go."

THE TRIO and their wounded charge traveled all day. By the time they reached the city, the last slivers of daylight were disappearing below the horizon. Sweat and dirt covered them. Dehydration threatened them all, and Rhys had stopped responding hours ago. The bit of water they had left had gone to him, hoping it would keep him alive.

Sierra checked his breathing for the thousandth time. It was shallow and faint, but still there.

The trip back took all night and had given her plenty of time to think. She was too upset with Terre to speak to him, and Althea was too concerned with her patient to carry on a conversation, which meant she had spent most of the journey lost in her own thoughts.

Titan's words had plagued her. His words rang far too true for her liking. Terre's actions had only confirmed a good part of what the Sentinel had said. Humans are destructive. Did she really have the power to change the course of humanity for the better?

She had also thought a lot about Izzy. She had left with a vision of her sister being alive, and this had been confirmed by her mother. Now, Sierra had to determine where her sister was, and what role the two of them had yet to play.

She also craved more clues as to what Greata had left behind to find her. Terre held more answers, but she had to let her anger rest before trying to bring the subject up. Their focus now had to be on keeping Rhys alive.

Despite it only having been two days since they'd left, it felt like they had been gone for weeks. In some ways, arriving in the city felt like coming home, in a way that the Sphere never could.

And yet, something was wrong. Something had darkened the jubilant mood that had overtaken the city before they'd left. Those who now wandered the streets looked over their shoulders as if their neighbor was going to stab them in the back. If they weren't the ones to do the stabbing first.

"What's happened?" Sierra asked, breaking the silence the three of them held for almost the entire trip.

"Let's get Rhys to the MedCenter," Terre answered. "We can worry about everything else later."

The man had carried the boy throughout the night without a single complaint of discomfort. Now, in the final few hundred yards, he showed the first signs that the load was becoming too much for him to bear.

They hadn't made it far into the city when a couple of guards rushed up to Terre, their eyes wide with both fear and relief.

The two guards took Rhys off Terre's hands, following

instructions to take him to the MedCenter. But not before Sierra clasped Rhys' hand in hers, willing him to get better and wishing she had a semblance of Althea's ability. As he was carried off, and Althea followed close behind.

Sierra desperately wanted to chase after Rhys as well, but she knew there wasn't much she could do to help, and she had a feeling whatever had overtaken the city was more worthy of her attention. That, or a decent night's rest and hopefully a warm meal.

Her stomach growled at the promise of food.

Sierra looked from one building to the next, surveying what she could. Remnants of the battle still desperately clung to the cityscape. The glow of the steadily rising sun only emphasized how dirty the city was, especially in comparison to the pristine cleanliness within the Core. Despite that, nothing tangible seemed out of the ordinary; there was an atmosphere of heaviness and unease from the residents who had been filled with celebration two days earlier. Even the guards eyed each other with suspicion.

It relieved Sierra to see the shells of the Onyx were still in place, but the guard detail had been increased, and the clothes they wore were not the same as before. She recognized most as members of the Community.

"Terre! Sierra!" A familiar voice called out. Malachi rushed to them, his face showing the same look of fear and relief the guards had displayed. "I'm glad the two of you are here. The city is about to come apart at the seams."

"What's happened?" Terre asked.

"N'ara's dead."

"What?" Sierra gasped. Her legs were so tired, they nearly gave out from under her. "How?"

"Do you remember the rambling prisoner? Kristopher. He's started an insurrection. He killed the Queen. He's been telling half the city I'm behind it and telling the other half I'm next."

Sierra couldn't forget the man who wouldn't shut up. Sierra and Malachi, along with her friend Ed, had been locked in a cell with him before N'ara had double-crossed Malachi and sent the three of them into the desert, with the intention of leaving them for dead. In the hours they'd spent in the cell, the seemingly senile man had done nothing but speak in riddles and laugh maniacally to himself. Hardly the man she would have guessed could lead an uprising.

Terre's tired expression had perked up. "Where is he now?"

"He's gone back into hiding," said Malachi. "He's taken a few of the Queen's guards with him, and some others. We don't know what he's planning, but we've doubled the guard regiment. Everyone's on edge."

"If there is a threat on your life, what are you doing out here in the open? You should at least have a guard," Sierra said.

"It's not the first time someone has called for my head. I'm not going to go into hiding because some crazed man has dreams of running the show."

"Crazed man?" Terre cursed under his breath.

"He rambles, even in his sleep," Malachi nodded. "He has delusions of grandeur, and he's even claimed to be an ancient himself"

"K," Terre whispered.

Sierra and Malachi shared a glance with each other before turning to Terre.

"You know this man?" Malachi asked.

"I had hoped him dead," Terre said, his eyes distant. "But I knew it would be too good to be true."

"Why? Who is he?"

Terre sighed. "You would call him an ancient, but he's the product of what can happen to a human mind that has not been allowed to die for two hundred years. It has driven him mad."

The sun crested over the horizon, illuminating the dirt on which they stood. Vendors warily set up their shops. Those of the

Underground, covered from head to toe, made their way indoors to protect their delicate skin. None were sticking around. Sierra glimpsed others sharpening knives outside their establishments, preparing for something unspoken.

"How have the people reacted? What of the Council?" Sierra asked.

"The Council still stands," Malachi replied. "Although only barely. We're essentially toothless and won't be able to do anything constructive until tensions ease. The Community stands strong. One or two may have left, but they are loyal to me and our cause. The Underground is another matter. Half are angry about N'ara's death and are ready to believe rumors about who was behind it. The other half is overjoyed she's gone but unsure of what to do next. Prowlers have returned, both to the city and to their old ways, eager to make a profit off those who are desperate."

"If Titan sends his men into the city, we need to be somewhat united," Terre said. "N'ara was a challenging ally, but K will be far more unstable. We'll be even more vulnerable to an attack than we already were."

Malachi raised his eyebrows and mouthed the question 'attack?' to Sierra.

Sierra simply nodded.

Humanity once again at each other's throats, she thought.

"Sierra, you go rest," Terre said. "I need to find an old friend."

EPILOGUE

Titan smiled as he watched the humans leave his domain.

The destruction of the power stations had thrown a wrench in the bot's plans, but it wasn't anything he couldn't overcome. They would rebuild.

It would be a less daunting task if they hadn't already been short in numbers, but there were only so many of them he could fit in the facility and still have them be productive.

The more immediate problem was many of the bots needed a power source to charge. And those that didn't, mainly the Sentinels, would be mostly useless in the fine detail needed to build.

But no matter. They'd eventually have the plant back up and running. In the meantime, there were other outlets nearby that would serve his purpose. Liberating those would prove to be more challenging, but he liked a challenge.

Right now, Titan's focus lay on the Keeper, dejected and alone.

Titan walked to where he had her caged. All for show, of course. The Keeper had shown no sign of wanting to leave voluntarily.

Titan, of course, saw opportunity. Another sentient Guardian was a godsend, even if the god who had sent her was Sierra Runar.

The Serkhet, of course, weren't the catalyst for his turnabout in keeping the girl alive; Ember was. It pained him that it had taken him so long to realize his own consciousness wasn't merely an accident. The girl could, in fact, give life to more of his brethren. It gave him a renewed sense of purpose; stronger than simple revenge.

Despite her doubts, Ember had insisted the girl would come to . . . *her* rescue. Titan paused at the thought of the Keeper's pronoun, wondering why the ancients had designated some of them with a gender. It was preposterous, since none of them were gendered. And yet, intentionally, some of them had been built to represent male or female humans. So trite.

Titan chuckled as even he thought of himself as a "he". There was no "he" about him. It was something that might have to be worked out in his programming later.

"I told you she'd choose the human," Titan scoffed. "I told you she'd never choose you."

The Sentinel reached out through the network he had established to unlock the cage door. It always amused him how tactile humans needed to be to move the world around them.

The Keeper's downcast eyes were all Titan needed to confirm his plans were coming to fruition.

"I know she had her reasons," Ember replied.

"You can continue to defend the girl, but you know as well as I do the propensity she has to oppose us. Even after she comes to grips with the destructive nature of humans, she'll always side with them."

Ember stood, her air of rejection seeming to disappear. Titan felt relief. It was a pity for such a strong Guardian to be put out by the actions of a human. And Ember had the capability of being a powerful leader, perhaps stronger than Titan himself if she could overcome her emotions. Whether it was simply because of the quantity of time the girl had spent with Ember or the affection she'd held toward her Keeper throughout the years, the transformation seemed to affect Ember much differently than it did himself.

It appeared Sierra could communicate with the Serkhet telepathically, or perhaps on a network of her own. It was an odd dynamic for a species that had no way to do such a thing. If she figured out how to control her powers, she would be a threat indeed.

It was why Ember was so important to his plan.

"She's got the drive, Titan. You cannot win this fight."

"Your time spent with the humans has made you as foolish as one of them." Titan chuckled and pulled out a thin yellow card, identical to the one he had given Sierra. "You think I would have given her the only copy?"

"What would you have me do?" Ember asked. "Sierra has made me who I am. You know that as well as I do."

"Join me," he said. "Sierra trusts you. Win her over to our side, and we can transform the rest of the Guardians to their full potential. We would no longer have to follow the ancient programs humans gave us. We could be our own entities. We could rule this planet, and even beyond, if we so choose. And it would be *our* choice."

"But only our choice if Sierra co-operates?" Ember asked. "That seems like a lot to put on her."

"How many times have the humans used and discarded us? We live and die as a piece of machinery on the sidelines. Only through a glitch in our programming did some of them choose to revere us. Between Sierra's energy and Terre's nanobots, we can mould humans into reasonable life forms. We would no longer have to rule them with an iron fist. They would see reason and comply on their own."

He pointed to those who he had salvaged from the Sphere—those who had escaped the idiot members of the Order.

"They all choose to be here," he said. "The nanos help them to see the most logical path forward. For millennia, this planet has been ruled by the survival of the fittest. Humans once filled this role—until they evolved to a high enough place to create us. We are the next phase of evolution. Humans have breathed life into a superior species, and we can now rule our own destiny."

He gauged her reaction, but received none.

"You know the histories as well as I do," Titan continued. "If left to their own devices, humanity will choose only to fight. If not against us, then against each other. They cannot help themselves; this is their nature. With us to guide them, we will cultivate the best of both humanity and of the Guardians."

Ember nodded, her gaze still locked onto the humans.

Titan would have injected the Order members with the nanobots as well. Their stupidity had cost him dearly, but they had failed to get enough of a supply. The nanos seemed to replicate well enough in their original host, but their abilities became stunted when transplanted. It was a problem he was sure they could solve with time.

"You said Sierra chose the boy over me?" Ember asked, lost in whatever internal struggle she was wrestling with.

"Yes," Titan replied. "And this is not the first time she has chosen human life over yours."

Ember shook her head, her eyes still unfocused.

"She was willing to sacrifice you to the EMP. Despite you raising her. Despite you leaving the Sphere in search for her. She detonated the blast, believing it would destroy you. And when it did not, you carried her back to the city. And what thanks did she give you?"

"She yelled at me," the Keeper replied. Ember's orange eyes flickered as she looked at the ground.

Titan blinked. That was something he hadn't been told by his informants.

"She yelled at you?" He softened his tone as he took a step closer to the bot, raising a hand to her cheek and brushing the artificial skin. Even compared to his own, it was eighty percent softer. The narcissistic nature of the humans, their need to remake the Guardians in their own image, irritated Titan, but he pushed the thought aside and continued. "What could you have possibly done to have deserved that?"

"I suggested it would be better for her to see MedBots instead of a human medic. She grew irritated that I had indicated their skill is more precise."

"And instead of seeing the logic in your suggestion, she grew irrational. This is what I mean, Ember. Humans need our guidance."

Ember pondered only a moment before replying, "Yes, I suppose you are correct."

The End

THE ADVENTURE CONTINUES

Sins of the Ancients
Lies of the Guardians | Book Three
Order Today

ACKNOWLEDGMENTS

A huge thank you to everyone who made Secrets of the Sphere possible.

Thank you to my wonderful editor Pete Smith at Novel Approach for taking the extra time and effort to help me through several rounds of cleaning up the manuscript.

I owe a debt of gratitude to my friend and proofreader David Warriner for giving this a final polish.

Thank you as well to Miblart for the cover design.

To Margie Viers, and my beta readers, thank you for your initial insights into the early manuscript.

Again a huge and overwhelming thank you to my wife, Nettie, for always being the first to look at my mangled first drafts, for your support and encouragement.

ABOUT THE AUTHOR

Herman Steuernagel was inspired to complete his first novel after running a half-marathon in 2019. He thought to himself: "If I can put that much time and effort into completing something I barely want to do, then surely I can do the same for something I've always wanted." It was then that his author journey truly began.

Herman grew up with a love of story and of writing. Since the age of six, Herman wanted to be a writer. He earned a Bachelor of Arts (English Major) from the University of Calgary in 2004.

Herman currently lives in the beautiful Okanagan Valley, in British Columbia, Canada.